The Sound

BRONA NILSSON

Copyright © 2021 Brona Nilsson

All rights reserved.

ISBN: 9798506082439

DEDICATION

To Des Collins, an exceptional father, who crossed many seas and lived to tell the tale.

ACKNOWLEDGMENTS

Rebecca Millar, development editor, did an incredible job whipping this manuscript into shape, teaching me so much about crime writing in the process. Rayann did a great copy-edit. Daniel Brenner advised on the cover art. Writing is a lonely job, but some people make it less so. For encouragement and advice along the way, thanks to my writing pals, Tracy Fahey, Dan and Laura Martone, Gary Jonas, Audrey Sharpe, Vicki-Lewis Thompson, and Jamie Davis.

Finally, thanks and love to my family, Ulf, Fionn, and Skye, who somehow manage to keep putting up with the crazy author in the room at the end of the house.

# *1*

Lyra Norton's phone buzzed two minutes before 8:00 p.m. disturbing the evening lull of her third-floor apartment in Rathmines, Dublin. The paintbrush she had been coaxing down a doorframe wobbled off course and slashed red across her knuckles. *Whoa, this may not be the best color for a baby's bedroom.*

"Phone…phone."

If this was a student, she was going to fail them. Those essays on plagiarism detection software were due tomorrow, and many of her charges were pulling all-nighters just as she had done in her own student days. Calling her lecturer, though? Never. She batted the sheets of *The Irish Times* on the floor until she located the device underneath.

Caller ID showed Olive. Her students were off the hook. For her best friend in Sweden—an hour ahead of Ireland— this counted as late. Whatever happened to her regimental routine of bath and meditation before nine hours of beauty sleep? Then again, in these pre-wedding days, normal rules did not apply.

"Lyra, it's me," came Olive's voice which always made her smile. After fifteen years of Sweden, her Roscommon

1

accent was still robust with only a frosting of Nordic crispness. Lyra's own had warped into a Dublin South dialect ages ago.

"Hey you, excellent timing. I need a break." Lyra cradled the phone between her ear and neck, rubbing her knuckles with a spirits-infused cloth. "That poppy color I chose to impress the adoption people? It looks like blood. What's new?"

The pause lengthened.

"Lyra, I'm afraid this isn't—It's…It's um…" Olive's breath came in gasps.

"Olive, what?" Was she *sobbing?* Lyra's temples started pulsing, as they tended to do when something was up.

People often cried to her on phones—as a former police officer, it came with the territory, and as subsequent university lecturer, arguably even more so, the dramas of young people being so much worse than everyone else's—but Olive, not so much. Hers was a charmed life since emigrating to a better country, dating "up", as in multimillionaire up, and securing a high-flying job. It had to be an attack of wedding nerves.

"Olive, take it easy. Look, whatever it is, nobody's died, right?"

"Um…" A muffled sniff.

"Is everything all right with you and Arvid?" She hated to go there, but could this possibly be cold feet on either side, two weeks before the wedding?

"It's Arvid's father." Olive's voice trembled. "H-Hedvig."

"What about him?"

"He's gone! Dead. He was on the f-ferry, and he..." Sobs wracked her friend's voice again, making her incomprehensible.

"Oh no. Oh, Olive, I'm sorry." Lyra frowned and settled her spine against an unpainted patch of wall.

Hedvig Sammland didn't often feature in their chats, but whenever he did, Olive spoke warmly of her father-in-law.

Or, future father-in-law, now late future father-in-law. Lyra tried to picture him—a vague memory emerged of a good-looking, impeccably tailored, older Nordic man.

A man could have many reasons for not returning from a ferry trip, the most obvious being that he hadn't been on the vessel at all. She needed to hear more. Gradually, Olive's breaths slowed down to the point where it seemed reasonable to get her to talk again.

"When did this happen?" Lyra asked gently.

"This afternoon. I wanted to tell you before you read about it in the papers. Ever since they found his body—"

"Wait. They found his *body?*"

"Yes, the police divers pulled him out."

"Holy shit. Oh, Olive, this is terrible. You were quite close, weren't you?"

A pause. "Yes."

Lyra grappled for the arm of the couch and sank into it. She had so many questions. Firing them off would be insensitive to Olive, though.

"There's something weird about it," Olive continued, her voice regaining some of its usual clarity. "Everyone on that ferry must have been blind, or drunk, or in on it. Nobody saw a thing. But how could they not have seen a man go overboard, Lyra? Hedvig would have put up a vicious fight. He was in good shape."

"Then how did they know? Someone had to have seen it to report it, right?"

"A boy spotted his cap floating on the water and alerted the ferry crew. Then someone said they saw him before he went out."

"Wow. Who ID-ed him?"

"What? Oh, Arvid. He's in the other room. I don't know what to say to him."

"Christ, Olive. Poor Arvid. That must have been galling for him."

"Mm. I should've gone, too, but I backed out last minute."

"I don't blame you in the slightest. You poor dears. At the worst possible time, as well. This is supposed to be a joyful time for you all. Did Hedvig have any health conditions?"

"None, fit as a fiddle."

Lyra hummed in sympathy. "Which ferry was it?"

"The 16:00 Oresund from Helsingor to Helsingborg. Literally a fifteen-minute trip."

The Oresund was a sliver of water a couple of kilometers wide—the narrowest point in the strait separating Sweden and Denmark. If she remembered correctly, it held brackish water which wasn't as lethal as salt water in terms of drowning, but then again, it was January, so if anyone fell in, there was little chance of swimming to harbor alive before freezing.

"Hedvig was what, sixty-ish?"

"Sixty-two. Sixty-three next month." Olive's voice wobbled again.

"Did the police mention that anything had been taken from him? Wallet? Briefcase?"

"No. He only had a credit card with him and a bag with some Royal Danish porcelain. They didn't take those. He had a Rolex on, but they didn't take that. We think the porcelain was our wedding present. Some elaborate, custom-made vase. Hard to tell for sure. It was in smithereens. Poor Hedvig."

"So, nothing was taken?"

"No. Just his life."

"Has anyone official suggested his death might be suspicious?"

"Nobody's telling us anything." Olive said. "The police don't want to speculate. I get that, but this is torture."

Lyra softened her tone. "Hey, I'm not surprised. Listen, how can I help? Is there anything I can do from here? Or perhaps it mightn't be a bad idea for you to come on home?"

"No, I'm staying here. Arvid needs help with the

arrangements. He's all alone. He's got the company to run as well. I have to stay. Besides, I've a full calendar to deal with, and I'll feel even worse if I let things slide." Determination had crept into Olive's voice.

"Of course."

Arvid was orphaned now, his mother having died when he was twelve, and he had no siblings, so this was going to be especially tough on him. Not only was his father gone, but the CEO of his company, too, and Arvid was probably expected to step up and become the new Sammland CEO in his most vulnerable hour.

"Is there someone else who can take the helm? Isn't there an uncle?"

"Uhm, not really. I mean, there is, but it's complicated."

Sammland AG—was a chemical and consumer goods company headquartered in Helsingborg, Sweden, run by the Sammland brothers, Hedvig and Klemens, with a Cain and Abel affinity for each other. They produced brands such as *Freshlife* shampoo and *Puritee* skin lotion. Lyra had listened to enough practice presentations on Olive's journey up to Executive VP of Beauty Care to rattle off a credible marketing pitch of her own. Yes, it was a cutthroat environment, but surely a man could take a day off when his father died-slash-got murdered? It was all terribly un-Swedish.

Lyra rose from the sofa, restless. "Who's handling it—Swedish police? Or the Danish?"

"I don't know. All our dealings have been with the Swedish police so far. But maybe Denmark's involved because some passengers were Danish, and they boarded the ferry over there." Olive's voice petered off, the mere effort of speaking seeming too much for her.

"They'll keep questioning until they get someone who saw something," Lyra said confidently.

The two police forces had cooperated on crimes before—from car chases across the Oresund bridge connecting both countries to high profile murder cases. It wasn't as though Hedvig Sammland was a nobody. He was a prominent local businessman that people would be curious about.

"I don't know." Olive let out a sigh. "Arvid overheard a journalist talking at the station. Apparently, they did round up all the passengers, like you say, but they were under so much pressure because of timetables, missed connections, and then the press hullabaloo at the harbor that they let most of them go."

"What? All of them?" This was making it seem like the police had ruled out involvement of another party, but what made them so confident?

"Well, the foreigners they took straight down to the station, of course, but the Swedes and Danes, yeah, they collected the names and addresses to contact later. Who knows if they'll even bother?"

Lyra stifled a groan. If anyone was involved, then it was more likely to be a fellow countryman than a foreigner. But speculating on this was hardly helping Olive. "Have you told your folks yet, hon?"

"Yes, I'm just off the phone to them. They're in shock. Especially Dad. He pestered me for two hours. Drove me crazy, trying to persuade me to abandon Arvid and come home, like that'll solve anything."

Lyra nodded to herself, picturing the argument only too well.

"Will you drive over and see them, Lyra, please? I can't go home any time soon, but it would help if they could see a friendly face. Just to let them know I'm OK and that things will go ahead as planned—eventually. Chat about the wedding or something normal to get them to calm down. I'd so appreciate it."

"Of course, I'll go over." She had never refused a request from Olive, and now wasn't the time to start. "But can I wait until after sunrise?"

Olive produced a sniffling chuckle which was the best Lyra could have hoped for. *Going over* entailed crossing three counties to Roscommon and dealing with Olive's parents, both in a state of agitation. And then there was Olive's brother, Liam.

"Thanks, Lyra. They'll be thrilled to see you. I can't deal with them right now. But…there was something else. I hate to ask you this, but I can't help it."

"Tell me."

"When you read the reports, could you let me know if you spot anything…out of place? You know, the way you do?"

The way you do. Ever since the Howley-Murphy case, when as a young Garda, she'd busted an international pedophile ring centered in Dublin, Lyra's civilian friends thought she was a miracle sleuth, as in, she only had to read the newspaper headlines of a case—any case—and she would solve it faster than you could say Enola Holmes.

"Sure, if I see anything out of place," she said lightly. "Um, I have to ask, what's happening with the wedding plans? Are you still going ahead?"

"Postponed, for now. I just can't."

"Hm, probably for the best."

Lyra eyed the blue chiffon monstrosity that was her bridesmaid's dress hanging in the wardrobe.

"But hold on to your dress. It will go ahead."

Lyra grimaced. If the planning was complicated, the re-planning was going to be a whole other quantum level of complexity, and it still meant she had to wear that thing. "For sure. But deal with this first. Start by putting your phone on airplane mode and trying to get some sleep."

*

After the call, Lyra reached up, grabbed her laptop from the desk, and placed it down on the newspapers. The Post-It sticker had fallen off her camera lens, probably ages ago—proof, not that she needed it—that academic life was making her sloppy in the cyber-vigilance department. The paint on her fingers had hardened to crusty scabs, like eczema spreading up her hand. She rose to scrub it off. The bedroom re-do would have to wait another while.

As a rule, a successful, wealthy man preparing to attend his only son's wedding did not commit suicide. Could he have been so careless as to topple over the side railings of a ferry, though? It wasn't an easy thing to do. Assuming it was an accident. Alternatively, if someone had attacked him, how did they manage it without being seen or heard?

Settling back down on the floor, she pulled up a browser and searched for local newspapers from southern Sweden. After her policing career had come to an abrupt end, she'd studied Germanic languages and linguistics in her first years of university, so she had enough Swedish to get the gist.

For now, she was keeping an open mind, casting a wide net, checking to see if Hedvig Sammland had any grief with anybody of late—individually, or on behalf of his company. But no court cases, litigation, or legal wrangling of note showed up. No scandals appeared in the gossip rags. All very clean—very proper newsletters, meeting memos, and success stories in the business sections. Kind of boring.

An employee was quoted, presumably before their HR department had put a blanket ban on talking to journalists, as saying, "He was a powerful man; he had to be firm with people at times, but he was nice." Another said, "He was kind, even to those at the bottom of the food chain."

The Hedvig Sammland ferry death story hadn't just hit the south—it was front page material in the national papers, too. A wealthy CEO's sudden, mysterious drowning was juicy clickbait from Kiruna at the Arctic Circle to Ystad in the south. Frustratingly, most sites were paywalled. She signed up to the best ones, hoping she'd remember to unsubscribe later.

The stories all quoted the same text from the TT news agency featuring the same photo of the *ForSea* ferry parked in Helsingborg harbor thronged by camera crews and emergency services. Most showed the same image of Hedvig Sammland, CEO, taken from the company website. He had the looks of a gracefully aging movie star—deep-set, startling, crystalline eyes, prominent cheekbones, and well-defined jawline. Not bad for sixty-two.

The consensus on the cause of death on one less reputable site, awash with disclaimers, was that the perpetrator had been a lone madman who had attempted to negotiate money from Hedvig but had gotten frustrated and somehow tossed him overboard. This was greedily taken up on a notorious internet forum for armchair sleuths where the speculation had gone way out of control. Hopefully Olive or Arvid didn't read that forum.

Two hours later, Lyra put the laptop aside and cleaned off her paint brushes to get ready for round two—yes, she had started, so she'd finish the damn room in red even if made her look weird in the eyes of the adoption agency. Amateur research on the Hedvig Sammland case was pointless. The full autopsy, witness statements, and DNA tests would sort it all out, if they hadn't already. The Swedish or Danish police would do their job. Her job was to support her best friend by supporting her family.

So, to County Roscommon she would go.

2

The next morning, with sleet clouds hanging heavily over the motorway, Lyra took the exit west from Dublin toward Roscommon. Her sleep had been fitful—unusual for her—so she felt cranky and could only imagine how badly poor Olive had slept. It seemed wrong to be heading west to Olive's parents' place while Olive herself was over in Sweden having to deal with this away from them all. There had been no phone calls from her which meant nothing new had been uncovered. No doubt she and Arvid were inundated with calls from concerned friends.

Kiltomb was a minuscule parish north of Athlone in Ireland's mid-west tucked behind some gently undulating hills. Lyra couldn't call the remote village home since her mother had moved down to Kerry five years ago, and her brother had emigrated to Sydney two years before that. Their family home had been renovated by an energetic young family of five who had bought the bungalow. So her mother had informed her, anyway. She felt no particular inclination to drive past the stone bungalow of her childhood.

The turloughs were still full of water. Winter hadn't

shaken off its mantel yet. But as the Maguire farm came into view over the crest of the low hill on the N61, the sun peeped timidly out, and it made her feel better. Lough Ree sparkled in the distance, the constant backdrop to her childhood. Every turn in the road yanked back fresh memories—friendships, dogs, bikes, schoolbags, trips to and from mass, the wonders of the local newsagents on pocket money day.

The Maguire holding consisted of a traditional farmhouse painted in grays and whites, a farmyard with a medley of sheds, and a renovated stone lodge that generated a healthy Airbnb side income—Olive's idea, of course. The fields stretched down to the protected wetlands at the shores of the lough. Half her childhood had been spent there with Olive.

Olive's parents, Pronsious and Una Maguire, were working-class farming people with upper-middle-class aspirations. Their kids hadn't disappointed them. Ella and Dermot secured cushy jobs in Dublin. Olive was doing very well for herself in Sweden. Only Liam, the eldest, had stayed at home to toil the land. In Lyra's childhood, the Maguires had been like a second family to her, but once Olive moved away, she'd had little reason to go there, especially seeing as her own mother no longer lived in the village. So, there was going to be that initial phase of awkwardness.

She parked her Kia beside Pronsious's ancient but well-maintained Subaru. He'd kept it all this time. The air was damp and smelled of peat moss burning—the scent of Western Ireland.

The front door swung open before she reached it.

"Lyra Norton. I'll be damned." Pronsious, standing in the doorway, held his arms wide. His stature was still tall and proud. His shock of once-black hair was almost white, and the lines on his craggy face had deepened and merged like a join-the-dots puzzle.

"It's been a while, indeed," Lyra said, taking his cue and playing along with the faux politeness.

"It most certainly has. Well, well, well, come on in. Here's Lyra," he hollered out to whomever was in the house and the neighbors four fields away. "There now, sit yourself down." He pointed to the faded floral settee in front of the window which was still the guest place of honor.

Lyra's gaze roamed the pale pink and cream wallpaper and landed on a gold-framed photo of Olive in her ponytailed student days holding up a trophy from the debating society. Another beside that showed her posing beside the President of Ireland, with a newspaper clipping above it reading, 'Green Award to Student Council Leader.'

Una, a small, plump woman with a serene, freckled face came in and hugged her.

"I'm not staying long. I've a lecture in the afternoon," Lyra said apologetically.

"But you've time for a cup?" Una asked.

She nodded. "Always."

"How's Mary?" Pronsious asked as Lyra settled against the cushions.

"Living life to the full. She's head of the school committee." Lyra's widowed mother was so healthy and her life so regulated that she rarely had news to report from her.

Pronsious looked faintly disappointed. "Perfect life, right?"

"Pretty much."

"And yourself?" He winked. "Married yet?"

Lyra shook her head. "My brother tells this joke, he calls me bus bait, as in, I've more chance of getting hit by a bus than getting married. I'm thirty-seven and counting. I take crosswalks seriously."

"Oh, Lyra." Una held her hand to her chest.

Pronsious seemed to be still working it out.

"But academic life is suiting me," she added. "It's quiet."

"Don't you miss getting the bad guys, though?" Pronsious asked. "And being on the news all the time?"

"I was hardly—"

"There was another one yesterday, wasn't there, Una?"

Pronsious wagged his finger at the TV in the corner of the room. "One of those chatrooms with those disgusting images. Horrific sexual abuse, they said. What did they call it...live streaming? Just...babies, and little ones. I can't fathom…"

"I know," Lyra said. "They all deserve to go to hell."

Pronsious polished his glasses. "But the Gardaí—they're slow off the mark, not like when you were there."

"I'm sure they're working hard on it. It's like whack-a-mole trying to get rid of these criminals. I was only part of a team as well."

"But it was you that made the big breakthrough and found the main guy."

Pronsious didn't seem to want to let this narrative drop.

"I was just doing my job."

Una re-entered the room with a teapot and cups and a plate with a pyramid of fruitcake slices.

Lyra used the distraction to change the topic. "So, uhm, Olive called me last night."

Una wrung her hands and sought Pronsious's gaze. "Ah, yes."

"Mm-hm?" Pronsious, with a mouthful of tea, bobbed his head up and down and winced as he swallowed.

"Yes, and I came here to offer my condolences for Olive's would-be father-in-law, Hedvig." Awkward as it was, she couldn't think of a better expression for their daughter's connection to the deceased or a better way of saying that. It sounded rehearsed.

Pronsious swatted at an invisible fly and settled back on the couch. "Sure we hardly knew him. Did we, Una? Never met the man in my life."

"No, we didn't," Una said. "Not in person." She fidgeted with her apron.

The room went silent. Lyra followed Una's cue and looked to Pronsious.

"I can't reach her on the phone at all this morning," he continued. "She has her mother all worried."

Una, sipping her tea, nodded obligingly.

"I know she'd come home in a heartbeat if she could," Lyra said. "But at the same time, there are all the arrangements to take care of first—the funeral, the—"

"I don't see why she can't come home." Pronsious's jowls quivered as he reached for cake. "They have their whole family over there to deal with such matters."

"Arvid's kind of on his own."

"Bollocks! It's our Olive that's on her own." Red blotches erupted across his cheeks. "Can't you make her come home, Lyra? She listens to you the most."

"She will, as soon as she can. I can't persuade her until she's ready."

Pronsious hummed. "She hasn't been herself at all, has she, Una?"

Una shook her head. "Not for a while now."

"How do you mean?" Lyra asked, looking from one face to the other, although she didn't expect Una to do anything but parrot Pronsious. That was simply the way they talked to outsiders.

From her own observations, Olive hadn't been any different recently. Conversations had revolved around itemizing wedding tasks—invitations, musician vetting, menu planning, dress fittings, correspondence with guests and the registry office. The only alarm Lyra had felt was at the list growing exponentially longer every time they spoke. This was all normal for Olive.

"She's what's the word now... jaded," Pronsious said. "The spark is all gone from her. She used to be happy, ready to take on the world. The past year she's been staring into space for so long that I have to I wonder if she's turned to marble."

The light in the room changed, and she heard a creak behind her. She turned. A man had entered the doorway, silhouetted in the morning light. Liam. Tall and stockier than she remembered, there were threads of silver in his hair, and his face seemed craggier around the cheeks and chin—hints of his father there. The tobacco-brown eyes—unique in the family—burned with the same intelligence as ever.

She held his gaze until Pronsious's voice interrupted with a loud, "There's himself."

"Hi Liam," she said lightly.

"Hi Lyra. Alright?"

"Yeah. You?"

"Mm. Heard you talking about Olive there." Liam directed this at his father, who was looking between them with a sly twist of his mouth.

"Listening in, were ya?" Pronsious asked.

"Didn't have much choice." Liam moved inches into the room. "What do you make of it, Lyra?"

Lyra shook her head. "It's terrible, of course. An awful shock to Olive and Arvid. It's so sad when this should have been a joyful occasion for you all—"

"But what do you think happened?" Liam broke in.

Lyra looked around. The intensity of their focus suggested they didn't want her comforting as much as they wanted her answers. To them, once a cop always a cop.

She reached for her cup of tea. "It's not my position to say. I'm not on the case. I've no information."

"But just between us," Liam pressed.

Damn it, if he was going to ask such awkward questions, then he could at least commit to coming into the room, but he seemed only too happy to linger on the threshold while he threw out the questions. She got the impression that their mid-morning routine rarely involved everyone sitting around together in this room drinking tea.

She took a long sip.

"Go on there," Pronsious said. "Give us the professional opinion."

It was manifestly *un*professional to speculate with the little information she had, but if it made them feel better, she would. As they didn't seem close to Hedvig, she didn't have to be overly subtle. "I have my doubts that it was an accident. I just don't see it."

That elicited eager nods all around.

"On the other hand, there was no apparent attempt to steal from him, so it doesn't seem to have been some random attack, either—a mugging for money or whatever. There's no clear motive at this point. Even if we were to assume foul play, it's darn near impossible to see how.

"The police are still interviewing passengers," she went on. "But no suspects have been singled out yet. That's all I got from what Olive said and from reading publicly available information. If I do see anything, I promise to raise the issue with the Swedish police."

She looked at each of their faces in turn, bearing various degrees of skepticism. "What do you know about Arvid's father?"

"Not much," Una said. "We were going to meet him for the first time the day before the wedding—a family evening, to get acquainted." She gave a self-conscious wiggle. "I was a bit nervous at meeting him, but I got used to that idea, and now it doesn't feel right that we won't be meeting him after all."

Pronsious snorted. "Waste of money, the whole shebang. We can't get a refund or postpone the flights. It's an absolute disgrace."

Lyra put down her cup. "Sometimes the small print on airline reservations is purposely hard to navigate. I could look into it for you. You should at least be able to get vouchers for replacement flights." The Maguires didn't travel outside of their own county, let alone Ireland. They probably didn't even have passports until Olive's wedding forced the issue. "When exactly had you planned to travel over?"

"Next week. And I may yet." Pronsious looked pointedly at Una, who looked at the floor, shaking her head.

"I think a girl needs her father at a time like this," he added.

Lyra mentally recoiled. Pronsious tramping cluelessly

around Southern Sweden was the last thing Olive needed. Pronsious believed himself to be independent, but he didn't know what he didn't know. Starting with the fact that to get to where Olive lived in Helsingborg Sweden, the nearest airport was actually in Copenhagen, Denmark, so there were border checks to navigate. She glanced at Liam, who was studying the carpet, apparently having discovered whatever his mother had found so fascinating there. Some help.

Pronsious broke the silence. "Olive's done fierce well for herself, though, hasn't she? She could find a job anywhere else in Sweden now. Nothing tying her down."

"Ah, but she's got no plans to move," Liam said, returning to life.

"I'm just saying she could, son, hypothetically speaking." Pronsious's volume rose. It sounded like an argument they'd had before, more than once. "She could choose to walk away from it all, and I wouldn't blame her in the slightest."

Lyra frowned. Olive had no intentions of leaving Sammland AG let alone Arvid himself, and Hedvig's death made no difference there. Pronsious was deluded if he thought his daughter was fundamentally unhappy. She was thriving in her own high-powered, control freakery way. He was probably projecting his own dislike of Arvid onto the situation. Olive had mentioned that they didn't get on terribly well.

Liam flashed her a brief look and exited the doorframe. The sunlight came flooding back in. Where was he running off to? And what was that look supposed to mean?

"Of course, she could get a job anywhere," Lyra said. "But I can't see her ever leaving Arvid. She's been happy and excited about the wedding, like any bride. You should see how much she's throwing herself into the details." She forced a chuckle. "We spent literally hours deciding on the perfect floral arrangements for the tables. She even insisted on doing a live stream of the bridesmaids' dress fittings last Saturday."

Una nodded, her dimpled smile returning.

"Hmph." Pronsious slumped back against the cushions and took a piece of fruit cake from the tray, chomping it noisily. "She should come home straight away with all this going on. For all we know, there's a what-do-you-call-it—a psycho killer on the loose."

"Oh, no, no, no." Una splayed her stubby fingers against her chest. She looked at her husband reproachfully. "Don't be saying such things, my love."

It was a rare, wifely admonishment, and it brought all conversation to a crashing halt again.

"It's very unlikely to be anything like that," Lyra said in her most placating voice. "I mean, there may be people who've thought about it. You don't get to be rich and powerful without making some enemies along the way. However, we've no reason to believe that he didn't just have a heart attack or slip on the wet deck or something. I hope that the investigation gets wrapped up quickly and that Arvid and Olive can put it behind them and move on with their lives."

"Please God," Una agreed, her smile reappearing. "Arvid's a good boy deep down, I know he is. Don't you think so, too, Lyra?"

"Yes, absolutely."

Olive had first shown the handsome blond Swede off a week before the engagement on a trip to Dublin. He might have been a little stiff and formal, but he treated Olive like a princess, and he'd managed to sit through a conversation of girly talk and feign interest. On subsequent occasions, he'd handled Lyra with an easy familiarity without being effusively friendly or striving for deeper connection. Olive had said that was about as good as it got with Swedes.

"Were you there when you all went to Youghal for that boating trip?" Pronsious asked.

"No dear, that was Hugo," his wife said gently. "That was before Olive got her promotion. That's how she had all that time off."

"And I wasn't there for that," Lyra confirmed. That was

the year her life had been turned upside down because of what happened to her own ex, David. Social events had been out of the question, so much so that she missed out on meeting Olive's charming ex, Hugo.

She rose, glancing at her watch. "Thanks for the tea. I'd best be going now, or I'll be late for my students."

"Oh, of course." Una leapt up. "You're great for coming, Lyra. It's been lovely to see you."

Pronsious followed her to the hall. "Will you come back when she's home? Keep her company? Keep her spirits up."

"I will, of course."

"We'll be holding you to that. Take care now."

Waving, Lyra walked the paved path between shrubberies toward her car. In her periphery, she detected movement behind a tree. She froze. Her hackles rose. She braced herself to flee, not taking her eyes off the trees.

"Just me." Liam emerged from the shadow of a double-trunked hawthorn. "Christ, twitchy, aren't you?"

"Comes with the job," she said. Then she realized her mistake. Where was her head? In which decade? She could almost feel the press of the stab vest against her chest.

He looked at her curiously. "Why? Do students sneak up on you and demand better grades?"

She decided to play along. "The operative verb is whine."

"Hah. Uhm, sorry about…in there." He nodded back to the house. "Dad thinks he knows best for Olive, needless to say."

"He's worried about her."

Liam dug his hands deeper into his jacket pockets. "I think he always assumed that she'd get sense one of these years, come home, get married, and settle here. Not that there was any chance of that happening. The wedding was pushing his face in it. He'd just about come around to accepting reality when this shite happened. I bet in his mind, it's a deliberate act of God."

"Right, I'll add that to the list," she said. "Makes about

as much sense as anything else."

"So, you've no idea?" He had a conspiratorial glint in his eye.

"None beyond what I said in there."

Liam nodded. "I feel guilty for not being close enough to Arvid to call him up and tell him how sorry I am, or better still, go over there and get him drunk. I'm not even invited to his stag party if he's having one."

"He's not. And if it makes you feel any better, we're distant, too," she said. "I've only talked to Olive about this, not him."

He winced. "I sent him a text. Shameless, I know. We're just not on that level. Hugo was a lot more fun."

"Exes usually are," she said. "Especially those that haven't stuck around to deal with much."

He looked away for long enough that she suspected she'd hit a nerve. "Yeah, I don't really see myself as your ex."

She grinned at how defensive he sounded. "You don't?"

"No. It was a non-starter so soon after the David thing. What technically didn't start, didn't finish."

She met his gaze again. "That's a charitable way of looking at it."

"It was a difficult time." He settled against a wooden fence and cleared his throat. "And as for Arvid, I don't mind that he's a bit hard to get to know. It's more the effect he has on Olive that bothers me. She's always a bit snappy these days when I call her. She wasn't like that when she first went over."

"That was fifteen years ago. Few of us get chirpier as we age."

"Has she been like that with you?"

"Not really, no. Then again, maybe I haven't noticed because we talk so often. She's dealing with big decisions and a lot of job responsibility."

Liam drummed his fingers against the fence. A frown appeared then cleared again. "For what it's worth, she did mention Arvid's uncle, Klemens, quite a bit recently."

"Ah, the Cain and Abel situation. Mm, she mentioned that in passing."

"In passing? What do you talk about?"

"Men."

Pink seeped into his cheeks, or perhaps it was her imagination. As it happened, they had discussed him, too, but that was a long time ago.

"Just kidding," she said. "We talk guest RSVP lists, cancellations, dress-fittings, cake decorations, florists, makeup rehearsals. Come on, the wedding is in two weeks. Or was meant to be."

He held up his hands in surrender. "It must be a nightmare being her maid of honor."

She chuckled. "Yeah, but imagine being maid of honor to someone disorganized, especially at a time like this."

"Fair point. Anyway, beyond the wedding malarkey, I think work's getting her down. Whenever she's home, she's all tensed up, even when she doesn't bring him."

"Him, being Arvid?"

"Yeah. When he comes here, we're all tensed up."

On reflection, Olive usually came home alone. She'd never explained why. The implied excuse was that Arvid was too busy, but it was clearly more than that.

"I wish she'd come home," Liam said. "It would be the best thing for her."

He sounded all too much like his father. The patriarchal streak irked her.

"I'm sure she knows what's best for herself," she said.

"Hm."

Like his father, Liam clearly had difficulties accepting that Olive may have a support network in Sweden that catered to her emotional needs as well as, or better than, her own family.

She jangled her keys. "Don't worry. I'm going to keep a good eye on her and make sure she's doing OK at all times, and to see to it that we can postpone the ceremony without stressing her out."

Liam's face broke into a smile. "I appreciate it. We all do. It's a lot of extra hassle for you and,"—he slid her a look— "I suppose you have a life?"

"Are you a-digging for info, there, Liam Maguire?"

His chin bunched up into a sheepish smile. "Sorry I asked. It's been years since we talked."

"Five, to be precise. I was here when I was helping my mam to move that time."

"Ah, yes."

She debated whether to tell him about her current personal situation. Olive had been sworn to secrecy, a promise she'd obviously held. But now that things were moving forward, she could afford to relax a little. If she and the Maguires were going to be mingling at the wedding soon, it may even be for the best to broach this in advance. "Actually, I'm trying for adoption. I have a first interview on Monday to determine if I fit the requirements to be a parent. Crazy, huh?"

Liam seemed to lose control of his facial muscles. "But...why?"

"Just something I want to do."

She waited for the *shouldn't you find a man first?* Or, *shouldn't you try to have one yourself?* –as in, the questions that always followed that admission.

He remained silent, biting his bottom lip. Perhaps his patriarchalism didn't extend that far.

"That'll keep you busy."

"Out of trouble," she said with a grimace.

"Is that what you want—the quiet life?"

She shrugged. "No one's getting any younger."

"True." He rubbed the back of his neck. "Look, can we—would you mind if we—stayed in touch? About Olive, I mean. About this whole thing? You never know, you may find out something before we do." He pulled out his phone—a battered looking Nokia—and thumbed the screen. "Look, I'm 087-"

"Oh. Are we…exchanging numbers?"

He shrugged. "You have my old number. We're just updating."

"Updating." She opened her contacts and entered his digits under "Liam." The old profile photo was there of a smiling, younger Liam—it also needed updating.

She rattled off her number to him.

He typed it in and shoved the phone into his jacket pocket. "If something develops, call me?"

"Yeah, I want to stay on top of this until it's solved." She was surprised at how easily that popped out of her mouth. "But understand I'm only the messenger," she added.

"Understood."

"Good," she said, backing away toward the car before things could get any more awkward. "It was great to…update."

She got in and slammed the door and reversed out, avoiding looking in the rear view at him.

*

Back on the motorway, she calculated she had two hours until the lecture on copyright law. She'd just about make it if traffic stayed at this level.

She hadn't managed to comfort the Maguires much, if at all. Then again, comfort hadn't been what they wanted. They wanted answers. She did, too. Starting with: was Olive more miserable than she was letting on? Why was Arvid so tensed up? Why did Hedvig and his brother fight so much? And what the hell happened to Hedvig on that ferry anyway?

It was starting to bug her. How could there be no answers to a man falling overboard on ferry between Denmark and Sweden? A niggling voice whispered that the answer was there—somewhere inside the Sammland empire, and that only somebody with close links to the family had a hope in hell of uncovering the truth. Of course, she couldn't get involved. Once next week rolled around, she could be one step closer to being a parent of a squawking, needy infant that demanded her attention around the clock.

But…she still had this weekend as a carefree, non-attached individual. One weekend to root out the source of potential trouble in her best friend's life. It was arrogance on her part, expecting to gain an insight into a murder—or whatever it was—but what the hell, her best friend needed her. Olive had been there for her in the worst of times—after David, so she wasn't going to let her down now.

Already she knew she was going search flights to Copenhagen after her lecture today.

Call it her duty as a best friend.

3

Copenhagen Airport was subdued as Lyra got in at 1 p.m. the next day, mid-January being a quiet time in Denmark seeped in post-Christmas blues and dark, freezing days, which accounted for the dirt-cheap last-minute flight from Dublin. Passengers on outbound journeys were bundled up in puffer jackets, hats, and scarves. It amused Lyra to watch the optimistic incoming passengers saunter in with their trendy hoodies and even a Hawaii shirt or two. Once they got a blast of that icy eastern wind outside the revolving glass doors, they'd learn to bundle up.

Nobody knew she was coming here—and that was on purpose. Catch people by surprise if you want information. Her first boss, DC Tony Mullen, had taught her that. Someone had to know more than they were saying. Not only on the ferry—the Swedish or Danish police would take care of that—but among those closest to Hedvig; his colleagues and family. That was where she came in.

She picked up the car rental and navigated her way out of Kastrup's traffic circles muttering, "Drive on the right, drive on the right." All the focus on driving Continental-style left no mental room for the case. She followed the signs for Malmo and the Oresund Bridge linking Denmark and Sweden. She could equally have driven up through the island, Zealand, and taken the Oresund ferry across to Sweden, but under the circumstances, it was better to avoid that one.

Cruising across the majestic bridge, she put the local Danish radio on full blast—the guttural, talking parts were almost indecipherable, but the music was good—she shook her hair out and felt like police detective Saga Norén. Half way across, the Welcome to Sweden sign greeted her on EU-signage, followed promptly by the border passport check.

Of everyone, she was most curious to meet Arvid in his native habitat. He was ambitious, like Olive, and passionate about his work and his two hobbies—sailing and hunting. She'd been initially surprised when Olive broke up with the fun-loving Hugo and let herself be swept off her feet by Arvid, but within weeks, Olive had started to speak of concrete plans in the future, and that was when he turned into a serious contender.

Olive and her were very different and so was their taste in men. Olive was Hollywood Irish with her red-gold hair, lively green eyes, and waif-like figure. Lyra was what would be called Reality Irish—dark auburn hair, hazel eyes, and a figure that was, well, robust. They'd been friends for thirty-three years ever since the first day of primary school when Lyra, aged four, had told Olive, aged four, that it was OK, they could run away because she knew the way home, and Olive had dutifully informed Lyra that nobody had to go anywhere because she had planned out what games they would play at lunchtime. Instant bonding.

The flat plains of the Malmo region gave way to gently undulating Scanian landscape—hills with contentedly grazing horses and pretty wooden houses straight out of Astrid Lindgren. It was all picturesque, but compared to Ireland, it was like someone had placed a gray filter over the trees and grass.

An hour's drive later, she checked into the Clarion Hotel in Helsingborg, a process she managed to her satisfaction in rusty Swedish. On her way to the elevators, she liked the look of the velvet lounge chairs, so she sank into one of them and called Olive.

Olive picked up on the second ring. "Oh, hey Lyra."

"Before you say anything, I want to tell you I'm here in Helsingborg. For the weekend."

There was a pause. Then a gasp. "Oh my God, you're here?"

"Yep."

"You shouldn't have. I definitely wasn't expecting this. OK, maybe I was hoping it deep down."

Lyra smiled at the sudden energy in her friend's voice. "I sensed you could use some moral support. I won't be in your way. I'm staying in the Clarion."

"You won't be in the way. Listen, I'm at the office. We had to go in and deal with the staff—you don't want to know. I've a bunch of things to wrap up before the weekend, but do you want to come over here?"

That was music to her ears, as it offered an opportunity to snoop. "If it's OK?"

"Of course. Plug in Fältarpsvägen 500 in your navi. Just tell Lasse at reception, and I'll come down for you. You'll need to sign in and collect a badge."

Lyra checked her watch. "I'll be there in an hour."

*

Lyra was pleased to see the hotel had given her the twin-bed room she'd requested. She dumped her suitcase on the bed nearest the window and got busy turning the second bed into a makeshift case board, spreading out the A4 print-outs and mug shots across the bed-cover. It was an old habit from her policing days, and it helped her to think. Of course, it may all be for nothing if it turned out he had died of natural causes or tripped over his shoelace or something, but her gut feeling was telling her there was foul play involved.

Hedvig's mug shot was in the middle, surrounded by images of Klemens, the brother, Arvid, the son, and Olive, the daughter-in-law-to-be. Everyone was a suspect until proven innocent, and that included Olive herself.

She looked down at Olive's black-and-white image. "Sorry, Olive, I know you don't belong there, but you know how it goes."

Klemens, the brother, had, in theory, the same motive as Arvid, the son, namely, become the immediate CEO of Sammland AG. It wasn't inconceivable that Klemens felt the top job ought to be his. Also, in several newspapers she'd read about a spat inside the company due to environmental policies. Hardly a reason for murder, but context was everything.

If the Swedish police were doing their job, Hedvig's computers would have been taken by now and his phone records pulled, but if she was lucky, she could scavenge some scraps by asking some IT employee to recover backed up data. Beyond that, her main mission was simply to talk and get a feel for how the key people related to Hedvig, and to keep an open mind.

*

Sammland AG, like most Swedish industrial buildings, was low and long, constructed in nondescript, off-white bricks that blended in with the sky. The only color that popped was the cyber-blue of the window frames and the signs. It was the company's brand hue which suggested cleanliness and modernity, as Olive had informed her. They'd paid a branding company twenty thousand Euros to select it for them. Lyra had laughed and asked who needed law enforcement when people allowed themselves to be robbed voluntarily.

There was no security gate, so she parked and entered

the glass atrium at the front of the building. A refreshing aroma of something fruity hung in the air—watermelon perhaps?

Judging by the employees sporting trendy haircuts, muted colors, and jeans, the Scandi aesthetic was in full force. Her faux leather jacket, black skinny jeans, and dark green turtleneck fit in perfectly, as she'd anticipated. People huddled in small groups and spoke in subdued tones, with much shaking of heads. Clearly, this was a group of employees coming to terms with the mysterious death of their chief.

She walked right up to the front desk which was back-lit and under-lit in the same cyber blue. A mid-twenties guy with a curly, red beard manned the desk.

"Lasse?" she asked. "Olive Maguire is expecting me."

He made a "aw," sound, which Lyra remembered was the Swedish abbreviation for *Ja*, yes, which was apparently too long. He took her name and email with glacial speed.

"Thank you, uh, Lyra. I shall let Olive know." He pressed his desk phone and drawled out in Swedish, *"Vi har en Lyra Norton här i receptionen."* He pronounced Lyra as two stressed syllables, making her name sound dramatic, like a super villain.

He swung back to her. "You shall need a security card."

He clacked on his keyboard. *"Legitimation?"*

She handed him her passport. "I need access to everywhere."

"Everywhere...?" he frowned.

"Everywhere. I'm helping Olive and Arvid with a full professional services audit." Which was complete bullshit, but he seemed more anxious to return to playing Hitman Sniper Assassins on his phone than having a protracted discussion.

"Aw." He nodded and got busy clacking again.

Lyra regarded the décor. Massive back-lit posters depicted happy families splashing about in baths and showers, creating froth that was as bubbly as their lives.

Behind those, sexier ones were on display with supermodel types showing a good deal more skin, advertising more expensive body lotions.

Olive appeared at the double doorway in a body-hugging tan suit, delicate purple scarf, and pointy-toed ankle boots. Her famed red hair was tucked away in a prim bun. From far away, she could have been the same eighteen-year-old Lyra had shared an apartment with in their first year of college. As she came closer, taking elegant, firm strides, the fine lines around her eyes and shadows under her cheeks hinted at her real age and her recent bereavement.

"Hey!" Olive's greeting worked equally as an Irish "hey" or a more formal Swedish *"hej"*.

"Hey."

They hugged.

"You look great." Olive pulled back to inspect her, much like Liam had done, only she was more obvious about it.

"So do you," Lyra lied.

Her friend was becoming scrawny, and it didn't suit her. The hollows under her cheekbones made her look old, not glamorous. Her head seemed too big for her neck.

"Wedding diet...you know?" Olive grimaced. "At least I can lay off that for a while. Anyhow, Liam said you went over to them—thanks so much, Lyra."

"Don't mention. I was happy to."

"How were they?"

"Your father seemed quite upset. Your mam was fine. Liam was...Liam."

Olive exhaled. "Yes. Come on, let's head to my office where we can talk."

"Hang on, I'll grab my wee blue card here."

Lyra smiled at Lasse as he laboriously attached the card to a lanyard. Finally, he handed her the security card. Thanking him, she nicked a branded USB stick from a bowl full of them, seeing as it was just sitting there—*You never know when it might come in handy*.

Olive led the way through into a spacious corridor. The

walls on both sides were lined with more attention-grabbing ads for hygiene products—body scrubs, face masks, face scrubs, body masks, and a cornucopia of conditioners. Every body shape was represented, in skin tones from dark to light, and everything in-between, including one featuring two black women with white patches over their faces and shoulders.

"Two percent of the population have vitiligo," Olive explained. "It develops when melanin-producing cells are damaged, though no one knows why."

"I have learned something new today," Lyra remarked.

"Indeed. Here we go." Olive pointed into an office with her name and title on the door.

Executive VP Beauty Care. It was space-age minimal, mostly grays with accents in cyber blue. A white, faux leather sofa sat against the wall—an area for casual meetings. It felt like stepping into a dentist's office and did nothing to represent Olive, who loved fey florals in warm colors and who in their childhood had an entire bedroom decked out in Holly Hobbie patchwork and lace. This felt a lot more like Arvid's aesthetics.

Now they were alone, Lyra felt she could relax. "Come here." She hugged Olive tightly. "Are you OK?"

Olive looked away, shaking her head. "No, no, I'm so not." Then the façade crumbled—her face went lax, her rigid stance slackened. Clasping her arms around her torso, she lowered herself down onto the sofa.

"Poor thing. Come on, tell me." Lyra took a seat beside her and laid a hand on her shoulder.

Olive exhaled a long breath. "It's the wedding and everything. I just wanted to get it over with, you know? Have the family over, get it done, and then settle back into it." She stared up at the ceiling as if willing gravity to pull her tears back into their ducts. "Oh Lyra, everything's tainted."

Lyra hummed sympathetically. This was the stress talking. On the list of the worst last minute wedding planning disasters, the death of the father-in-law was right up there.

She decided to change the subject. "I just decided to come. Nobody knows I'm here."

Olive's eyes widened, but then she nodded.

"It's only for the weekend."

"I appreciate it. Did you—did you find out anything?"

"Hey, I just got here. All I can do is poke around like a child in an attic before Christmas."

Olive gave her a wan smile. "And I seem to remember you doing that."

"Of course. Not only my own attic—yours, too."

Olive's smile lit up at the memory, but it faded quickly, her gaze darting around as if enumerating items on a to-do list.

"You OK?"

Olive straightened. "Oh yes, of course." But her eyes had lost focus, staring into the middle distance.

"You knew him well," Lyra prompted. "He was your boss and future father-in-law."

Olive sighed. Her hands gripped the sofa seat, squeezing it. "He is sorely missed. We had the staff meeting today, and the employees are all disorientated, and they have a billion questions, and there are all these conspiracy theories floating around. It's borderline toxic. And everything's on hold. I'm going through the motions for their sake, but I can't work. Arvid's clearing up some essential contractual stuff with the legal team, but once he's done with that he's going home."

"It must be particularly hard on him."

"Mm, it's hard," she said tersely.

Lyra didn't press further. She knew what losing a father suddenly was like, and she didn't want to dwell. Instead, she gazed out at fields and a distant golf course—a bucolic view for an industrial office. Under normal circumstances, she'd feel proud of her friend for having made it so high in the corporate world, but right now, she wouldn't want to be in

Olive's shoes.

Olive pulled out a compact from a secret pocket inside her blazer and inspected her makeup in the tiny mirror, dabbing translucent powder on her cheeks and under her red eyes. She gave her reflection a critical frown and snapped the compact shut. "All right then. Why don't I give you the grand tour?"

"I don't need a grand tour. I'm happy just to talk to specific people without them getting a big introduction to me first, if you know what I mean."

"Then let's do that." Olive rose and led the way out of the office.

A tall, blonde woman approached them. Olive rattled off an instruction to her in fluent, tonal Swedish.

"You're fluent now," Lyra remarked when the woman had walked on again. "I could just about follow that."

"Yes, I've had the full immersion treatment. They stopped talking English to me in my second year. I'm still trying to master the tones, though. Work in progress."

"Sounds perfect to me. What do you and Arvid speak privately?"

"English, mainly. He likes to keep it up for international business purposes."

"How romantic," Lyra said.

"Hah, yes."

They had come into a quiet section of the building, devoid of employees. Olive paused at a minimalist painting on the wall that she must have seen countless times. "Normally, we'd invite you over for dinner tonight, but under the circumstances..."

"I don't need a red carpet, Olive. Not while you're swamped with funeral arrangements and a police inquiry."

"Yes, though I must say it's been quiet on that front." Olive didn't sound pleased or annoyed.

"What have they done so far?" Lyra asked, trying to better gauge her friend's mood.

Normally, Olive would be on top of this, badgering the

police to produce results faster, or at the very least, complaining of their inefficiency and detailing it with gusto. Then again, she was probably overwhelmed.

"They took Hedvig's laptop and paper files from his office." Olive prodded her dainty front teeth against her bottom lip. "I don't know what they were looking for."

"They likely don't, either. It's just procedure."

They had reached another security door.

"Allow me," Lyra said, pressing her card to it. It opened with a satisfying click. "How was Arvid when he came back from identifying the body?"

"Calm. Taciturn."

"And certain it was his father?"

"God, yes." Olive wrung her hands. "No doubt whatsoever."

Lyra nodded. Olive herself was being strangely reticent. Perhaps it had been a mistake to come here, because the usual method of talk therapy didn't seem to be working. Too soon? Or maybe such a conversation needed to happen outside of corporate walls. At a bar, say, or in Olive's own living room. Nevertheless, she had to extract some basic facts before she gave up.

"Did the police question you both yet?"

"Yes, they took all the details. Who was where, when, *et cetera.*"

"And…" Lyra lowered her voice though the corridor was empty. "Where were you when it happened?" She tried not to use her old cop tone of voice.

Olive blinked rapidly. She stared at Lyra. "Right here, of course. Same as Arvid. I didn't even know Hedvig was out of office."

"I'd imagine a CEO is pretty hard to keep track of. He must have a slew of appointments all over the place every day, right?"

"Not Hedvig. He liked to stay in the building most of the time if he could help it."

They'd come to a junction, and Olive pointed toward the

right.

"So, leaving the office and hopping over to Helsingor was actually unusual for him, would you say?"

Olive bobbed her head vigorously. "Very much so."

"OK, hypothetically, if someone were to have had a hand in his death, have you any ideas as to who?" Lyra tried to adopt an offhand voice. "I know it's a weird question, but hey, you know me."

Olive straightened her neck scarf. "No clue. Sorry. It's mindboggling that it might be someone he knew."

"What about Hedvig's brother?"

"Klemens?" Olive scoffed. "No. Just no. It's true they fought a lot, but he's family."

My point exactly.

They had entered a slightly more luxurious section of the building with polished wood and abstract paintings that looked like originals. A faint whiff of expensive cologne and coffee lingered in the air. Gold plaques hung beside each door bearing the titles CEO and CFO—the international acronyms of power.

"The C-suite?" Lyra asked.

"Yes."

Lyra lingered by a glass cabinet displaying vintage cleaning products. "All right, here's what I'm going to do over the weekend if I can get your blessing on it. I'm going to try to talk to all employees who have been in contact with Hedvig recently. Should anyone ask, tell them I'm a friend of yours, working as your, um, professional services auditor."

Olive produced a wan smile. "Whatever that's supposed to be."

"I'll wing it. I'll also need to talk to whomever has access to his appointments."

"Mm. That would be Berit, the Admin Coordinator, and Arvid."

"Perfect, let's start there."

"Let's start where?" A man in a gray cashmere sweater

and blue jeans appeared out of nowhere behind them. His ash-blond, wavy hair framed his delicate face with high cheekbones and the kind of eyes that Lyra could imagine staring moodily into a distant horizon. Almost cyber blue.

"Hej Arvid," she said.

4

"Hej again, Lyra."

Arvid shook hands with her in the perfunctory Swedish fashion. His grip was firm, dry, and cool. His gaze followed her unabashedly as she resumed her position by the wall. He moved in close beside Olive. Sadness lingered in his slightly hunched stance and the dark semicircles under the eyes.

"We were talking about where Lyra should start her investigation," Olive said, clearly feeling his question required an answer.

"Informal investigation," Lyra emphasized.

Arvid fixed her with his direct gaze. "Start with me then."

Lyra hesitated. She'd rather warm him up first. She only had one chance at this, and she didn't have enough facts yet to catch him out on a lie.

"How about later?" Olive said. "I'm sure you're busy, Honey."

Arvid dragged his fingers through his hair. "Yes, my love, but this should not be delayed."

"Lyra literally just got here."

"It's fine," Lyra said. "Let's do this."

"Good. Come with me to my father's office," he said in the voice of someone used to having his orders followed.

Olive, apparently sensing dismissal, said, "Fine. You two go on then. Catch you later."

Lyra followed Arvid, slowing down her normal fast walk to keep in pace with his strides. Arvid had a caustic edge that reminded her of several former police colleagues. Here was a man she could talk straight with.

"My sincere condolences for your father," she said, feeling it was somewhat belated.

"Yes, thank you." Arvid stopped, then continued walking. "What can I say? He's gone and I have to accept it. I wake up, and then I wish I hadn't. I've never been this way before. Everything seems stale, and flat, and useless without him. And then I'm supposed to shake it off and play the same old politics? I owe it to my father to get to the bottom of this, even if it kills me."

Again, he came to a standstill and stared at Lyra in a way that few Irish people would dare to do. "Olive tells me you're good. Are you? Or was that just talk?"

She blinked. "Depends on what you mean by good."

"You solved that big pedophile case in Ireland."

"That was a long time ago. Plus, this case is different. I'm here as support to Olive and as a favor to the Maguire family. Please don't expect anything beyond that. I'm not a cop anymore."

"I understand. I have no experience with this sort of thing. But I can get you into any office here, IT department, CCTV recordings, wherever you think will be useful. Even if you're only doing an informal investigation as you say, I want to help."

"Do you think any of that would be useful? It happened on a ferry."

He didn't answer for several moments. "Here's where he spent most of his time."

"Come on, Arvid. What are you trying to say?"

Arvid hovered outside the door with the gold plaque,

HEDVIG SAMMLAND, CEO as if reluctant to open. Perhaps he felt the ghost of his father lingered within.

He gave a sad shrug and fingered the plaque. "Getting killed on a ferry was rather ironic."

"Why ironic?"

"Because he never went anywhere. Except the golf course." He pushed the door in. Lyra followed him inside to the impeccable office with soft taupe carpet, wooden wall paneling, a large pine desk, and neatly stacked shelves. Gold-framed photos adorned every surface. Old-fashioned and elegant.

"And yet he'd been in Denmark to pick up a wedding present for you," Lyra prompted.

Arvid took the seat behind the desk and motioned for Lyra to sit opposite. "That's it, you see. My father doesn't do things like that. Didn't. Why would he? I don't need a gift. I need him to be here."

The raw pain in his voice sent a wave of empathy through her. "What do you think happened?"

"All I can think of is that somebody must have been following him. Probably somebody that was paid to do so. Either that or somebody forced him to take that trip somehow, and he walked right into a trap."

"Assuming the latter, who might have such power of influence over him?"

He brushed a speck of dust off the desk top with his forefinger. "Nobody on the planet could touch him. When you have high principles, you are immune to that sort of thing."

Pride shone in the depths of his blue eyes.

"Arvid," she said gently. "I don't know how many opportunities we'll have to talk in private." She paused to let that sink in. People reacted differently when assured they were speaking in complete confidence—without a spouse or partner around. "If there's any aspect of your father's dealings that I should know about, no matter how trivial it may seem, or potentially sensitive, please tell me and it will stay strictly confidential. It may help the case."

"I appreciate that, yes. Of course, though, I hate to speculate without facts. There is enough of that going on already. Gossip from all sides."

"Yes, it must be annoying," she said, hoping to catch up on this gossip soon. Gossip often held a strand of truth.

His wavering gaze suggested he needed more reassurance, but not too much more.

"I'm here to find out what happened, who killed your father, and to make sure he pays," she said. "I'm sure Olive told you my story. Some bastards robbed my father of his life savings. I joined the force because of that. Eventually, I got them and I made them pay."

"Yes, she told me about that." Arvid ran his fingers though his hair. "She also told me about your boyfriend. Did you make them pay, too?"

Lyra looked away. "No."

He exhaled. "I'm sorry," he said in a kinder voice. "If I were to say anything, I'd say start looking at Klemens."

"Klemens?"

"Yes, my uncle. He's happy this happened. He's moving in fast, using the opportunity to boost his own position, to steal it all from me in my weakest hour. You see, he and *Far*...I mean, my father...have always had differences of opinion."

"Call him *far* if it feels more natural. I do speak a little Swedish."

He nodded. "They had always been rivals, even in school, that's what *farmor* says."

"Your grandmother?" Olive had mentioned her years ago but not lately.

"Yes, she's in a nursing home. She's ninety-six and doesn't know what's going on in the world."

"I see. Well, sibling rivalry is commonplace. But to actually take pleasure in a sibling's death—that's another thing entirely. Are you sure your uncle isn't simply dealing with it in his own way?"

He stiffened. "You don't know what it's been like." He rose from the chair, and strode around the room, raising his arms high, mimicking throttling someone. "For years and years."

"I'm trying to get a sense of it," she said, shrinking in her chair.

He spread his palms. "Question him then. The police don't seem to have the time or inclination to do it."

"Oh, I intend to." She knew better than to comment on the Swedish police's competence. That said, she was beginning to wonder why they hadn't at least taken Klemens in for questioning yet.

Arvid let out a pained breath and returned to the desk, pressing the heel of his hand against his forehead. "What's taking them so long? Who *för fan* did it? What do you think? It couldn't really be Klemens, could it? Why would he? After all these years of fighting? That would be ridiculous. He should have done it in the beginning in that case and saved himself all that trouble."

He'd used the worst Swedish swear words she knew, *fan*, the devil—laughably mild by Irish standards—and he'd contradicted himself. This was good; emotional, confused people tended to let things slip.

"Tell me what they fought about," she said softly, perusing the photographs on the wall of Hedvig with various prominent members of society.

"A lot of things. Everything. Mainly, I suppose, the handling of microplastics waste."

"The Baltic Sea microplastics pollution scandal?"

That had been a feature of most news articles, piling new scandal upon old, as news outlets never failed to do. Microplastics traceable to Sammland products had been found in large quantities in the Baltic Sea. Lyra was no marine biologist, but she knew that the tiny balls of plastic were bad news for the fish and other sea creatures. Various EU countries had proposed bans on their manufacture, but they had yet to come into effect. Meanwhile, fish in the

Baltic were choking on them.

Arvid's jaw tightened. "We followed all regulations."

"Mm, no doubt. Bear with me for a moment. How did your father and your uncle disagree on this?"

He let out a harried breath. "Klemens wanted a complete and rapid overhaul of the products, our bestselling ones, the bread and butter of our business. We—Father and I, we felt we could adapt and improve, gradually, conservatively, without the brand damage, or the job losses. Our manufacturing plant is in a dirt-poor region in Norrbotten, and it employs fifteen percent of the residents of a small town up there. Many families depend on the income. You see, people often forget that saving the environment can destroy communities."

"So, there was an impasse in company policy. How did this difference in opinion play out between your father and Klemens, I mean personally?"

"They hid it well in public, I suppose. They remained civil when they sat in the same meetings. Even if they never agreed, they kept it professional. Every time there was a vote, though, they came down on opposite sides, for as far back as I can remember."

"What about family gatherings? Birthdays? Christmas?"

He shook his head. "Far and I gave up inviting him to anything like that."

Lyra rose to examine a photo of a beautiful, blond, smiling couple with a small boy standing in front of a boat. With a start, she recognized the boy as Arvid, probably about eight or nine—cherubic and delighted, his expression unguarded, clutching his mother's hand. She tore her gaze away.

"Does Klemens have family?"

"No. Just us and *farmor*."

"How well do you yourself get on with him?"

He paused to consider. "When I was a child, he was a generous uncle. As I grew older, we used to spend hours talking business strategy. I suppose I liked him. Eventually, however, I became aware of the issues he had with my father, and I had to take a side." Arvid trailed his fingers down his jaw and frowned as if surprised to find stubble there. "And now I can hardly bear to look him in his face. Has he shed a single tear for his brother? Not at all."

"Does he know you suspect him?"

"I think so. I hope so." His tone was cool now. Cool as in cold war.

"Very hypothetically, what would Klemens's motive be?"

"Being CEO now, he can push his green ideas through no problem. They have traction that they wouldn't have had five or ten years ago. The board is rotten, exactly like him." He banged his fist on the desk. "But tell that to the employees in Norrbotten. They and their families expected those jobs to be for life. We gave them a promise in the Sammland name, something Klemens doesn't give a shit about."

"Did you want the CEO position yourself?"

"No. Maybe? I don't know." He clenched his jaw and stared out the window. "I didn't think I would have to think about it. I certainly didn't want him to have it."

"But he grabbed it?"

"Of course he did. They're all dinosaurs on that board. They voted for Klemens to become interim CEO, and to be sure, he'll become permanent CEO at the next vote. Most of them still see me as Hedvig's little boy."

She let that hang there as she surveyed Hedvig's desk but nothing seemed distinctive. Heavy pine top. A glass in-tray, a jar with pens, a mousepad. A high-backed leather swivel chair. Behind his chair a shelf of folders in neat rows. "Where were you exactly, Arvid, between 4 and 4:30 p.m. last Wednesday?"

"Next door." He cocked his head toward the wall. "Board room. 3 until 5 p.m."

"Klemens?"

"There too, but he left the meeting early. He said that

there was no point in his being there if the main decision-maker wasn't present. He was right—it felt strange not to have far there and for nobody to know where he was. I stayed on because we needed somebody to chair. We had important items to address. You can ask Berit—the secretary."

"I'll do that. What time did Klemens leave the meeting?"

"It would have been around 3:15 p.m."

"Where does Berit sit?"

"Across the way. She's taken a few days off. The shock, you know? At least somebody is in shock."

"Has she been questioned by the police?"

"No idea. Seriously, if you think Berit had anything to do with this…" He shook his head, smiling in fake mirth.

"I think nothing," she said.

5

Klemens's office door, straight across the corridor, looked similar to Hedvig's with the same style of gold name plate, this one bearing the name and title, *KLEMENS SAMMLAND, CFO*. Two alpha brothers separated by a mere two meters of wall and carpet? Little wonder they fought.

Standing outside the door, she shook out the tension from her shoulders and arms. That conversation with Arvid had been tricky. He was defensive of his father and suspicious of his uncle, but these seemed to be ongoing everyday issues rather than clues to his father's sudden death. Hopefully Klemens himself could shed some light. She knocked.

"Ja...?" came a gruff voice.

She marched in. The man at the desk looked up from his keyboard. He had a full head of white hair, swept back from a high forehead and thick black glasses that gave him an intellectual vibe. He seemed to have made every effort to look distinct from his brother, but the bone structure was undeniably Sammland. He seemed thoroughly unsurprised to see her standing there.

"Lyra Maguire, Olive's friend," he announced, producing a smile that had all the charm of a shark that ate people for breakfast.

She acknowledged with an efficient quirk of her lips. "Correct. Is this a bad time for you?"

"Not at all." Klemens took off his glasses and rubbed the bridge of his nose and then replaced them. "There have been so many unplanned meetings this afternoon that I have not managed to start anything," he said in flawless English. "In other words, a typical Friday afternoon."

She nodded. "I'm sorry for your loss, Mr. Sammland."

"Thank you. Call me Klemens."

His demeanor was neutral as he indicated an empty chair on the opposite side of his desk. He shut down his laptop and faced her head on with steepled fingers, in full attention mode. It reminded her of being interviewed for the police cadets.

When she had settled, he let out a sigh. "Yes, it is a bad business with my brother."

"Bad business," she echoed, intrigued to hear no emotion in his voice. "Has Olive told you why I'm here?"

"I suppose you're here to ask me if I killed my brother?" he asked, avoiding the question.

Well, yes, but... "That would be a ridiculous question to ask."

"Would it?" He adjusted his glasses. "Some people seem quite convinced on the matter."

"I'm here for Olive's sake as a friend. I was, or am, going to be her bridesmaid, but I came over early. At times like this," she continued, "families can often feel the strain and—"

"Point fingers at each other?"

She held his gaze steadily. "That has been known to happen."

Klemens smirked. "What rank were you over there in Ireland? You were with the police, were you not?"

"Detective Sergeant. I left and switched to academia."

"Interesting." He sat back in his chair. If he was surprised at this career progression, and most people were, he didn't show it. "It's true, Ms. Norton, that Hedvig and I had differences in opinion over policy. Everyone knows that. Kill him, though? Or have him killed? No. Any fool knows I loved him." A hint of warmth entered his voice. "He was my brother. Why on earth would I kill him? How idiotic of Arvid to suggest as much."

Lyra tilted her head to encourage more. He didn't seem the type to pour out his feelings to a stranger, so it had to be some kind of act.

"How intense were your differences with Hedvig?" she asked.

"Not intense enough to kill him."

"How often did you meet him outside the office, say, for family occasions?"

He winced. "Not at all of late. Of course, he hadn't been the same since Greta's—his wife's—death."

"But she died a long time ago, didn't she?"

"True. Yet, it seems like yesterday. Arvid was most affected, of course, losing his mama at that young age. No wonder he's unstable."

"Unstable?"

"Shouting accusations, those horrendous mood swings. It has been creating a toxic atmosphere around here."

"Do you have the authority to do anything about it? You're technically his boss now, aren't you?"

"Yes. I'm interim CEO. Oh, he'll say I grabbed the position from him, but ask anyone in senior level management, and they'll tell you they wanted me here. He's unfit."

She had to hand it to him. Klemens's instinct for what was being said behind his back was spot on—a useful quality in a CFO ascending to position of CEO.

"I will handle it. This is between my nephew and me."

His phone buzzed on the table. He flipped it around. "I apologize, Ms. Norton, but I must take this one. "Pleasure talking to you."

"Of course." She rose. "Thanks for your time."

Klemens answered the phone while she crossed to the door and closed it behind her. She left the C-Suite and retraced the journey she'd made with Arvid back down to Olive's level.

Something about the conversation bothered her. She couldn't quite put her finger on it, but it was something about Klemens's insistence on Arvid's instability. It needed more thought. She'd figure it out in the hotel.

She hadn't eaten since Dublin Airport, and it was making her feel light-headed. As if on cue, her stomach grumbled, echoing down the long, empty corridor. The hotel bar better serve decent food. Olive's door was shut when she walked past, so she headed straight for the parking lot. She'd call her later.

*

Like any woman who often travels alone, Lyra was pretty used to dealing with unwanted attention in hotel bars. It usually came from older men—slimy types, often married, and always with delusions of their own attractiveness. But the figure that sat in the corner of the hotel bar spying on her as she wolfed down meatballs and fries was female, stocky, with a round face and blonde pixie cut. Lyra watched her reflection in the dark mirror behind the bar between bottles of vodka and gin.

She tried to read the newspaper. The long Swedish words danced before her eyes in convoluted sentences. It was impossible to focus with Ms. Pixie Blonde gawking. She debated leaving, but the bar was warm, the music good, and she had her favorite position—right in front of the serving counter with full view of the entrance via the mirror. If it were a creepy man watching, she would leave. This was merely borderline uncomfortable.

Ten minutes of half-hearted reading attempts later, Lyra

gave up and pushed the Helsingborg Dagbladet aside. She asked for the bill. As the bartender returned her credit card, Lyra glanced into the mirror. The mystery woman was gone. She spun around. Where had she gone to? She was only just there— Lyra whipped back around. There was the mystery woman, taking the bar stool next to her, hanging a jacket on a hook, calm as you please.

She had white-blond hair and eyelashes, pale gray eyes, and delicate Swedish features in a face that seemed too big for them. Her sweatshirt was faded pink and boxy with an Under Armor logo emblazoned across ample breasts.

"Will you have a drink?" the woman asked, looking directly at Lyra.

Lyra shook her head automatically. "No thanks, I was just leaving."

"Hang around. There's no one upstairs in your room."

It wasn't even a question. Lyra frowned. "And you know that how?"

The woman grinned and patted the counter top. "Otto Brydolf, Helsingborg Polis." She reached into her jacket and pulled out a wallet which opened up to show police ID.

Lyra scanned it, taking her good time to absorb name, date of birth, rank. It seemed legit.

"I know. I'm gorgeous," the woman said, pocketing it again.

"Otto, you say? Unusual name for a woman." And it didn't match the ID.

"Full name is Karlotta, as you probably saw. I didn't want to be called Lotta, did I?"

"What's wrong with Lotta?"

"Despicable!"

Otto's drink, something clear, had arrived in a shot glass. "Sure you won't? I thought you Irish girls drank?"

"So, you know all about me then?"

"Just a little, Lyra Norton."

Perhaps this was worth hanging around for. She caught the barman's gaze, pointed at Otto's drink, and then at herself. He reached for the Absolut vodka.

She downed it in one swallow out of some dumb need to impress, and reeled from the burn. "Whoa."

"Same again?" Otto asked.

"Not quite yet. Waiting for this to hit."

Otto shrugged and pointed at the glass to the barman. He was now hovering expectantly, in recognition of serious customers. He dutifully filled Otto's glass.

"I only drink on Fridays," she explained. "But when I do, I do."

"Do you have any Guinness?" Lyra asked him.

"No. We have Murphy's."

Lyra pulled a face.

Otto snorted. "Same thing, no?"

"I'll have a Carlsberg, please." Lyra side-eyed the policewoman. "What else do you know?"

Otto grinned. "The basics."

"I'm listening."

Otto leaned in toward Lyra. "OK, here's the picture. I'm involved in the Hedvig Sammland case. The call came in to dispatch at 16:17, Thursday. I was in the first patrol car on scene at the harbor at 16:31. I preliminarily ID-ed him from his ID card as Sammland, 62, of Björnstigen 1, Ingelsträde. Not that it was necessary—I knew Sammland from the media, of course. The physician arrived after a while and declared him dead. I then summoned the family. His son, Arvid, formally identified him two hours later."

Lyra nodded along.

"And I've been waiting an hour for you to show up. Ask him." Otto nodded at the barman.

He took the hint and shuffled further away.

"How did you know I was here?"

Otto twisted the shot glass between her stubby fingers. "Followed you. I went to Sammland AG to interview employees and was told at reception of someone coming in to talk to Olive Maguire."

Damn Lasse.

"I checked your background and discovered you've got close links to the Maguire family, you've got a law enforcement background, and moreover, academic credentials in forensic linguistics. If you were me, wouldn't you at least ask?"

"Ask what?"

"What you've figured out?" Otto's voice maintained its playful edge. She was one of those cops who used their happy-go-lucky shtick to fool suspects into revealing more than intended. Lyra wasn't a suspect, however, and she didn't enjoy being on the receiving end of a surprise visit.

"Not much. I'm here as moral support for Olive. We go way back."

"How far back?"

"Primary school. She called me up yesterday morning. I'm just doing what any friend would do. I'm her bridesmaid, you see, and we had to reorganize—"

"You were a good cop from what I've been able to dig up."

Lyra shifted her position. "That was a while ago."

"And you came here to check out this mystery death for...the weekend?" There was a particular glint to Otto's smile that told Lyra she wasn't going to drop this line of inquiry until she received a satisfactory answer.

"No, like I said, I came as a friend to Olive."

"Nothing else?"

Lyra regarded the policewoman. Technically, they were on the same side. They both wanted answers. "Obviously, if I could pick up any clues about Hedvig's death, it was going to be a bonus. Having a mysteriously dead father-in-law is a right downer when you're trying to plan a wedding. Bad enough that they decided not to have it in Ireland."

"Ah, and they expect you to wrap it up by Sunday afternoon?"

Lyra had to smile at her accuracy. "Something like that."

"This is fortunate then. We're in the same boat. If I and my team don't produce something by Monday morning, my boss will bring in the boys from Malmo, and I won't get a look in. You see, we don't have time for homicides in this town. We have personal ID cards to issue and stolen bikes to return to their owners."

Lyra heard bitterness in the woman's voice, a bitterness she could identify with. "You're assuming homicide?"

"Forensics hasn't found anything to suggest a heart attack or any other medical explanation. And I doubt he dove voluntarily into that freezing water."

"Was there any evidence of a struggle?"

Otto straightened her arms, pressing her body away from the counter. "Tell you what. Let's do a deal. A little information swap, if you like. Did you get access to Sammland AG?"

The policewoman probably knew this from Lasse, so there was no point in denying it. "All-areas access card."

"Very good. Here's my proposal." Otto's voice sped up. "I have access to the ferry passenger transcripts, divers' reports, forensics, and data from the Danish side. You have insider access to the family and the premises. We collaborate over the weekend, and we may get some good leads by the time you have to check in for your flight on Sunday. Then I can hit my boss in the face with this on Monday. Are you in or out?"

Why was this policewoman so eager for her help? Why go to the trouble to come here? What did Otto possibly think she could do that the police couldn't? The all-access card to the Sammland AG premises wasn't the issue—the Helsingborg police could secure warrants to check out anything they wanted. That was just Otto playing the charm card. More likely, it was her intimate access to the family that the policewoman valued—as though she'd already decided that Hedvig's death was somehow family-related. If that was the case, Lyra needed to know more. And the best way of finding out anything was to cooperate.

"Yeah," she said. "I'm in."

Otto nodded and tipped back shot glass number three.

"That's my limit. Come on, let's take a stroll around the harbor. It's on my walk home."

They paid up, coated up, and headed out into the bitter wind, heading downhill on the cobblestone sidewalk to the harbor. The chill seemed to creep up into the marrow of her bones. Irish sea breezes were mild, salty, and refreshing. Swedish sea breezes froze the scalp, watered the eyes, whipped around the ankles, and made one long for the nearest doorway.

"It was a ferry like that one." Otto pointed at the back end of a huge *ForSea* passenger ferry parked in the dock.

Lyra stared into the concrete-colored water that stretched out to the horizon. Lights twinkled on the Swedish and Danish sides. The wind slashed hair across her face, and she had to force herself to stop shivering. "How cold is that water?"

"Almost freezing. About 2 degrees Celsius."

"Jesus."

"Yeah. Even if Sammland could've swum in, the hypothermia would've got him half-way. See those lights?" Otto pointed across the water to an imposing building jutting out on its own peninsula. "That's Kronborg Castle, or Kronborg Slot. The Danes are terribly proud of it. It's positioned at the narrowest point of the Sound between Denmark and Sweden, only four kilometers across. That's why they built the fortress there—to control this outlet of the Baltic Sea and gather all the taxes from passing ships."

"Was Hedvig on his way back from visiting that?" Lyra asked. Olive had indeed mentioned in the past that the castle was worth a visit at some stage.

"No. He only went into the town and straight back out to the ferry again. His stay was less than an hour." Otto twisted her head and regarded her with an amused expression. "You're freezing. I should let you get back to your room. Let's meet tomorrow. I'm off-duty, so I won't be answering my radio all the time."

"You don't mind working a case in your time off?" Lyra

asked, teeth chattering.

"No. One of the most eminent businessmen in my district mysteriously killed? I want to know exactly how and why. I sure as hell don't want some asshole from Malmo or worse, Stockholm, to solve it for me."

"I hear you," Lyra said with feeling. As a young policewoman, she'd been pushed off cases, too, as soon as they got more interesting. "What about your family, though? Don't they mind you working on the weekend?"

"I just have Moses, my sambo. He likes his space on the weekend." She rolled her eyes. "Musician."

"OK. How do we proceed?"

"I'll pick you up at the hotel at eight sharp tomorrow. Sleep well." Otto pulled up her collar and faced the breeze, waving backward as she went.

Lyra was almost sorry to see her go.

*

After two hours, her hotel room looked like a bomb had hit it. Creative mess was a habit formed in childhood that, despite her mother's efforts, she never shook off. Now, instead of Lego and makeshift farms, she had case notes all over the place—not just on the extra bed but also on the desk, the bedside table, and parts of the floor. Her clothes were mostly in the suitcase, but some were strewn on the bed. She'd had several coffees and worked her way through three chocolate bars, the wrappers on the window sill where she'd stood as she mindlessly wolfed them down. She'd seen on Twitter that chocolate consumption and Nobel prize distributions were highly correlated. What better country to test that out in than Sweden?

She'd been down to the hotel's small but adequate business center and printed out website articles she could find on the Sammlands. She ran through the facts, muttering to an imaginary audience. Officially, the Helsingborg police were keeping "an open mind", but unofficially they regarded Hedvig Sammland's death as suspicious and were keeping tabs on the family. No suspects had been identified on the ferry. Nobody had witnessed Hedvig's fall into the water. Before his death, Hedvig had been having heated discussions with his brother over environmental policies—Klemens wanting to radically clean up the company's practices, Hedvig calling for a more conservative rollout in order to preserve jobs in vulnerable communities. Against this backdrop, Arvid, Hedvig's only son was getting married to a high-ranking Irish employee, Olive, in two weeks' time. Hedvig's last action in life was to purchase a gift for the couple in Helsingor.

She couldn't see any links. She'd quiz Olive and Arvid at home tomorrow—surely they wouldn't be in the office on Saturday. Maybe she should organize lunch. Olive seemed too distracted to be able to organize anything as she normally would. So, it was up to her.

Right as she'd reached for her phone, it buzzed. Liam.

She hesitated before answering. Was he updating?

"Hi. Is it a bad time?" His voice sounded unexpectedly mellow on the phone. Without the surly looks, his human warmth came bursting to the fore.

"Nah, heading to bed soon." She yawned. "Nice to hear from you."

"This isn't that type of call."

"What type of call is it?"

He laughed. "So, you decided to go over. I wasn't expecting that, but it's great, thank you. Olive must be thrilled."

"She's—" Lyra grappled for the correct expression "—coping as well as she can, and I hope I'm supporting in some small way simply by being here."

"Well, you're not alone."

"What do you mean?"

"Hold your breath. Pronsious is going over."

"Holy cow. When?"

"Monday."

Lyra groaned in relief.

"Once he'd heard you'd headed over, he decided Olive needed her dad over there. I tried to convince him otherwise, saying that you'd be better qualified to handle it, but he was having none of it. Mam's not going, needless to say. She has more sense. Will you keep an eye on him? I can see him poking his nose in everybody's business."

"Uh, sorry, Liam, I'll be back in Ireland by then. Return flight on Sunday. I've classes on Monday." That was a lie. She had the adoption interview on Monday, but he didn't need to know that. Only Olive knew about that.

He was silent. "Forgive me, it was presumptuous of me to think you'd babysit him. How's my sister?"

"She seems to be holding it together pretty well, all things considered. I met her at her workplace earlier. Arvid's a bit of a nervous wreck, though."

"Course he is. So, how come you're not with them now?"

"They need their space. I'm at a nearby hotel. I'll see them tomorrow."

"See? This is the kind of thing Dad would never understand. Right, well, if you're looking for good company, you could always check in on Hugo. He texted me out of the blue today."

"Hanging out with Olive's ex may not be the best idea. He's not even on the guest list, so I'll pass. Thanks, anyway. I do quite well in my own company." And with a strange policewoman.

"I'm sure you do."

There was a pause in which she could almost hear his brain whirring, trying to find something to say. Despite the warmth of his voice, she didn't want to be chatty and give him any notions. "Hm, it's getting late over here," she said, wincing at how clumsy it sounded. "And I've an early start tomorrow."

"OK, please warn Olive about Dad, will you, in case you get talking to her first? Tell her under no circumstances to let him stay with them. He needs a hotel room. If you can get a hotel room, then so can he."

Liam's bossiness had returned. Indeed, that was probably the true reason for him calling. "Sure. Will do."

"By the way, early start for what?"

She smirked. He was no slouch. "Oh, nothing much."

"Come on. You're snooping, aren't you?"

"Maybe."

He laughed. "OK, but promise to swing by Kiltomb for a debriefing soon?"

"If I discover anything," she said. "But don't hold your breath."

6

Saturday at 8:10 a.m. it was still dark when Lyra and Otto pulled up at the Sammland AG building. Otto had picked Lyra up outside the hotel at eight sharp in her little blue Honda. Along the way, the policewoman explained that she wanted to talk an IT guy into giving her a dump of Hedvig Sammland's emails dating back a year or so. The deceased's laptop had been useless—too new. When they arrived, the parking lot was deserted except for an old black Saab. Lights were on in the reception area and on the third floor.

Otto cut the engine and peered up at the window. "That's the IT guy, doing weekly backups. Name's Rasmus Ismat. He has speeding tickets outstanding if we need to be persuasive."

Lyra raised her eyebrows. "Sure this is a good idea?"

"No, but I need that data, and I can't wait 'til Monday. I need a lead, or else my boss Eriksson is going to dump a ton of petty crime shit on me. That's where you come in—helping me read through all these texts—company language is English—and you're a forensic linguist, right?"

"R-ight," Lyra said. That sounded like the kind of drudgery she'd assign her students as a term project. In fact, she'd love to call up her forty MA students and tell them to get their keyword spotting and intent analysis tools ready for some serious data crunching. "But what if I want a piece of the action?"

"You want to do the talking?"

Lyra sat up straighter. "Why not? I've got my auditor excuse. You have none."

"If you're sure." Otto handed her a box of latex gloves. "Deniability may be useful. In fact, it's best to say you're a PI trying to solve the murder—he'll sympathize with that a lot quicker than saying you're an auditor. Definitely don't say you're with the police. I'll stay here and keep an eye out."

"Got it. Shouldn't take long." Lyra took a pair of gloves and pocketed them, took her takeaway coffee from the holder, and got out.

As she stalked in through the glass revolving doors, her veins thrummed with the old thrill of clue hunting. If Hedvig rarely left the office, then chances were good that there was some clue in his correspondence as to who might have wanted to kill him. At the very least, it may provide a starting point for a later discussion with Olive and Arvid.

The guy at the reception wasn't the curly-headed Lasse but some much older guy with gray hair, engrossed in *Motorsport* magazine. He barely looked up as she flashed her card. With her harried air and takeaway coffee, she looked the part of overworked executive.

All the doors beeped and slid back precisely as they had done with Olive's card. Inside, she scanned the list of departments: *Sales, Accounts, Marketing… ah IT. Third floor.*

Rasmus, a short, sinewy, mid-thirties man of Middle Eastern descent, was doing disk-based backup. Everything about him was neat—chiseled haircut, perfectly circular glasses, trim beard, sharp shirt collar. Not your stereotypical IT guy.

He Looked up, startled. "Hej?"

"I'm Lyra. Do you speak English?"

He smirked. "Of course."

"Cool. I'm a private investigator from Ireland, as you've probably guessed from the accent."

His blank look told her he hadn't. She'd been laying it on thick.

"I'm working on behalf of Arvid Sammland and Olive Maguire. Didn't they warn you I was coming?" She wandered to the back of his chair, knowing how irritating this was, banking on him wanting her out of there ASAP.

He shook his head without turning around.

"No, they forgot? Well, sorry for the intrusion." She looked at his screen from behind. "Ah, you're encrypting your backup images. That's smart. I guess you transfer to the cloud?"

He looked around. "Yes, for security."

She grinned widely. "Then you're exactly the lad I need to talk to. See, the Sammland family want to check some questions internally, you know, before the police start poking around? There's sensitive information in Hedvig's account, and we need access to that."

Rasmus's forehead creased in confusion.

"It won't take you long. We need a dump of all emails Hedvig received in the past two years. Then I promise, I'm out of your hair. Would that be technically possible?"

"Technically, uh, sure, but—"

"Oh, you're worried about legitimacy. No problem." She took out her phone. "We can call Arvid at home. Oh—he and Olive may still be in bed, but as this is so important to them, I'm sure they'll be happy to discuss the ins and outs with you. Now, let me see, maybe a video conference would be best."

"No, no, it's OK," he said hurriedly. "I can dump the data for you." Seeming glad to have a concrete task, he swiveled his chair and faced another monitor and clacked away on his keyboard.

As he worked, she nosed around. The place was insanely tidy for an IT department—no clutter, no cables, no obsolete hardware, or nerdy gimmicks. Just stacks of well-labeled backups and well-maintained manuals on shelves. If only she could be more like that.

She strolled to the window and looked down to the parking lot. It was still only the black Saab and Otto's Honda there. Otto gave her the thumbs up. Lyra nodded back. "Oh, can you retrieve them all? Company and private, or just company? Are you running a proxy?"

"Sure. It handles all connections in and out, no matter from where, so yeah, we can track it all."

"Can you dump it onto this?" She produced the Sammland USB stick she'd nicked from reception.

He glanced at it. "Uh-huh."

It wasn't surprising that they had access to every bit and byte of data flowing in or out. What was surprising was that this relatively young man seemed to be in charge of the whole IT department. At no stage did he say, "I have to ask my boss if this is OK." Perhaps he knew more than he was letting on. How could she warm him up?

"You didn't come by car, did you? I don't see many cars in the parking lot." She reckoned the black Saab belonged to the guy at reception.

"No. I cycle."

"In this weather?"

"All weathers. I live nearby."

"How long have you worked here?"

"Ten years, give or take," he said, still without looking up.

"Good place to work?"

"No complaints."

"What do you make of all this infighting between the Sammland brothers?"

A shrug. "It's all corporate politics. It doesn't affect me."

"You never felt you had to take sides?"

That was enough provocation to get him to lift his gaze. "I'm just IT."

Rasmus, she guessed, was the kind of guy who would stay up all night arguing over a technical point on Reddit but who would never get his ass out to vote. It wasn't in his job description.

"Here you go." He held out the memory stick.

"Excellent. Thanks."

"No problem." He gazed longingly at his other computer where clearly some tasks were waiting.

"Back to the grind?" she asked.

He nodded.

She called Otto once she was out of hearing range of the IT office. "I got the emails. Now I want to snoop around Hedvig's office."

"Yeah? What for?"

"I want to get a feel for him."

"Yeah. I'll just be here feeling my ass freeze off."

"I'll be quick. Call me if the reception guy moves, will you?"

"You got it."

She opted for the stairs down to the VIP corridor. Lights pinged on as they detected her movements and went off again thirty seconds later—very environmentally conscious, but eerie. Her card worked for all doors, even into the C-suite. Yes. Once inside, she stopped at Hedvig's office, put on her gloves, and tried the door. It swung open. She was surprised that Arvid hadn't locked it.

Turning on all the lights, she gazed at the photos again. The body language of the people suggested he was loved. There was one of Arvid and Olive on their own, perhaps an engagement photo. Olive was in a yellow pinafore dress, smiling at the photographer, looking absolutely stunning.

Her attention moved to the bookcase stacked full with business tomes that, judging from the dust on top, nobody had read since the internet was born. The middle shelf had ring binders sitting in a neat row. They had that classic design with an empty circle two-thirds way down, all circles lining up with anal precision. Accounts Payable They dated from 2009 to 2021. So far, so boring.

She recalled that the company had been restructured in

2014, which seemed to have been the genesis of the strife between the Sammland brothers. Was there anything interesting in these accounting files to explain the rift? Gingerly, she moved her hand toward the 2014 folder.

Then she thought she heard a noise. She drew back, heart beating fast. Straining her ears, she could hear nothing. As she reached for the 2014 folder, she noticed something. Accounts Payable 2016 showed subtle signs of having been moved—a trail in the dust on the shelf surface. She hooked her middle finger inside the hole to tug it out. Rather than her finger brushing against paper, her nail hit against something hard and plasticky.

What?

She pulled out the folder and opened it up on the table.

Her heart started to thump. Stuck to the inside the folder's spine was a tiny microchip surveillance device. An *Endoacoustica NANO2* micro recorder—one of the world's smallest—law enforcement grade—the type that could be operated remotely via Bluetooth via phone or PC. *Holy shit.*

She poked her gloved finger in each of the holes, but 2016 was the only one. The ring binders were placed at head height for someone sitting down at Hedvig's desk—optimal for speech pickup.

The conversation she'd had with Arvid yesterday in this room floated back to her, and Arvid's impassioned speech, *'Did Klemens do it or not? And if not, then who* för fan *did it? What do you think? It couldn't really be Klemens, could it?'* Whoever planted this must have heard all that…and everything else ever said in this room dating back to God knows when.

Pulling off the gloves with her teeth, she took hurried photos with her phone. They were blurry, but they'd have to do. She pulled the gloves on again and quietly replaced the folder. Then she smoothed her hands under the desk, around every lamp shade, on top of photo frames. She didn't know what she was looking for exactly. One listening device was as damning as ten. There were no sneaky cameras as far as she could tell.

THE SOUND

That noise came again, but this time louder. It was a door opening and closing in the room directly below her. Was the guard doing the rounds? Had Rasmus alerted him?

Shit, oh shit.

Could she make it out of the room, out of the C-suite, and into the main stairwell without being caught? Or was it better to hide in there? No, she couldn't get caught in Hedvig's office. Arvid would never trust her again.

She bounded for the door, stumbled into the C-suite corridor, and raced to the security door. Pressing her card up to the card reader, it flashed an indignant red.

"Come on, Come on!"

She twisted the card around and slapped it up again. "Please."

Meanwhile, the elevator shaft rumbled. Someone was coming up.

The light switched to green. She gasped and pushed through the spring-loaded glass door. The ping of the elevator opening on her floor sounded out the millisecond she reached the stairwell door. Half falling on the analog door handle, she crashed through to the cool air of the stairwell. Her legs operated at triple speed getting down those stairs, and she came out into the atrium.

Flicking back strands of hair, she crossed the reception area with quick but unhurried strides, putting on a good show for the cameras. Then she was out in the cold again.

She sprinted to the car.

Otto, clearly sensing trouble, started the ignition before she reached the car.

"Hedvig's office is bugged." Lyra gasped as they drove away from the premises.

"No way."

Lyra clicked her seat belt with still trembling fingers. She was so out of practice. "Klemens's doing, I'll bet."

"Why do you think that?"

"I found no other components, nothing that would boost the signal; therefore, it has to be someone within fifty meters for the Bluetooth, and he's right across the corridor. No other office is quite that near—it's all meeting rooms."

"How'd you even know to look for a bug?"

"Just the eerie way Klemens knew I was coming to him yesterday? And he used the exact same words Arvid had used."

"Well done, Dirk Gently."

"So, Klemens has no doubt that Arvid suspects him. The conversation I had with Arvid yesterday was bad enough. I can only imagine what things were said when Arvid and his father thought they were on their own."

"Yeah. What about the emails?"

Lyra held up the USB stick. "We need to search through a zillion."

"Great. Your place or mine?"

Lyra imagined Otto's partner, Moses, skulking around barefoot with a guitar, practicing his music. "Mine. I've got a nice big room."

"As long as it's heated," Otto said, turning out of the parking lot and speeding off.

7

"Nice room," Otto walked in, carrying the laptop she'd taken from her car. "I like what you've done with the bed." She gestured to the organized chaos that was the second twin bed.

Lyra grinned. "It's my case board."

Otto studied the printouts, nodding approvingly. "So, you think the environmental policies spat between the brothers is worth noting. What are these?" She pointed to the handwritten notes Lyra had scrawled under Klemens's picture.

Lyra paused in her erratic tidying up of her clothes. No representative of the Swedish police needed to see her tattered underwear. "That's from our chat yesterday. It went nowhere because I had nothing on him. If only I'd known of his little surveillance operation at the time."

"Don't worry. We'll make sure to use it during our next chat with him...down in the station." Otto clapped her palms together. "Ready to rock and roll?"

"Let's do it."

Lyra pulled the USB stick from her jeans pocket. They were typical business emails—mediocre, jargon-filled, ass-covering verbiage explaining why targets or forecasts hadn't been met, interspersed with banalities like birthday cakes in the canteen or wellness reminders. It made Lyra glad she didn't work for a corporation. On the vast majority, Hedvig had been cc-ed, but it was others doing the communicating. She focused on those that were addressed specifically to him. More perusing resulted in nothing juicy.

Otto headed onto the tiny balcony "for a sneaky cigarette."

"You smoke?" Lyra asked, joining her on the balcony that had a view over a side street—the back of a clothes store.

Otto exhaled a plume into the freezing air. "Only when I work overtime."

"You only drink on Fridays, and you only smoke doing overtime. You should do overtime on Fridays, then you'd get to do both at the same time."

"Yeah, I'll definitely think about that." Otto blinked at her through the smoke. "Do you ever make rules for yourself?"

"All the time."

"Like what?"

"Oh...I have to stop obsessing about the past, and I only have certain days when I'm allowed to dwell. I have to let students solve their own problems. I have to stop reading too deeply into things people say. I have to keep my house clean and tidy even though I'm chaotic by nature. I have to...be a mom by the time I'm forty."

"Wow."

"Yeah, wow."

"You have a partner?"

"No. I'm going down the adoption route."

Otto appeared unbothered by this announcement, which made Lyra like her even more. The stocky policewoman smoked another few drags. "You're good at investigating. Why'd you stop?"

Lyra gripped the railing tighter. "Long story."

"I'm not rushing off."

"Well, not now."

"Aw." Otto flicked ash over the balcony and watched it sail to the ground below. "Babies. Not for me. Moses has zero interest—he's from a family of eleven, and we're not talking a delightful, happy family here. Me, I'm not the maternal type. Never was. Never will be."

"I'm not so sure I am either," Lyra said. "I'm just scared of regretting not doing it."

"My advice? If you don't regret it right now, you won't regret it later either."

"Yeah, maybe." She shivered and went back inside to tackle the next couple megabytes of data. Tedious though it was, it beat having that conversation.

*

It was two p.m. already. They'd been sifting through emails until their eyes blurred. Empty potato chips and chocolate bar packets lay strewn around—they had ransacked the minibar. One empty beer can—Lyra's. Otto had stuck to her Fridays Only drinking rule even if she'd gone to town on the smoking. The stale smoke in the air from Otto's breath and the dim room lighting were making Lyra feel headachy.

"What are you thinking?" Otto asked.

Lyra realized she'd been staring into space for some time. One part of her wondered why Olive hadn't gotten in touch by now and whether she should call her. Another part of her wanted to wrap this up first.

"Here's my take. Something nasty's been festering between the brothers over the years. It may have started as a business dispute, but then it grew into stone-cold hatred. Klemens overhears something said in Hedvig's office that makes him explode with rage or maybe start fearing for his life. He sets up an opportunity to get Hedvig on his own on a ferry, and hires a professional to take him out."

Otto nodded. "It fits better than anything we have so far. The passengers we interviewed knew nothing, saw nothing, heard nothing. It has the mark of a professional job—someone who could quickly overpower a fit man and toss him overboard and leave no marks on his body. That would take serious skill. Judo or jujitsu, perhaps. They may have disguised themselves as tourists or a family. I am sure no expense was spared."

"Of course, if this were to fly, we'd need to find an email where Klemens is actually corresponding with the contract killers."

"That would be nice, wouldn't it?" Otto said wryly. "We need to get at Klemens's emails, but that's not quite so easy seeing as he's not dead."

"There's still another seven gigabytes of this guy to go," Lyra said. "Maybe we'll find something."

Otto groaned and flopped her head back on Lyra's pillow. Any reserve between them had been ground down by their confinement in that small room for four hours.

"I should call Olive soon," Lyra said.

"Ten more minutes, then we give it a rest," Otto said. "I'll get my minions to continue. We'll get a warrant to search the premises, so we can officially find the surveillance equipment, and if we're lucky, some recordings too on Klemens's phone or computer, and take it from there. I reckon it's enough to convince my boss that my team should keep going."

Lyra shook her head. "No, hold off on grabbing those recordings. Best if Klemens doesn't realize what we have on him. At least for the moment. It would only prompt him to start deleting data."

"Good point. And we won't pull him in for questioning until we have a stronger case, because he'll bring an army of the best lawyers. He'll have slipped up somewhere. Everyone does. You keep quiet to the families, right?"

"Not a word."

They settled back to reading.

"This is weird," Otto said, pointing to her screen after five minutes.

"What?" Lyra moved over to Otto and hovered over her shoulder.

"All right, here we go, Berit is asking Hedvig, 'did you approve the Marketing meeting agenda sent by Olive yesterday?' This is February 10th, 2019, see, and he says yes, everything is in order, blah blah blah.'"

"What's weird about that?"

"There's no mail from Olive on February 9th."

Lyra shrugged. "He must have deleted it. Or maybe she printed it out and handed it to him."

"I don't see any emails from Olive. None directly from her."

Lyra frowned at her own screen full of emails. She did a quick text search. Indeed, none were directly from Olive. She'd been on cc in many, but there was no direct correspondence between Olive and Hedvig—in either direction.

"That's strange. You'd expect mails between the CEO and a VP. It's not like she was avoiding him. They got on pretty well. Yes, I know for sure she's sent him presentations, because I remember her telling me she'd gotten good feedback from him on a storyboard she did for some expensive TV ad not long back."

They looked at each other. From Otto's expression, Lyra could see the same thought forming. "Unless someone deleted those emails. I mean, deleted them from his machine, presumably hers, too, and from the backup."

"And why would they do that?" Otto asked. "Has he confided something in his VP of Beauty Care that he couldn't share with anyone else? Were they using stem cells from embryos for reverse aging or something?"

"Doubt it. But I'm going to ask her."

"Let's check if there's the same pattern with anyone else's mails," Otto said.

Now there was no question of stopping. They called for

a room service dinner and re-scanned the mails.

It was after six p.m. by the time they were satisfied that the anomaly concerned Olive's emails only. That made Lyra nervous. Had she opened a can of worms that didn't need opening? Surely, it had nothing to do with the case.

"You've been a big help in getting us these leads," Otto said, tidying up some of the mess from their dinner. "I'm extremely grateful." Her movements were more efficient than before, and she seemed reluctant to look Lyra in the eye."

"Glad to have helped. I wish I could stay longer."

She really meant that. The adrenaline was flowing again—it had been absent for years. She longed to stay another week and to help make sure Otto's team got to solve the case. It stung to have to abandon it just as she was getting started, but she'd made her life rules, and she was sticking to them.

Otto acknowledged with a tight smile. "Are you going to talk to her before you go?"

"Yes, if she's on for meeting."

"Good. Let me know how that goes, and I'll keep you updated on whether I get to stay on the case or not, and anything we find out."

They shook hands, and Otto left the room. Lyra went out onto the balcony and watched the tail lights of the blue Honda disappear down the narrow streets toward the harbor and then into the night.

*

Twenty-five minutes later, Lyra was sitting in a bar around the corner, where she'd agreed to meet Olive. Olive had sounded harried on the phone but agreed readily to meeting up. Lyra was early at the bar, wanting to get out of her hotel room and soak in the atmosphere of a Saturday night in downtown Helsingborg. It was a mid-level Mediterranean place with a cheerful ambiance and great views of the harbor from the second floor.

Her time there had flown. She'd seen the airport terminal building, the inside of a corporate building, and a hotel room, and instead of giving Olive comfort, she'd gone behind her back and uncovered some workplace shenanigans. Would she have done better to stay put in Dublin and catch up on correcting essays on tools for detecting plagiarism, and painting the bedroom wall? Had the whole visit been a self-indulgent trip down memory lane, playing cop for the weekend?

Olive looked impeccable in a fitted blue coat as she walked in.

They ordered gin cocktails. Olive took out the plastic straw from the glass and frowned at it. "In this day and age?"

Lyra laughed. "Now that's the Olive who spent her lunch hour between lectures volunteering down in the Greenpeace offices, making posters and sewing hemp tote bags and whatever else you did."

A smile lit up Olive's face. "Yeah, where is that girl? I'm sorry I haven't been here for you. I've missed you."

"Don't apologize. I invited myself here, after all. I should have visited you more often over here, as opposed to only in Ireland. You see, once you announced your engagement, I kept thinking, 'well, I'll see you at the wedding'. Can you forgive me?"

Olive raised her palms. "I'm every bit as bad. I'd always assumed we'd just bump into you in Kiltomb, but of course, with your mother in Kerry now, that wasn't likely unless I'd actually invited you over when I was there at Christmas, which I failed to do. So remiss of me."

"Never mind, we're all caught up now." Lyra paused. "It was good to meet Arvid again, too, of course."

Olive nodded. "And did you find out anything?" she asked in a half whisper. "When you talked to Klemens?"

"There's definitely some tension there that the police should look into, and I know they will. But I'd avoid discussing this matter anywhere inside that building." Lyra looked at her friend sternly.

Olive nodded. "All right."

"There was something I wanted to talk to you about before I left, though."

"Oh?"

Lyra swallowed a gulp of gin-fizz. "This may sound invasive, but I ran a check on Hedvig's emails. It's what the police will be doing, anyway."

Olive's hand froze mid-way to her cocktail glass. "And?"

"There's no other way to put this, but all correspondence from you to Hedvig—and I'm assuming there was some—has been wiped, and vice versa."

Lyra watched her friend lift the glass to her lips. Was that a tremble in the liquid?

"Who would have done this, Olive? Of course, I'll ask Rasmus if I get can get hold of him when I'm back home, but—"

"No!" Olive blurted. "Don't. That won't be necessary," she added in a quieter voice. She propped her elbows on the table and sank her face into her hands, shaking her head back and forth.

"Olive?"

Slowly, Olive lifted her head, took in a deep breath, and released it. Her expression had lost all its confidence. "I know who deleted them."

"Who?"

"I was dreading this," she said, barely audibly.

Lyra didn't move a muscle.

"You have to swear not to tell anyone."

"I swear."

Olive kept staring at her glass as she spoke. "I deleted them, or, I ordered them to be deleted."

"Why?"

"Because I was scared. Because Hedvig and I..." She shut her eyes. "We had a thing."

Lyra's stomach tightened. "What do you mean?" she

asked, although she knew very well.

Olive looked up. "An affair, Lyra."

"Yes, yes, just hang on a moment while I process this."

She pressed her fingers to her temples. Hedvig? Arvid's father? OK, he was rich and handsome, but he was sixty-two, old enough to be her grandfather. And now, dead. This turned everything she thought she knew about her best friend on its head—her best friend who was meant to be getting married in two weeks. The worst thing was, she hadn't suspected a thing.

"It was so, so stupid." Olive was talking to the glass again. "At the time, two years ago, things were rough with Arvid—he was so hot and cold, distant, you know, as if he was having second thoughts? I felt so alone any time we were together. So abandoned. Of course, it's no excuse. I was plainly stupid."

Lyra shook her head rapidly. "We all make mistakes. Remember Kevin Shaw?"

Kevin Shaw was a senior detective fifteen years her senior who Lyra had a fling with in her fourth month of police cadets. He'd turned out to be dating another senior officer, something her budding detective skills had failed to detect, although everyone else in the force seemed to know. It had all ended in tears—mostly hers.

Olive managed a watery smile. "God, yeah. At least Hedvig wasn't seeing anyone else."

"I know, right? So how did it start?"

"A-after my promotion to VP of Beauty Care, Hedvig and I were working closely together a lot. In the beginning, he was just this kindly older man to me, you know? A mentor figure? I was constantly traipsing into his office to ask him his advice on this and that, and he was always so friendly to me. I'd be standing right beside him, pointing at stuff on his screen and thinking nothing of it. I truly didn't…It was probably naïve of me. I-I'm sorry. I couldn't bring myself to tell you."

"It's OK, you're telling me now," Lyra said gently. "Go

on."

"So, there was this one time when we went to Portugal together for a client meeting in the Douro region. We had dinner, as always, and we'd drunk some local Porto, and after the clients left, we stayed on chatting in the lounge. When we stood up to go, he was putting my coat on me, and I turned to him to say something, and he kissed me and...I let him." She exhaled. "It was good. I can't explain it. We both felt terrible, so utterly guilty, but we couldn't deny the attraction that had built up between us."

"Oh Christ," Lyra said, swallowing hard. She thought of the monitoring equipment in Hedvig's office and what all Klemens would have heard. "How long did it go on?"

"It had gone on a year. We stopped it six months ago. Had to. It was dreadful, you know, with Arvid? I could hardly bear to be with him in the same house, and that wasn't fair to him. Hedvig had his own burden of guilt, cheating on his own son. Can you imagine? He took charge—he went away on a long business trip to Singapore without me. I sent a deputy. Then I moved my office downstairs, ostensibly to be nearer my team. It solved it."

Lyra gulped. "This...makes things complicated. Is this why you wanted me over?"

"No!" Olive's eyes widened. "This has nothing to do with anything. Nobody knows except you."

"And Rasmus?"

"No, his Swedish isn't that good, and he did a bulk delete. I told him it was about company secrets—that I was afraid of hackers getting at them."

"Did he believe you?"

"I don't know. I don't care, Lyra. Nobody else knew, and this has nothing to do with whoever killed Hedvig."

"Right." Lyra tried to keep a neutral face, but of course, it could be related. It called for a total overhaul of everything she thought about the case.

When the waiter came with the bill, Olive took it as a cue to go. "Sorry for dropping this bombshell. You're shocked,

I can tell."

"Concerned, more like. For you and Arvid."

Olive sniffed. "Don't be. In a strange way, this tragedy has brought us together. Despite how it may look, I want to start over, to be a supportive wife to him as he takes control of the company that Hedvig left him. It's my role in life now." She looked at Lyra, her face taut. "You believe me, don't you?"

Lyra nodded though it was plain Olive was protesting too much.

"Speaking of which, I need to get home now. He's not good when he's left on his own."

They hugged hard. *"Slán abhaile,"* Olive said. *Safe trip home.*

"You'll be seeing your father tomorrow."

Olive grimaced. "God, yeah. That's the next thing." She clutched her Hermes purse tighter to her side. "Now you understand why I can't deal with him, with anyone, but especially not Dad. Are you sure you can't stay?"

"I'm sorry. I've a meeting with the adoption rep on Monday morning. I have to fly back tomorrow."

Olive laid her dainty fingers on her forearm. "Oh, I forgot about that. Forgive me, I'm being so selfish. You must wonder what kind of person I've become."

"Not at all, I understand, I really do. Look, how about I check him into my hotel? They have rooms available."

"That would be fabulous. Thanks."

"One less thing on your list."

Olive nodded. "When this is all over, we'll go on a holiday together, hmm? Just us two?"

Lyra beamed. "I can't wait."

Back in the room, Lyra debated furiously as she packed her suitcase. Was Olive's affair a personal matter that belonged in the past, or could it have some bearing on the case? As in, did Otto really have to know? It felt wrong to betray a best friend's secret. Then again, Otto would ask what explanation Olive gave for those missing mails. She wanted to give Otto every chance possible to stay on the case. Lying wasn't an option.

Damn it.

She pressed Otto's number. No answer. It was 23:57 so she was probably asleep. Otto's voice recording prompted to leave a voice message.

"Otto, it's Lyra. Yeah, Olive explained the email thing. She, uh, was having an affair with Hedvig. It's over now. I'm flying tomorrow morning, but you can call me tomorrow evening or Monday."

She clicked off.

Now I feel like complete scum.

8

After a Sunday of travel, Monday dawned far too quickly. Lyra spent most of the morning pacing her tiny kitchen floor, anticipating tricky questions, pitfalls, a character assassination. She had cleared her agenda for the interview and it had to be a success. Only trouble was, her mind was in Sweden. With Olive, Hedvig, Arvid, and Klemens.

Just another few days in Sweden could have made all the difference, but it was impossible—she had this interview, responsibilities to her students, the faculty. Her life couldn't stop simply because her best friend's had. There had been no word from Otto yet on whether she'd managed to stay on the case.

The illicit May-December affair explained how distraught Olive had been after Hedvig's body was identified. It explained her gradual change of mood, as noticed by her family. Did Arvid know? And did anybody else?

The doorbell rang.

Mrs. Thompson, from the adoption agency, was more or less as Lyra had imagined her from their phone conversation: mid-fifties, gray-blonde bob, rectangular glasses. She marched through the apartment with a haughty air, clipboard clutched to her bosom, her beady eyes scanning all surfaces like a Terminator cyborg monitoring all manner of death traps for a tiny human. Now seated, she gazed at Lyra in a calculating manner from across the kitchen table.

It felt weird being on the other side of an interview, like her whole life was on trial. Lyra tried to picture her apartment from this woman's point of view. A tell-tale whiff of chlorine lingered in the air. The place had undergone a drastic de-clutter worthy of a YouTube video. All surfaces were clear, but if she opened a cupboard, a tsunami of stuff would topple out. Her workout equipment had left dents in the carpet. A movie poster for John Wick III had been replaced by one for Paddington II.

"Interesting color." They had stepped into the child's bedroom.

"Yes, I'm not a huge fan of pastels." Lyra adjusted her blouse, remembering why she never wore it—polyester suffocated the skin.

"I see you specialized in forensic linguistics," the rep said, as if this were somehow related.

"Correct."

"That's the study of liars, isn't it?"

"It's a broad field. We analyze language, written or audio, to help solve crimes, to find the guilty, but also to protect the innocent."

"Hm. Then before that, in the Gardaí, you had a high-profile case, with that pedophile ring."

"Ah, you heard about that."

Mrs. Thompson's lips rose into a faint smile. "I think the whole of Ireland heard about it."

Great. A conversation about pedophiles was exactly what she needed.

"How did that affect you?"

"The fame? Or the case?"

"Let's say the case."

"It's an upsetting topic for many, but as a professional, I had an important job to do. Nothing is more important than protecting kids from predators."

The agency rep nodded along. "Absolutely. We're glad we have the Gardaí keeping our children safe. Do you ever miss your service there?"

"Now and then." Was this a trick question? "It was a great job, but I had an interest in linguistics and I thought I could serve the community even better that way, combining them."

Mrs. Thompson nodded along, making notes. She looked up again. "Becoming a mother is also a role, one with responsibility for keeping children safe—from household dangers—stairs, electricity outlets, ovens, glass. Food allergies. Constant vigilance is needed. It will mean a massive change in your lifestyle. And you won't get to be on the TV at the end of the day." She smirked.

"I understand that," Lyra said evenly. "I'm prepared."

The rep walked out of the room into the hallway. The walls here were newly adorned with photos of her mother and her brother— happy outdoorsy snaps she'd dug out of the attic last night at half past three. Luckily, she didn't have to make that shit up; she came from a happy family. Normally, though, she kept her walls clear of any personal items that would make her vulnerable should anybody intrude.

"Why did you choose to adopt?" Mrs. Thompson asked, her attention snapping back to Lyra.

"I may find Mr. Right, but I'm not going to risk waiting for that. I want to be a mom more than I want to find the right guy."

Mrs. Thompson smiled. "What if you meet someone who wants to have kids with you?"

"Men are not a priority right now."

"You do realize that many, most, of these children have had difficult backgrounds and may be suffering some the effects of that? It's not an easy option by any means."

"I've had experience with such kids. Part of my reason for going for adoption."

"I see. How are your work hours?"

"Flexible and manageable, compared to most of the working population."

Similar questions followed until the rep finally said it was time to discuss next steps.

"I'll set up an interview for tomorrow. If that goes well, the wheels will be set in motion. A team will assess the data from our current set of applicants and come up with a ranking determined by the needs of the child, the agency, and you yourself. Your flexibility on age and sex and potential contact with the birth parents will stand to you and balance out other factors."

Like my single status. Lyra smiled. "That sounds promising."

"Indeed. We shall be in touch," Mrs. Thompson said in the hallway, buttoning her coat.

After she'd gone, Lyra slumped on the floor of the child's bedroom. It wasn't that she had a burning desire to have a child enter her life. It was rather that she was looking forward to the time—a year or so down the line—when that kid was a natural part of her life, like breathing. Then she could look back on these days and chuckle at how clueless she'd been in all matters of child rearing and croon about the newfound sense of fulfillment she had in her life.

But who was to say she wouldn't be happy on her own? It would be so much easier if she were with someone who desperately wanted children. Like David. He'd wanted them. Even at age twenty-five, he'd been so sure, and his enthusiasm had been contagious. It had taken the burden of decision off her shoulders. In that parallel universe where David was still alive and with her, life was so much easier.

Her thoughts were interrupted by a loud knock on the front door. Had Mrs. Thompson forgotten something? She scanned the hallway for anything out of place—a scarf or gloves. Nothing.

Shrugging, she went to open up.

Liam stood there in the rain, his face drawn and pale, making his eyes seem even darker.

"Liam?"

"Lyra." His voice was quiet and grave.

Something was wrong. That look in his eyes—she'd seen it before, too many times.

"What is it, Liam? Come in, out of the cold."

"It's Dad!" Liam's voice was thick as he stumbled in over the threshold. "It's Dad... He's *dead*, Lyra."

9

Lyra shut the door and followed Liam who had wandered blindly into the kitchen. "What the *hell?* What happened?"

"Shot through the heart by a lone gunman." He flopped heavily onto the same chair Mrs. Thompson had sat on.

"What? Where? In *Sweden?*"

"Yeah. In some disused cinema. Around four o'clock. I've been trying to call you. I drove straight here." His voice was shaky, but he was making a heroic effort to be factual. He cleared his throat and added, "Nobody knows what the hell he was doing there. I was on my way to the airport. My flight is at eight. I'm going to drag Olive home by the hair of the head if I have to. She's not staying in that country for one minute more."

"Did you talk to her?"

God, why did I have it on airplane mode? She was probably trying to call me.

"Yes, she was the one that told me. But don't call her. She's turned off her phone. She asked me to tell you. That's why I'm..." He broke off, leaning his forehead into his hands.

"Liam—" A wave of guilt overcame her. She should

have stayed in Sweden. Maybe this wouldn't have happened then. She placed her hand awkwardly on his shoulder.

He pushed back upright. "I have to go."

"No wait," she urged. "Is this the best thing to do? What about your mother?"

"She's at home, with her sister Rose."

"A-are you even sure it was Pronsious? Have they identified—?"

He looked away. "We're sure, Lyra. Olive went there. She saw the body. It's him. He's dead, and we just have to accept it, and it's my fault for letting him go over when it should have been me."

She sat down opposite him. "Tell me what you know."

"He left the hotel walking. He'd left his room key at reception. That was the last anyone saw of him."

She felt a chill in her whole body. Poor Liam. Poor Olive. Poor Una. Poor Pronsious. Yes, he was a bit of a buffoon, but whose father wasn't in some way? He loved his family. He didn't deserve to be shot through the heart. Who the hell would have done this? And why?

"You're not able to drive," she said, seeing the tremor in his hands.

"I'm well capable."

She looked down to where her hands clutched onto the doorway. Releasing it, she walked to meet him at the front door. "I'm coming, too."

"Then you'd better get booking. I got the last seat on my flight."

He left.

Otto. I need to call Otto.

No, first I need to get a flight.

She searched all possible connections, but Liam had indeed taken the last available seat on any direct flights. Flights with stopovers would take until tomorrow to arrive. She booked a direct flight for the next day, Tuesday.

Then she called Otto.

"Ah," came the Swedish officer's voice over urgent male

voices in the background. "I thought I'd hear from you. This Pronsious Maguire homicide has shaken up this place. Eriksson wants Malmo in on it. I'm hanging on by a thread. The evidence of Klemens spying was interesting, he said, and the Olive-Hedvig affair too, but he sees no connection."

"No connection? What is *wrong* with him?" Lyra exploded.

"That's how it is." Otto's tone was heavy with defeat.

"All right, listen, I'm getting a flight landing mid-day in Kastrup tomorrow. Please let me come to you to discuss what can be done to convince Eriksson."

There was a pause. "Fine. Come direct to the station when you land. I'm working at the desk then. I'll watch out for you."

"OK, thanks, Otto."

Next, she called the departmental secretary's number who she knew wouldn't answer at this hour, so she left a message. "Janet? Lyra here. Sorry, but I need to cancel my classes for tomorrow. Possibly for the entire week. Family issues. Very serious."

Cringe. This was the second week in a row. The departmental head, Prof. Yeates, was going to have a fit.

As she re-packed her suitcase, she checked around the apartment. The red walls reminded her she had one more thing to do before she took off to Sweden again. Shit. How can this all be happening at the same time? She pressed the adoption agency's number.

"Hello, this is Lyra Norton. I have a follow-up appointment scheduled tomorrow as organized by Mrs. Thompson, and I need to postpone it."

"Yes, ma-am. Let me look at your file. One moment please."

"Sure, sure."

It took a long moment. Lyra drummed her fingers against the phone until the voice returned. "Oh, but Ms. Norton, this is a *second stage* interview."

"Yeah, I know. I need to postpone it for a few days. Maybe a week?"

"A week?" The receptionist's voice was breathless with misgiving. She deserved an Oscar. "You know, it may be quite difficult to get a replacement appointment. Prospective parents usually don't reschedule these ones. Oh, the calendar is not looking good. Mrs. Thompson is going on vacation next week."

Lyra squeezed her eyes shut. "Well, could you try? It's a matter of life and death, at my work."

"You work in University College Dublin?"

"Correct," Lyra breathed.

"Hm," came the voice, degrees cooler now. "I will see what can be done for you, but this, as I say, is unusual."

Was this the universe's way of telling her she was never going to be a mom? Maybe she didn't need the universe to tell her what she already knew.

10

The atmosphere in the cabin of the SAS Dublin-Copenhagen flight was different this time round—everybody on the flight seemed dour. Of course, it was a Tuesday, not a Friday. It was mostly Danish businesspeople in smart black suits under expensive winter coats.

The moments alone without a phone connection gave her space to sort out her thoughts. Because there was no way the killings of two fathers were unconnected.

Had Arvid had gotten wind of Olive's affair and killed his father in revenge? Or gotten someone to do it for him? He had the money to hire a hit man. Then again, one look at Arvid when he was talking about Hedvig showed her how much he'd loved him. And even if one assumed that Hedvig's murder was Arvid's doing, it sure as hell didn't explain Pronsious's. A slight distaste for your future father-in-law was no motivation for murder.

If it was a case of Klemens being on a quest for ultimate power, why would he murder Pronsious—a man he'd never met and who had nothing to do with him or the company? Klemens was far too clever and self-centered to put himself at risk like that.

Maybe Eriksson was right and there was no connection. However, in isolation, Pronsious's murder made even less sense. Who, other than the family, could have known that Pronsious was in Helsingborg? Why would an Irish farmer who'd never set foot in Sweden be a target if it wasn't in some way linked to Hedvig Sammland's death?

Would there be another strike? And who would it be? Another one in the family? The thought made her blood turn to ice. She had no other choice than to go and ferret out any clues she could, even if it meant standing on some toes. Otto could help for now, but if she got shoved off the case, then it was time to go solo.

As soon as she got phone network in Copenhagen Airport Terminal 3, she found a quiet corner to make her first call. Olive answered immediately

"I'm so, so sorry about your dad."

"Oh Lyra." Olive sounded exhausted. "Thanks for coming over so soon again. Liam's just arrived."

"Are you OK?"

Olive made a sniffing sound. "No, Lyra, I'm not. Who'd want to kill him? He'd never harm a fly. It feels like someone's trying to destroy us. Both our families. Who's doing this, Lyra? And why? Is it all because of me? I'm scared."

Her plaintive tone sent an arrow though Lyra's heart. "I'll be with you as soon as I can. Are you at home?"

"Mm, yes."

"Is Arvid there, too?"

"No, he's at work. But Liam's here."

"Arvid's at work?" *What the hell?*

"He said he couldn't sit around. He's been like this since...it happened."

Was it guilt making Arvid jittery? Or was his workaholic behavior an attempt to numb his feelings with business as usual? Either way, he should be with his fiancée. The man was insane.

There came a sniffle and then a series of labored breaths

as though Olive was forcing herself to stay normal. "I don't know what to do. Liam keeps shouting at me, telling me I should go home, but I can't leave Arvid, not with him like this. Liam just doesn't understand. I wish he'd go away and leave us alone. He's not helping. Can you come and take Liam away, Lyra, please? He'll listen to you."

"Yes. I'll come over. You can't go to Ireland until the police here have given you the all clear."

"Oh. Yes."

"Tell Liam that to make him shut up."

"Mm, I will. Come straight to the house, please. Are you taking a taxi?"

"No, I'm hiring a car at Copenhagen. I'll be there soon."

Just a slight detour to the police station first.

*

Lyra parked near the police station on Rundgången. She stood looking at the white façade with its long line of windows. The doors opened, and Otto came out, with red eyes and a crumpled shirt that she was hastily tucking into her bulging waistline. "Welcome to Sweden."

"Yeah. I wish the circumstances were happier."

Otto raised an eyebrow. "In this business? Come on. You need coffee."

Lyra followed Otto into the station and down a corridor, the Swedish officer talking loudly most of the way. "Soon as this story hit, they called in a guy called Magnus Larsson from Malmo. He's heading the investigation now. No choice in the matter."

"I'm sorry."

"Yeah, but you know how it goes." Otto punched a button on the coffee machine with a ferocity that suggested she was stifling anger. "Eriksson dumped a load of drugs related burglary cases on me. I explained about you, and he said we can sit in on the meetings and give input. He's a lot more accepting of having a family consultant like you on it now that it officially involves the Irish side. They're not sending representation over, though. How long are you staying?"

"I've no return booked yet. I need to make sure Olive's all right first."

"Black, right?" She handed Lyra a black coffee and got one for herself. "But what about your job?"

Lyra grimaced, thinking about the lecture on authorship attribution she was currently missing and the post-grad mentorship meeting scheduled for right after. "I took a brief absence of leave." *Of my senses.*

"Good. Let's go somewhere quiet, so we can talk." Otto pushed open the door to an interrogation room. It was like the interrogation rooms in Dublin—bare walls, a steel-topped table with three plastic chairs around it, an observation window with one-way glass, and a video camera on a stand.

"Two homicides," Otto began. "Fathers to the same couple. Coincidence?" She sat back, watching Lyra.

Lyra shrugged, twisting her coffee cup. "Good question. My gut feeling is no, but I can't see the connection. You got my message about Hedvig and Olive, right?"

"Yeah…" Otto trailed off, looking into space, probably going through the same mental exercise of wondering whether Arvid could've killed his father out of impassioned revenge. The question was, why would he kill Olive's father, too?"

"It doesn't make sense," Lyra agreed. "Anything more on Klemens?"

"Fail-safe alibis—for both murders. He was in meetings both times. I have statements from the other attendees."

Lyra drummed her fingers on the table. "And yet all that tells us is he wasn't present."

"True. No-one's off the hook yet, especially not him. It's not the same MO though. Pronsious Maguire's decision to fly here was too last minute for a contract killing to have been organized."

"Right, but there is the commonality that both men went wandering off on their own to some place without explaining it to anyone. Which makes me think it may have been a threat, or an invitation they couldn't refuse?" Lyra surmised.

"Perhaps. We must find out why Maguire went to that particular cinema. Is there anybody who knew both these men well enough to persuade them to do something uncharacteristic?"

Lyra nibbled the edge of her empty coffee cup. The only obvious link was the couple themselves, but she couldn't see it. Not to mention that blaming them for their respective fathers' murders seemed unspeakably cruel.

"Maybe I'm too close to the case," she said, dumping the cup in the trash bin. "Where's this cinema?"

"Two kilometers east of here. He walked there from his hotel."

"Any chance I could check it out?" Lyra asked.

Otto glanced at her watch. Then she shrugged. "Oh hell, why not? I'm only on paperwork, and that can wait."

*

Ten minutes later they rolled up in Otto's car to the cinema. "Have you been here already yesterday?" Lyra asked, reaching for the box of latex gloves in the door compartment that she remembered from last time.

"Briefly, straight after the technicians left. It should be quiet now." Otto turned and gave her a piercing look through the gloom. "Honestly, how well do you know this couple? Would they have any reason to kill their fathers? Some weird religious rite of passage before they got married or something?"

Lyra shook her head. "God, no. They're not the happiest couple on the planet—they've had their issues—and he's certainly highly strung, but I can't make it square with what I know of them. They're not crazy. Of course, never say never when it comes to crimes of passion."

Otto shook her head vigorously and turned into Hjorthögsvägen, slowing down to 30 kmph to comply with the speed sign.

"Perhaps I should also mention that I was involved with Olive's brother, Liam, years back. It didn't amount to much, but in the spirit of full disclosure you should know, seeing as he's knocking about here and…" She wasn't sure how to finish.

"This is the farmer guy, right?"

"Yeah. Hey, any word on the secretary, Berit?"

"She got delayed. Some family issue. That lady is pushing it. One more day, and we will hunt her down."

"She's still the only one who might know why Hedvig went to Helsingor?"

"Yep."

"It would be really good to know that."

"No kidding."

Otto parked the car. It was an unremarkable side street—an Asian food emporium, a hairdresser's salon, and a dormant hardware store. The *Bio Royale* cinema was cordoned off with police tape, and a lone officer stood by the door.

"Hang on here a moment." Otto got out and walked up to the lone officer standing outside by the cinema's front window. She started talking and gesticulating toward Lyra. A conversation followed with staccato phrases and curt nods on both sides.

Lyra scanned the street up and down. It was a dim back alley with dumpsters, not an obvious street for an idle tourist to wander down. There were no CCTV cameras anywhere, which was unsurprising as they were far less ubiquitous in Helsingborg than in Dublin. The windows opposite that overlooked the cinema entrance all seemed to belong to business premises, and several were boarded up.

She tried to picture Pronsious wandering there, on the basis of something—a phone call, say—and then being shot. The image refused to come. Pronsious belonged in his comfortable leather chair in his living room in Kiltomb, or tending the cows in his dairy, or teasing Una in the kitchen, not lying on the floor in some cinema in Helsingborg with a bullet in his chest. It was a dreadful thing to lose a father. She'd lost hers when she was twelve. Imagine losing a father and a father-in-law slash lover all in the same week under highly suspect circumstances? One thing was clear; She had to get Olive home to Ireland as soon as possible.

Otto returned. "That's Wallström. He's one of ours. I had to explain what we're at."

Lyra looked at the policeman. "Everything all right?"

"All clear. Let's do this." Otto pointed with her gloved hand at the double glass doors with a vertical brass handle. "This is where Maguire entered."

"It was unlocked?"

"We think so. His fingerprints don't indicate any fumbling to get in. Rather, a clean yank outward on the door handle."

They entered. Dust motes sparkled in the beams of light from fake candles on the walls. The Moroccan-style floor tiles were so worn that they dipped into troughs in front of the ticketing booth and candy kiosk. A faded brown velvet carpet stretched from tiles to the two theaters. It smelled fusty, and the yellow ocher wallpaper was tattered in places. Polished, worn wood with faux gold details dated the décor back to the seventies, or earlier.

"How soon after coming in did he got shot?"

"Immediately, we think, from the postmortem. The killer stood somewhere around here." Otto walked to a position behind the kiosk. "Whoever it was probably looked through the glass, saw him, stepped out like this, and took the shot from here." Otto mimicked a gunman stepping out from behind the kiosk, cocking a pistol and shooting. "A 9 mm bullet tore right through his aorta, and he died within five minutes. Our killer was either a trained marksman or a lucky shot."

Lyra winced at how casually Otto discussed Pronsious's death.

"Sorry. Did you know him well?" Otto asked.

"Kinda. We're from the same village. I've known him since childhood. I'd been to see him recently."

"I'm so—"

"It's OK, Otto. Any fingerprints?"

"No. The killer had gloves on."

"Could you go outside to the door and come in again?" Lyra asked. "I want to see how it looks from here."

Otto nodded and walked back outside the main door.

Lyra regarded Otto standing by the door through the parallel panes of scratched glass at the front and back of the kiosk. She hunkered down out of Otto's line of sight and peered through again. In the dim light, she could just about make out Otto's figure, her stockiness, her blond hair, but her features were a blur.

She stepped out from around the left side of the kiosk and mimicked shooting.

"Easy there, Deadpool," Otto said. She cocked her head and regarded Lyra's pose. "I can see you plainly. Try staying hidden as you shoot."

Lyra crouched behind the glass and tried aiming at Otto. "Hm, I wonder if they're left-handed." She switched hands and pretended to shoot with the left.

Otto nodded. "That would make things easier."

"Did the inspection team find anything?"

"DNA results come tomorrow. Fibers, hair—we collected what we could."

"What kind of movies did they show here when it was open?" she asked, scanning the faded posters on the wall. *Casablanca, Gladiator, Star Wars IV, Avatar.*

"Blockbusters, and small local interest ones—the usual crowd-attracting stuff for a small, independent cinema."

Pronsious couldn't have any connection to this cinema, but the killer could. The question was whether the cinema and the ferry had any connection. And if so, why?

They prowled around, searching for more clues, but there was nothing that the crew hadn't already gathered up. That didn't surprise Lyra. In her experience, the crime scene crew usually did a thorough job that left little room for an enterprising detective to come along and discover something crucial.

Otto jangled her car keys. "I need to get back. You need to get to Olive. Let me know if you find out anything—call me after you talk to them."

11

Fjälastofta was a scenic coastal village north of Helsingborg. Lyra had to slow down to 30 kmph as she drove through the center. Many of the old half-timber fishermen's houses in the harbor had been preserved for what looked like hundreds of years and gave the place a timeless appearance. Although it looked desolate and windswept now, she could imagine families with kids and dogs loitering on the promenade, eating ice-cream on a summer's day.

Arvid's and Olive's *villa* was a two-story wooden house perched on a slight hill outside the center with a view over flat plains of farmland in one direction and the sea in the other. The walls were painted in the traditional Falun red like most of the houses she'd passed on the way. Pristine white windows and shutters completed the traditional look.

On the porch she shook out her stiffened limbs. *What do you say to a friend whose father has been murdered?*

After a short wait, the door opened to reveal Olive in a white cashmere robe. Her face was drawn and anemic, the only color the red around her eyes. All the luster had extinguished from her skin and hair. She looked about ten years older. Lyra sucked in a breath.

"Oh, Lyra."

Lyra held out her arms. "Olive, I'm so, so sorry."

Olive fell into the hug. Lyra didn't let go for a long time. No words seemed appropriate. Nothing expressed the essential hopelessness of the world, the ultimate futility of living, of loving, of caring, of all the things that Pronsious had done in his life for the love of his family—all the sacrifices, all the emotional effort, all the pride, the planning, the scheming, the decisions, big and small, that defined him as a father and as a man. She squeezed her friend's shoulders tight.

Olive finally drew back.

"Who's here?" Lyra asked, listening out for noises but hearing none. "Arvid? Liam?"

"Just Arvid." Olive padded the way through the hall.

Lyra removed her boots and followed. The décor was tasteful—taupes, beiges, and creams with silver accents. Scandi-minimalist—IKEA upgraded. The Olive of old had more adventurous taste. Her childhood bedroom had been patchwork heaven. Her dorm room in college featured fuchsia pinks and forest greens and vivid artwork from South East Asia. Where had all that color gone?

"And Liam?"

"He left earlier. He had a fight with Arvid."

"A fight?"

Olive's wan expression seemed to say *please, no questions.*

They entered a roomy sitting room. Arvid sat in a lavender sofa in front of a large, curtainless window overlooking a long field with tilled black earth as far as the eye could see. It felt a little too exposed to be cozy. The smoky air hit the back of Lyra's throat.

"Hello," he said, glancing up but then returning to gazing out the window. In the four days since she'd last seen him, his physical condition had deteriorated drastically. His body was taut with suppressed emotion. His veined hands trembled as he pushed down a cigarette into an ashtray that was on the brink of overflowing.

"He's taken up smoking again," Olive said, compressing her lips. "First time in ten years." She went to the window and eked it open, letting in a blast of chilly fresh air.

Lyra shrugged. "Whatever works."

Olive sat down beside Arvid and stared straight ahead. Lyra took the armchair perpendicular to the two of them.

Nobody said anything.

Lyra and Olive made eye contact, but Arvid refused to engage, preferring to hunch over his knees.

Then Olive sprang to life in a weird, jerky manner. "I'll get tea. Or would you prefer coffee?"

"Coffee, please." Lyra didn't offer to help, because she wanted this opportunity to get Arvid on his own.

Olive left the room, and as soon as the clanking of dishes in the kitchen filled the sullen silence, Arvid shifted his position on the sofa.

"Damned business," he said, clearing his throat. "A damned, rotten business. All of it."

Lyra nodded. "That's one way of putting it. I'm sorry, Arvid, this must be extremely difficult for you. Tell me, what happened with Liam earlier?"

He shook his head furiously. "I told him to go. He was upsetting Olive."

"Mm, as if she needed that," she said warmly. "What was he thinking?"

Arvid met her gaze. "He's thinking he has to act like her father now. I'm her husband, and we're a team. Liam's not welcome."

"Where'd he go?"

"I don't know, and I don't care." Arvid's gaze met hers. "Does it matter? Someone's out to ruin us. You see that now, don't you?" His emphasis on *now* sounded accusatory. So he'd expected her to reach some conclusion before this, did he?

"It looks that way," she said carefully. "What do you suppose Pronsious was doing at that cinema?"

He rubbed his forehead with the heel of his fist. "That's

what I want to know!" His face flushed. "You must find out who told him to go there. That's the key. Don't waste your time on interviews and whatnot with all the wrong people. Get to the sender of the message, and there's where you'll catch your man."

"Or woman," she said with enough steel in her voice to let him know he could drop the mansplaining. For good measure she added, "You're talking like someone who thinks he knows who the sender was. Come on, tell me."

He frowned. "No, I don't know. But we're the only people Pronsious knows over here, and we certainly didn't tell him to go there. So, who did? Who would he trust enough to follow their instructions? No one. Unless, it was someone in authority. The police, maybe?"

"There may be other reasons for him to enter a disused cinema." She couldn't think of one—she was just throwing it out there.

He sniffed derisively. "Someone lured him there."

"Why would he be out on his own, though?"

"We asked him to come here for dinner."

Olive came into the room with a mug that she set on the table in front of Lyra. "We told him to get a taxi straight out to us, but he likes to walk around. Said it was good for his circulation."

She sat down beside Arvid, closer this time. Arvid didn't react.

"We waited and waited, and he didn't come." Her voice hitched. "Little did we think…little did we think he was in some kind of trouble. This is all our fault. If we'd only picked him up ourselves like we should have, then…then this wouldn't have happened!"

"You were both here the whole time?" Lyra tried to keep her tone casual, but there was no earthly way she could ask that without sounding like a cop.

The couple nodded simultaneously.

"I was cooking *coq au vin*, his favorite, and Arvid was in the wine cellar, choosing something for the table."

"Was anyone else invited to this dinner?"

Arvid leaned forward, lit up a new cigarette, and took a deep drag. "You mean, do we have alibis? As we already told the police, no, just each other."

They exchanged a quick glance. They were colluding on the delivery of information. Lyra wanted to shake Olive and get what she really thought out of her.

"My God, to think we even have to defend ourselves about this." Olive huffed in a way that resembled her father.

Lyra felt sorry for her friend, but she couldn't make it easier if she was going to get to the bottom of this. "And what time exactly was he due to arrive here? What time did you tell him dinner was at?"

"6 p.m. He wanted to mosey around the hotel area first, he said, seeing as he'd paid so much for it. And then he'd get the hotel to call him a taxi out to Fjälastofta when it was nearer the time. He was all excited. He had it all planned out. We didn't think anything could go wrong." She trailed off miserably. "He insisted on us not picking him up. You know what he's like. Wants to do everything himself to have control over every situation."

"Yes," Lyra said softly. Olive was still talking in present tense about her father, which made her account all the more heart-wrenching. "And when was this conversation?"

"Around 3 p.m."

"And that's the last you heard from him?"

Olive nodded. She seemed incapable of speaking.

Arvid shifted, pulling out a cushion from behind his back and dumping it on the space beside him. "Will you be able to get his phone records? Do the Swedish police have them?"

"Me personally? I don't know. But I'm sure the investigation team is looking into them."

He nodded. "Because that's the key. Find out who told him to go there and the case will be closed—both murders, as far as I'm concerned."

Again with the mansplaining. He wanted to direct her—

or was it misdirect her? What made him so sure that the murders were linked?

Olive nodded weakly.

They both stared at her.

"I'm going to try my best," Lyra said.

"I hope so." Arvid's voice had turned loud and querulous. He stubbed out the cigarette which was three quarters full. Butts and ashes in the ashtray spilled onto the table. "*För hellvete...*"

Arvid didn't finish the "to hell with this" thought or clear up the mess. He rose and paced the room behind the sofa. The sun hit his white shirt and highlighted his gaunt frame. The light cast deep shadows on his face, highlighting the skull underneath. As he walked, he glared sporadically at Lyra, perhaps to elicit a response, but she refused to be drawn into a discussion on where the investigation should start, especially not with someone who thought he had it all figured out.

Lyra took a sip of her coffee. It was cold. She glanced up. Olive, staring into space, clearly had no idea that this wasn't fresh coffee.

Strangely, Arvid seemed more shaken about the murder of Olive's father than his own. Of course, that could be down to the delayed response and the cumulative effect of two murders. Olive seemed disconnected to the world. Maybe she had already entered the denial stage of grief. Whatever she'd been expecting coming here, it sure as hell wasn't this eerie sense that she was being excluded from something.

Lyra continued to take pretend sips of the terrible, cold coffee, letting the silence draw out. She could handle awkwardness longer than most people. It was her secret weapon, because most people abhorred silence and tended to fill it, often with useful information. However, neither Olive nor Arvid seemed inclined to offer a lead back into the conversation. She couldn't stay there all day. She needed to find Liam to find out what he had got out of them.

"How many times have you been questioned by the Swedish police?" she asked Olive, thinking it was best to start with an easy question again.

Olive wrapped her hands around her knee and rocked back and forth. "They'd been here about Hedvig, and they came by here yesterday again," Olive said. "About Dad."

"Were you both here at the time?"

"Mm-hm. They questioned us both."

"Together or separately?"

"Together," Olive said. "I-I was in a bad way, and I couldn't say much. I was so glad Arvid was here and I didn't have to go through it alone. They ask so many questions when you're at your weakest and most vulnerable. It's not fair."

"I know," Lyra said softly. "It's definitely not easy. On either side. But especially on you."

The grandfather clock in the corner bonged out twice. Lyra glanced at her watch, which was still stuck in Irish time, 1:00 p.m. She twiddled the button and moved the hands forward an hour.

They stared at each other through the smoke.

Lyra took the coffee cup out to the kitchen where she dumped it down the sink then gathered up her coat and her phone. There was a message from Otto telling her to come to the precinct ASAP as they were having a meeting she could sit in on as Magnus Larsson, the Malmo lead investigator, was eager for any input. *Good.*

"I'll call in on you in the morning," she said to Olive, who had come out into the hall. "You're not going to work, are you?"

"I'm not. Arvid might, though. Look, thanks for coming over so quickly. I'm sorry we're so…"

"Grief stricken?"

"Mm, yes." Her eyes filled with tears again. "I'll try to get it more together for next time, I promise."

"No, take your time. You can't rush the grieving process, so don't even try. Take it from me. Just look after yourself and Arvid," Lyra said, hugging her once more.

Olive nodded.

With her hand on the front door handle, Lyra asked casually, "Oh, yeah, what did Liam say?"

"He's in bits," Olive said with a full body shudder. "I've never seen him like that. I didn't know what to say to him. He seems to think that me leaving is the only way to make this better, and he's focusing all his energies on that. But it won't make anything better."

"Leaving Arvid?"

"Leaving Arvid, leaving Sammland, leaving the country. He needs to mind his own business. He doesn't know what he's dealing with."

"No, he doesn't. Nobody does. You have to do what's right for you, Olive."

Lyra got into her car and glanced in the rear-view mirror. The curtain in the kitchen twitched. If she wasn't imagining it, they were glad she was gone. Olive had acted like some kind of demented Stepford wife instead of the capable champion of matrimonial equality she used to be. Arvid was as caustic as ever. And the smoking?

In a way, though, she couldn't blame them. After David, she'd spiraled, too, taking refuge in some bad habits like late night drinking, hookups with unsuitable people, and sporadic weight training sessions to undo the alcohol, all of which made her feel worse. Olive and Arvid were at their wits' end, each dealing with their own father's death, and Olive dealing with a terrible secret that she couldn't share with him. It would take a lot from them to recover from this. Solving the crime would be a good start.

12

"Cause of death."

Lyra watched from the back of the room as the tall, sinewy supervisor, Eriksson held up a plastic bag with a 9 mm bullet inside. He was debriefing the investigation team—Otto, Otto's colleague Andersson, two other officers from Helsingborg, Larsson from Malmo, and Lyra herself, listening in.

"One shot into the right ventricle," Eriksson announced.

"Professional job?" Larsson asked.

"Could be. Not necessarily," Eriksson said.

"Any other connections to the Sammland murder other than the fact that it was another father of the same couple?"

"No. We're researching all avenues. Green activists, animal activists, IRA links, Nazi, Antifa, you name it. Oh, Freemasons, too."

Otto glanced at Lyra and discreetly shook her head. Lyra agreed. Whatever this was, it wasn't any of these groups.

"The deceased entered the *Bio Royale* cinema building at around 15:30 according to a delivery man to the Asia Emporium food store," Eriksson continued. "The homicide happened minutes after. He was shot by someone who was waiting there for him. Visibility was low."

"Does this cinema—Bio Royale—have any significance to either of the families?" Larsson asked.

"Not that I know of. It shut down in late 2018. It hadn't been doing well before that point, so the owner never reopened. We questioned him this morning."

"Anything else from the DNA?"

"Not yet."

"Phone records?"

"He called his daughter at 15:01 and had a brief conversation with her which she herself has confirmed. He also received and read an email at 15:05. We don't know who sent the message. The email was blank."

"Blank?" Larsson asked.

"Yes, we believe it was a disappearing email."

"Where did it disappear to?"

Eriksson's eyes darted around the room. "Uhm…where's Martin?"

"He has the flu," Otto said. "Disappeared," she muttered under her breath which made Andersson smirk.

Lyra cleared her throat. "Perhaps I can explain?"

Eriksson's gaze landed on her, at first tight with misgiving, but then he relaxed. "Yes, go ahead."

"It's fine in English," Otto muttered.

Lyra rose from her seat. "OK, most email providers have a confidential mode which allows you to assign an expiration date to a message. The provider hosts this self-destructing message on its own server instead of passing it to another one. This allows them to delete it after a specified period.

"If both sender and recipient use the same provider, Gmail, say, this process works seamlessly, and a message in confidential mode will look like a typical email. But once the expiration date or time comes, the body text will disappear, though the recipient will still be able to see the subject header in their inbox."

"Can we track the sender from the email header then?" Eriksson asked, looking at Lyra.

"Depends. A search warrant to the internet service provider of the originating IP address would lead to the suspect's account information, but if they've used any kind of anonymizer, such as TOR, then all bets are off. It's likely that if the killer sent the email, they would have used one. Still, it's worth checking out. What would be really interesting to know is whether Hedvig Sammland also received such a disappearing message before he left for Helsingor."

"Yes, get IT to cross-check," Larsson said, addressing Otto. "We also need to question Olive Maguire, Arvid Sammland, and Klemens Sammland again. Plus, we need to find this Berit Ehrling."

Lyra found it heartening that Larsson was prepared to dig deeper within the family.

The meeting was adjourned, and the officers dispersed to tackle their tasks. Once they were alone in the meeting space, Otto asked, "How was it in Fjälastofta?"

"Inconclusive. Olive was in a bit of a daze, poor thing. Cold coffee, blank stares. Doesn't know whether she's coming or going. As for Arvid—I don't know. I get the sense he knows more than he's saying. What did he say in his interviews here?"

"Eriksson interviewed him yesterday, and he seemed to be quite responsive, but low-level paranoid, going on about Klemens mainly. The other interview yesterday in their house was merely to inform them of the death. Nothing particular came from that."

"Do you have the transcripts?" Lyra asked. *Nothing particular* was usually anything but.

Otto went to her desk and pulled out a sheaf of pages. "Sorry for the dead trees. I don't trust email. Don't expect much. He mumbled incoherently a lot of the time, like he was half insane. Going on about Klemens yet again."

Lyra took the pages. "Thanks. Let's see."

THE SOUND

"He's convinced his father's death and Pronsious's are linked, but he keeps stopping short of saying Klemens shot Pronsious."

"What about Klemens? Hasn't he been taken in yet?"

Otto sighed. "It's Larsson's call, and he hasn't done it yet. If I hassle him about it, Eriksson is sure to throw me off the case for good."

Lyra shook her head. "Two fathers of the same couple are dead, and we can't even link them. The killing may not stop there. I think that's what's really wrong with Olive and Arvid—they fear they're next. I have to admit, I'm starting to get worried too."

Otto's expression clouded over. "Yeah. We're stationing an officer out there today. Check the transcripts and let me know if you discover anything. Now I gotta run, but stay in touch, right?"

*

Arvid's interview transcripts in Swedish were disappointing even to Lyra's judicious eye. As Otto had said, Arvid had raved on, hinting at an unnamed assailant, without actually ever naming Klemens, although it was pretty clear he suspected him. He'd spent the rest of the time asking why the police hadn't gotten further with the inquiry. Lyra could easily imagine his peevish tone and belligerent stares.

In the notes from the interview informing them of Pronsious's death, Olive had said little. Arvid had been more specific and urgent, outwardly claiming that they needed to check Klemens's correspondence, in particular with regard to professional contract killers. His single-mindedness indicated an unhealthy obsession with a single theory that Arvid just couldn't let go of.

Now she had to find Liam. That overdue shower would be good, too. Her hotel was within walking distance of the precinct, so she called him as she walked.

"What are you doing?" she asked.

"I'm in my hotel room," he said, sounding grumpy. "Arvid and Olive threw me out last night."

"So I heard. Don't take it personally, Liam. They're in a bad way."

"Yeah, I know. No worries. Hugo was in town, and we went out for drinks, so it wasn't all bad."

"I'm glad. Hey, want to meet?"

"Sure. I need to get outside. Let's meet at the entrance of Kärnan—that tower thing, it's near my hotel and probably yours, too."

"When?"

"Uh, four-ish?"

"Good." She hung up. That was enough time to grab a shower.

*

At five to four, she saw him by the old entrance way, hands thrust deep into the Barbour jacket pockets, marching over and back like a sentry. There were no tourists, so he stood out. Kärnan, or the Helsingborg keep, was an odd-looking red-brick tower on a steep hill overlooking the old town, accessible via several flights of stone steps—the only remains of an earlier medieval fortress built by the Danes when both sides of the Oresund were controlled by them.

She swiveled to see the Danish side—Kronborg Castle barely visible through the fog. Both edifices faced each other like warlocks. So many power struggles over that little stretch of water.

"Liam," she called out, walking up to him and smiling.

When they hugged, she felt a rush of tenderness. Although she was irritated with him for hassling Olive, he'd just lost a father. He'd dropped everything in his life to be there for his sister. It was only natural to want to whisk her away from an environment where fathers were dropping like flies.

"Are you OK?" she asked when he let go.

"I'll survive," he said gruffly. "How about you?"

"Fine, yeah. I'm so sorry you have to go through this."

They started climbing up the broad, white steps.

"Yeah, it's shite," he said. "What have you managed to find out?"

"Not much," she said. Then, as the spark of hope in his dark eyes extinguished, she added, "it's not all hopeless. The police are doing all they can, and they're stationing someone out at the house today."

"How do you know this?"

"Oh, I have a contact there," she said hurriedly. "What's the situation in Ireland? How's your mam?"

He groaned. "She's in a bad way. Just been on the phone to her. Floods of tears one moment, unresponsive the next. Nothing I say or do seems to help. She doesn't know how to live without him. She doesn't know who she *is* without him. They were married for forty-one years."

"It's so hard on her. You're doing great, Liam. Are the rest of the family home yet?"

"Ella arrived last night, and Dermot's going over this afternoon. They've both managed to take a few days off from their incredibly important jobs in Dublin."

"It'll be good to have them both there."

"Oh, they're mainly worried that the funeral won't happen in the time slots they've marked off in their calendars."

"Jesus wept."

"And Dermot expects Mam to cook for him, Christ's sake."

"Unreal," she agreed.

"Mam needs Olive home."

"But you know that's not possible. Maybe best not to hassle her about it?"

He stiffened. "That's between me and her. It's a family matter."

"I'm her closest friend. She's practically family to me."

He looked away. "Being around Arvid is doing her no

good. He's not right in the head."

"Would you blame him, though?" she said. "Hedvig's funeral is the day after tomorrow. That's already disorientating without this on top. In his shoes, I'd be a wreck as well."

They had reached the top of the first flight of stairs from where they had a good view over the rooftops, but in unspoken agreement, they kept going to the park at the top.

"Any word on when we can start to plan Dad's funeral?"

"It'll be at least a few days before they get the…your father home."

"Say 'the body', Lyra. That's all he is now." He sounded defeated.

She climbed more steps in silence. She was making a mess of this. Had Liam been merely anybody, she could be professionally empathetic and conduct the conversation more smoothly. However, as things were, she was pretty choked up herself, and it was only hitting her now exactly how much. When she was running around on police business with Otto, she could pretend it was just another case. But it wasn't. It really wasn't.

"I'm sorry, Liam, it could take a while. As soon as the police here are ready to release him, I'll let you know."

"Is there anything you can tell me?" he asked.

"We don't know what we're dealing with yet. We don't even know if there's any link between Hedvig and your dad. It could be a psychopath hellbent on destroying both families, for all we know." Her voice hitched. "It's weird because that's one of the things Pronsious said when I was in Kiltomb. He said it could be a psychopath on the loose."

Liam dipped his head. "Yeah, for all my slagging off of him, he often had this sixth sense. God, I could have been nicer to him, especially in the final days."

She patted his arm. "Your mother needs you more than she needs the others by the sounds of it."

He sighed. "Trying to get rid of me, too?"

"That's not it, and you know it."

"I'm sorry." He shook his head. "That just popped out. I can't seem to do or say anything right anymore."

They were at the top and had entered a beautiful park elevated above all else in the town, with paths winding through grassy lawns in three directions from the central tower. Although the trees were bare and the flower beds filled with brown stumps of flowers, she could imagine its colorful glory in the summer. The view was even better in the fourth direction—all the way across the Sound to Denmark.

Lyra regarded Liam's side profile as he stared out at the view. She pointed out the harbor and Kronborg Slot, repeating what Otto had told her about the majestic building.

"Hamlet's Castle, right?" he said.

"Yes, but to the locals, it's more significant as some Danish king's military powerhouse from the eighteenth century."

"More significant than Shakespeare? Who'd have thought."

"I know, right." She chuckled. "And now I wish I could quote something from it other than 'to be or not to be.' Shame on me, I even did it in school. You?"

"No. We did Macbeth."

They stared in silence at the imposing castle. She peeked a look at Liam's face. She was glad he could be distracted, even if only for a fleeting moment. Nothing would reduce the pain of losing his father, but from experience, the best thing would be to make him feel useful. "Listen, is there anybody that Pronsious was in contact with of late? Any unusual conversations you might have overheard or that he might have mentioned?"

"Not that I can think of. He didn't talk to anyone outside the home except for the lads down in McNally's."

"Do you know who they are?"

"Yeah, all regulars."

"If you're up to talking to them, could you check in with

them, just in case? Ask them to tell you anything that he told them about his trip to Sweden."

"Mm. Will do." He turned to her sharply. "Come on, what's your gut telling you? Could it have been Arvid?"

"Liam, take it easy. Arvid had no motive to kill Pronsious, or did you ever notice antagonism when he was there?"

"Not antagonism. Avoidance, mainly."

"Besides, it would be a stupid thing to do, especially as he hadn't been cleared off the suspect list for Hedvig. His alibi checks out. He was with Olive the whole time."

"So you're saying it definitely wasn't Arvid?" He curled and uncurled his fist.

"I can't say that for sure, Liam. I can't say anything for sure. What we need to find out is who told your father to go to that cinema. It had to have been someone he knew. Either that, or somebody threatened him with something if he didn't do it. It's more likely it was someone he knew. Hence, my request to you to ask the crowd in McNally's.

"Yeah, I get it," he said quietly. "Sorry, I'm just trying to figure it out. There's a lot in my head."

"I know."

They walked up to the entrance of the tower which was closed.

"I think we've done enough sightseeing for now," he said. "You look cold. Are you up for getting brunch or something? I haven't eaten since Ireland. I haven't been able to, until now. Apparently, my hotel does a mean fry-up."

"Then it's a good idea," she said. He would need energy to deal with the next stages—denial and anger.

They walked in silence down the stone stairways back to the street level, over the old square, and down two streets to his hotel. The facade was brightly lit with potted plants hanging in the windows.

"Not bad," she said.

"Mm. I got lucky."

"Of course, you must have left home in a terrible hurry."

"It was pretty frantic, yeah." He laughed bitterly. "I think I broke the land speed record from Kiltomb to Dublin. I have to say, it wasn't how I imagined my first view of Sweden or Denmark."

She made a show of studying the menu on the board in the entrance, but she couldn't focus. Having him standing there so close beside her with his solid, comforting presence awoke all kinds of feelings—some old ones, some wistful memories from the past, and some new ones. Her stomach was in a tight knot. She had no desire for food.

"What are your plans for the next few days?" he asked when they sat down at a table.

"Hedvig's funeral on Thursday. Tomorrow I'm just going to sit in my room and figure this out. Do my homework, in other words. I also need to catch up on coursework corrections from home."

"That sounds like a full schedule. Should I come with you to Hedvig's funeral?"

"No, Liam," she said firmly. "I'm going there with Otto, my police contact."

Liam nodded and fiddled with the cutlery. "They were quick to arrange that funeral, weren't they?"

"They wanted it done quickly and in private to minimize press interference. Hedvig's a high-profile man around here."

"Yes, I know. Olive used to boast about him. So what about after? Should I meet you somewhere?"

She regarded him with sympathy. He wanted to feel useful, but there was nothing he could do over here. She could suggest he try talking to Olive again, but that would be going against Olive's wishes, who just wanted to be left alone. Liam's best option was simply to go home again. Did she have to spell it out?

"You need to rest," she said. "I bet you haven't slept since—"

"No, you're right, you're right."

"And consider, maybe, going home?" she added.

He shut his eyes and opened them again. "It was a mistake, me coming here, wasn't it?"

"Well..." she hesitated.

"By the time you come back from that funeral, I'll probably be gone to the airport," he said.

"You're doing the right thing."

"Yeah. Promise me you'll get Olive home as soon as possible and then come home yourself, too?"

Her heart melted at his woebegone expression. She reached across the tablecloth and squeezed his hand. "I promise."

13

On Thursday, Lyra unpacked a black dress from the bottom of her suitcase. She hadn't worn it since the last funeral she'd attended as a civilian—David's. *Christ.* She pressed the wool to her face and breathed in the faint whiff of cigar smoke that she remembered from his funeral reception. God, she missed him.

David had been killed by Howley-Murphy's gang two weeks after the main culprit—Sean Howley-Murphy was identified in the pedophile ring. The despicable ring-leader been taken into custody, and it caused a media hullabaloo. She and David had gone out to celebrate the successful closure of the case which had eaten up eleven months of her time and a bunch of nerves. Never once had she thought she might be in danger.

They'd gone to see a play in the Gaiety theater. Not that they were theater aficionados by any stretch, but David's cousin had been playing the part of Peggy in *Philadelphia Here I Come,* and he'd wanted to support her.

The gunman appeared out of nowhere as they'd crossed Parnell Square, heading north to Phibsboro where David lived at the time. It had been a balmy night, and they walked

THE SOUND

without a care in the world. Her fellow officers had warned her that retaliation was a fact of life, but part of her hadn't believed it, or thought that it could only happen when she was on duty. She'd learned that lesson the hard way.

To this day, nobody could ascertain whether he'd aimed at her and missed or killed David to torment her. They'd never found the killer. Either way, that part of her life was over. She handed in her letter of resignation from the force the next day. Her superior wouldn't accept it, but after hours of argument, he was left with no choice.

She went into the bathroom, splashed cold water on her face, and told herself, "You got this."

Her phone buzzed. It was a text from Otto.

"Berit's showing up at the funeral. Will you pick me up on your way? Moses is using my car today, and I don't want to take a squad to a funeral."

She followed it with her address.

*

As Lyra entered the funeral location into the car's navi—a place further north called Ingelsträde—she wondered if the killer would show up there. With 41 percent of male homicide victims being killed by someone they knew, it wasn't entirely unlikely.

On her way she swung by the address of Otto's place—a road on the edge of Helsingborg with many high-rise apartments of the lower middle class variety. Otto came running out onto the sidewalk, her coat tails flapping in the wind, her hand clamped on top of her head to save her dubious hairstyle.

"So, what's with Olive's brother?" Otto asked. "What did you do with Farm Boy?"

"Not much. Walked around Kärnan. Had lunch."

Otto stared at the side of her face.

"What?" Lyra hissed. "It's hard enough to drive on the right without you staring at me."

"You like him."

Lyra felt her cheeks flush. Her grip on the steering wheel tightened. "How do you know?"

"I just do."

"Well, he's going back to the farm today, so get off my case."

Otto coughed, took a sip of Gatorade, and sat back in her seat. "Let's talk funeral strategy, then. I say we split up."

"I agree. You keep track of Klemens. I'll watch Arvid and Olive."

They parked and got out. The sky was milky white, and the leafless trees rose up black and spindly against it. There was an incredible stillness in the air as if Nature herself had decided to do a minute's silence for Hedvig.

Otto slammed her door shut. "Make it look like we're chatting, but keep an eye out for anyone that's loitering on their own or showing up suddenly."

Inside the modest Lutheran church, the pews were only a quarter filled. Otto led the way and took a seat at the back on the left. Hedvig's casket lay mid-altar, surrounded by tasteful bouquets of flowers in whites and purples. Otherwise, the décor was pared back to a bared-walled minimum, a stark contrast to the similar sized Catholic churches of Lyra's upbringing.

"Were we supposed to bring flowers?" Lyra whispered, noticing that almost everyone had a bunch.

"Uh, yeah, probably."

"Now you tell me."

Lyra scanned the congregation from her vantage position at the back. They were dressed mostly in black. Arvid and Olive sat in the front row, on the left side. Klemens sat behind Arvid toward the aisle, positioned to make a quick escape.

Behind him sat a bunch of fashionable thirty-somethings, probably Arvid's friends. There was a wheelchair at the end of the pew on the opposite side. An old lady sat there, and beside her—a sprightly lady in her sixties with a silver pixie cut and angular, tinted glasses who looked the picture of efficiency.

"Berit?" Lyra mouthed at Otto, indicating the latter.

Otto nodded. "And Virginia Sammland in the chair, mother of the deceased."

"Wow. Fair play to her for showing up. Ninety-four?"

"Yeah. Not an easy thing to bury a son, at any age."

Everybody sat stiff and frozen. Only when footsteps alerted them to a newcomer did some of them stir and look around, as they'd done when she and Otto had arrived. It was another of the younger crowd—a tall, dapper-looking man. Lyra expected him to take his position in the young people's row, but he sat down next to Berit, and when he twisted his head to whisper something to her, she recognized him as Hugo, Olive's ex. Berit's face broke into a warm smile, and Virginia's into a gummy grin. Lyra blinked. This was the first sign of humanity in the whole damn place.

Klemens held himself erect, with little sign of giving in to emotion. Arvid, in contrast, kept glancing around, glaring at Klemens, who studiously ignored him. The hatred emanating from Arvid was palpable, but Klemens looked as unfazed as ever.

Somehow sensing the weight of Lyra's stare, Olive caught her gaze at one stage and smiled back sadly before looking down at her hands again. She was barely holding it together.

The ceremony dragged on. Although Lyra's Swedish was improving daily, she found it hard work to decipher the sonorous voice of the priest who looked almost as old as Virginia Sammland. The congregation followed the ritualized movements of the ceremony. The organ music blared out a rousing hymn that resembled a Catholic one from her schooldays. Some people dabbed their eyes.

Lyra and Otto were first out of the church. They positioned themselves strategically at a junction in the stone pathway where people would go their separate ways to the different parking lots. Lyra took a huge breath of the misty air.

Otto fumbled with the buttons on her coat and sighed loudly. "Hate funerals."

"Yeah?"

"My mom died last year, that's why."

Lyra swung to look at her. "I'm sorry."

"Cervical cancer. I've heard that all my life, you know, people saying, 'Oh, my mother died of cancer.' But you never think about what those words actually mean until it happens to your own mom, you know? Sorry."

"Don't apologize, Jeez. I know."

"Your folks alive?"

"My mother is."

"Your father?"

"Gone a long time ago."

"I'm sorry." Otto tilted her head. "But there's been someone else. Am I right?"

Lyra swallowed. Painful memories rose up close to the surface like a shallow grave. Confiding in Otto would mean explaining everything, and she wasn't ready for that. They had enough death to deal with. "Hey," she said. "You've been in this business longer than I have. There's always someone."

An old couple came up and shuffled off to their cars.

The younger crowd started coming out. Although they were the same age as Lyra, they made her feel middle-aged with their trim, woolen overcoats and chiseled blond haircuts blowing in the breeze to accentuate perfect bone structures and glossy complexions. Perhaps they wouldn't look out-of-place in Malmo, but in Dublin, that bunch of supermodels would stop traffic.

Out came Berit Ehrling, pushing Hedvig's mother in the wheelchair down the accessibility ramp.

But once the going got tricky on the gravel, Hugo took the handlebars of the wheelchair. He wheeled her towards some rose beds, stooping over to chat to her. That seemed to invigorate the old lady, and she waved her arms at the flowers.

"I'll grab Berit before she talks to anyone else," Otto said. "She's been dodging us for too long. You check in with Arvid's buddies over here."

The group of friends was chatting animatedly in that heightened manner of people reunited after a long time—jovial, but with an undercurrent of competition.

Lyra approached them and said in Swedish, "Hi, I'm an old school friend of Olive's from Ireland. Hej, Hej."

There was a chorus of polite—and surprised—*hejs* whereupon everyone switched to English mode, not entertaining for a second the notion of continuing in Swedish.

"Poor Olive," the tallest guy with curly, strawberry-blond hair said. He had a pink-cheeked face that looked like it would become permanently florid in a few years, and his voice was loud and authoritative. "She's taking it rather badly."

"Yes," everyone chorused.

"I'm Marcus. These," he indicated his cohorts, "are Jasper and Elsa, and that's Hugo over there with Arvid's grandmother."

Hugo, having clearly overheard, gave them a wave.

"It is terrible," Marcus continued. "I mean, with Olive's father gone now, too." He shook his head. "Who on earth would do this to them? Who?"

They all shook their heads and let out sighs of bafflement. Clearly, they didn't share any of Arvid's suspicions. Or if they did, they were excellent actors.

Hugo had left the old lady staring at the flower beds. He stalked over and offered his hand to Lyra, shaking it warmly. "I'm Hugo, old friend of Arvid's.

She eyed him up and down. With his tall, slim frame and unruly auburn curls, he was even more handsome than the other pair of friends. "And Olive's too, no?"

He grinned bashfully. "Yes, indeed, we had a moment.

Sadly, it wasn't to be. A better man found his place by her side."

There was a round of polite, muted laughter.

Olive hadn't shared a lot about her ex, but he was certainly different to Arvid.

Hugo waved a hand around, "It's a tragedy."

"It is," she agreed. "Did you know Hedvig well?"

He smiled wryly. "Yes, until he fired me in 2014."

"I'm sorry."

"Yeah. Restructuring, they called it. Capitalism. Whatever."

There was an awkward lull.

"I hear Arvid was very close to his father," she said to no one in particular. "Have any of you had a chance to talk to him?"

Jasper shifted uncomfortably and exchanged a look with Marcus.

Marcus spoke up. "To be honest, we haven't seen much of Arvid of late. You see, Klemens asked us to come here."

"Klemens?" she asked sharply.

"Yes, to distract poor Arvid from the fact that he wants to kill him," Marcus said deadpan.

"Excuse me?" Lyra asked.

Jasper elbowed him in the ribs.

"Figuratively speaking," Marcus added unconvincingly.

"Really?" Hugo said, frowning at Marcus. "That's in extremely bad taste."

Marcus held up his hands. "Is it? I'm sorry. I can't help it. I have dark humor. It runs in the family. My family are all doctors, except me."

"He does look like he wants to kill Klemens, though," Jasper said.

Nobody answered him. Nobody had to.

"Aren't we the cheerful bunch?" Hugo said. "I better get back to Virginia now. It was good of you, Lyra, to come all the way from Ireland."

"I'm here for Olive," she explained. "But Hedvig

seemed like a nice man."

"Ah yes, he was good to many people," Marcus said.

They all looked at the ground.

"Excuse me," Hugo said. He backed away from the group and returned to Virginia. Lyra watched him. He was engrossed in the process of packing the wheelchair into the van.

Spotting Otto chatting to a middle-aged couple, Lyra took leave of the group.

"Long-time investors," the policewoman said, watching them go. "Not interesting."

"Arvid's friends seem like a nice bunch," Lyra said. "But get this, Klemens *asked* them to come here today."

Otto frowned. "Like, otherwise it would be obvious Arvid didn't have any friends?"

"Maybe. Or, Klemens wanted to keep him occupied, so he wouldn't attack him and ruin the funeral. What did Berit have to say for herself?"

"Not a whole bunch. She's agreed to an interview at Sammland AG offices later with both of us."

"Great! Oh, here comes Klemens."

Klemens stood near the church doorway with hands tucked into his gaberdine coat pockets, frowning vaguely into the distance. Then, appearing to arriving at a snap decision, he made his way over to Hugo and Virginia Sammland. The two men chatted for a while, and Klemens patted Hugo on the back. Then Hugo walked off toward the parking lot, leaving Klemens and his mother by the flower beds. Virginia lifted a wrinkled hand to Klemens's cheek. He leaned in to the gesture, keeping his head bent, nodding a lot, but he seemed stiff and awkward.

Lyra felt a chill. Even when greeting his mother, Klemens didn't break down at the death of his brother. That should be the point at which he'd fall apart, if he had any soul at all. Then again, his mother didn't seem all that cut up about it, either.

"She's got dementia and barely knows what's going on,"

Otto said, reading her thoughts. "Berit said she didn't recognize her. She's been in a nursing home in Lund for several years. Apparently, before that, she was quite a fixture in the everyday life of Sammland AG."

"How so? Was she employed there?"

"Not officially, but she used to go in and out of the company all the time, bringing *fika*, raising morale, and generally keeping the two brothers from fighting. Everybody loved her. Berit doesn't think that the Sammlands visited her much in the care home, though. Definitely not Hedvig or Arvid. Too busy, you know?"

The mist then decided to evolve into rain which splattered against their faces. Umbrellas were produced. People clutched their coat lapels and zipped up puffer jackets. The forces of social cohesion that were already weakening snapped entirely at the meteorological provocation. People turned to look wistfully at their cars. The group of friends broke up, and Jasper was the first one to drive out.

"Arvid and Olive are still in there," Lyra marveled.

"*Ja ha*," Otto said. "It's like they're waiting for everyone to leave."

"How odd. Not to mention rude. They came all the way here to see him."

They watched Marcus get into his car, a lime green Tesla.

"He's connected to the Gyllenstierna family, one of the oldest noble families in Scandinavia."

Arvid and Olive finally appeared at the doorway of the church. Arvid came first, holding himself stiffly. He threw a murderous look in Klemens's direction, but turned away before their eyes could meet. Clearly, he didn't want to approach his grandmother with Klemens standing there.

Olive walked beside him. She looked bleakly ahead, unseeing, attached to Arvid rather than making a beeline for people, as she normally would. She had never looked so lost, or so forlorn. What must she be going through with a father dead, and a lover dead who happened to be the father of her fiancé? Could a woman *be* in a worse position? It made Lyra feel helpless that she couldn't console her.

Rather than veer off and join his group of friends at their cars, Arvid seemed to be making his way toward her and Otto. His murderous expression had mellowed to the haughty coolness she was most familiar with.

"Why come to us?" Lyra muttered under her breath.

"Good question," Otto answered.

Lyra nodded at Arvid and then hugged Olive tightly. She was trembling and didn't seem to want to let go.

They both nodded at Otto, who felt no compulsion to engage in any form of bodily contact with either of them.

"He came," Arvid muttered, darting a look at Klemens. "How dare he? Please put him behind bars soon, Officer."

Otto's smile was a borderline smirk. "Above my pay grade, Mr. Sammland."

"Have a heart, Arvid," Lyra said. "His brother's dead."

Arvid stared at her, through her. "And whose fault is that?"

Lyra wasn't going to get into it. "I met your friends. They seem nice."

"Yes." His smile was strained. "Come, Olive, we should talk to them before they leave," he said.

They trailed off toward the cars.

From this distance, the chorus of greetings in Swedish toward Arvid and Olive sounded more subdued than their greetings had been with her. Maybe it was the worsening weather. There followed a quick exchange, Marcus nodding a lot, Arvid shaking his head. A series of brisk nods seemed to close the conversation before it even got started. Marcus waved as he headed off to his Tesla sitting under a row of lark trees. The friends all took off in opposite directions.

When Lyra turned around again, Klemens stood by a silver van, helping Virginia to get in the back door. Clearly, he was driving her back to her nursing home.

"That's it. Show's over," Otto said.

Lyra rubbed her cold palms together. "Seriously, is there

not even an impromptu *fika* somewhere for the nearest family? What's wrong with these people?"

"I suspect that may be what Marcus was trying to organize, but Arvid was having none of it."

"That would be a crime in Ireland."

Otto smiled. "Not such a big deal here. The Swedish term for small talk is *kallprat*, cold talk, right? Or even *dödprat*. That tells you how much we like doing it. We'd rather be dead."

"You don't seem to have a problem with it," Lyra said.

"I know." Otto frowned. "I may look it, but I don't feel very Swedish. I think my soul is Greek…or Irish, maybe?"

Lyra laughed. "Very possibly."

The final two cars had left the parking lot, and the churchyard stood forlorn and empty. The priest lingered, chatting to a groundsman. A dog howled in a nearby garden. Even the traffic had died off. There was nothing more to do than to walk back to the rental car.

Lyra felt sorry for these people. Money, as was often drilled into her by her mother, didn't buy you everything. Right now, Arvid had little to be envious of. He hadn't even greeted his grandmother, for God's sake.

She shuddered when they got back into the relative warmth of the car. "What a dismal affair."

"It's a funeral," Otto said, strapping in her seat belt. "What did you expect?"

"I don't know, some levity in the face of the universal inevitability of death?"

Otto looked at her. "Come on. We still have a double homicide to solve."

14

Lyra started the engine. "Where to?"

"Back to headquarters. I want to know if they got the warrant to search Arvid and Olive's house yet."

"Expecting to find something there?" Lyra asked.

"Maybe, maybe not."

"Can it wait until after this funeral day?"

Otto shrugged. "Not up to me."

They got into the car, and Lyra set the navigation destination to the police station. She could have asked Otto, but in her experience, people were bad at giving directions in places they were familiar with.

After about ten minutes, Otto said, "Look up ahead. Someone's broken down."

Lyra slowed down abruptly.

Otto pressed against the dashboard. "Why are you slowing down?"

"Because someone's broken down."

"So?"

"So, we stop," Lyra said.

"What? Why?"

"To see if we can help."

"No," Otto wailed.

"Where's your Greek soul now?" Lyra rolled up behind the metallic red Volvo. "Wait a sec, that's Hugo."

Lyra stuck her head out the window. "Hej, need help? I'm not fantastic with cars, but not totally useless either."

Otto rolled her eyes.

He jogged to her window and flashed a wide smile full of white teeth. "That's really, really kind of you. It's the battery. It needs a jump start. I have cables and everything. Look, I'm so sorry, but if you have a few minutes to spare, I'll hook myself up, and it'll be done. You don't even have to get out of the car. In fact, just stay there. I don't want to be responsible for you getting a flu."

She parked so that they could connect the batteries. After a while, Hugo raised his hand to indicate it was finished.

Lyra reached for her door handle.

"You heard him," Otto muttered. "You don't have to get out."

"But I want to."

Otto narrowed her eyes. "Whatever."

Lyra went out in the drizzling rain. Hugo was unplugging the leads. He turned to her, water trickling down his cheekbones, his gray-green eyes sparkling. She couldn't help thinking he'd make a great actor for one of Olive's commercials.

"Thanks ever so much," he said. "I owe you one. I'd invite you both for a drink, except I've to head up north and get there before it gets dark." He looked up at the sky. "Hopefully."

"No problem," she said. "Another time."

He didn't mean it, and neither did she.

"And hey, thanks for looking after Liam," she added.

"Oh. I was happy to. He's good company."

Lyra nodded, warming up to him further. "How far d'you have to go?"

"Gothenburg. Over two hundred kilometers."

"What do you do up there?"

"Oh, I'm an actor in an independent theater. They money's terrible, but I like it."

"Better than Sammland AG? Olive told me you used to work there."

He grinned. "That was a while ago. Very different, indeed. Fortunately, it was a good move for me."

"Do you star in anything I'd have seen?"

He laughed. "Everybody asks that. No, theater mainly. A few smaller Swedish dramas, if you like that sort of thing."

"Uh, not really. I saw you being attentive to Virginia Sammland. That was kind of you."

"She deserves it. She was the grand old dame of the company in the early days, and she looked after everyone like we were her children. You know, she used to come in with massive wicker baskets full of homemade *kanelbullar*, the quintessential fairy godmother."

"Yes, I heard that about her," she said. "Do you think she even realizes what's happening today?"

A cloud passed over his face. "I hope not. Just imagine. A son dead. A grandson accusing the favorite son of fratricide? She doesn't deserve this after the good life she's lived."

"Favorite son?" Lyra asked.

"Klemens was son number one, not only in birth order."

"I see. Well, safe journey north. Hope the battery holds out."

He smiled. "We shall see."

She got back in the car. "Hm, he was nice—like all of Arvid's pals, weirdly enough."

"Yeah, yeah, *kallprat*," Otto said.

"The thing he said about Virginia is interesting."

"Which was?"

"Klemens is the favorite son."

"Why's that interesting?"

"I don't know."

As Lyra parked at the station, Otto said, "You coming

in while we wait for the interview with Berit?"

"Nah. I'm going to the hotel. I need to get out of these clothes and I want to look at all my notes again. Something big and obvious is missing; I can feel it in the ether, just beyond my fingertips. I need to stretch out and grab onto it."

"Yeah, yeah, call me if you do."

15

"She's waiting for us in Room 315," Otto said as Lyra walked together through the glass main entrance of Sammland AG. "Let's hope this leads somewhere."

Berit was waiting at a seating area in front of the reception desk. She was dressed in a white blouse with a navy pencil skirt. Sharp pleats were ironed into the sleeves of the blouse, and her hair was set in a sleek coiffure where every hair knew its place and obeyed. Lyra wondered how she'd gone from a windswept funeral to looking like this.

The older woman rose to greet them and shook hands with them. Then she led the way to the third floor and into a meeting room. She offered a *fika* of coffee and *kanelbullar* which they refused. Otto asked if the interview could be in English.

"I'll do my best," Berit replied in perfect but heavily accented English.

"You've worked at Sammland how long?" Lyra asked.

"For twenty years. I was here in the beginning when it was just the Sammland brothers, plus Mårten, Oskar, Hugo, and Katarina."

Lyra decided that this woman wasn't one to try to warm

up to, definitely someone for whom small talk was *dödprat*.

"What was your relationship like with Hedvig Sammland?"

"We had a good relationship, professionally and personally. I miss him very much."

"Would you say that he confided in you, trusted you?"

"Yes." She sighed. "He didn't have anybody else. He was a private man. He kept his feelings hidden from Arvid. The grief after the death of Greta, you know? She was his everything. It changed him forever."

Lyra wondered if Otto would bring up Hedvig and Olive. She didn't want to do it herself. It probably wouldn't help the case, anyway.

"Do you have the same level of friendship with Klemens?" Otto asked.

"No, I cannot say that I do."

"Did he ever threaten you?" Otto asked.

"Threaten me?" Berit's precise eyebrows shot up. "Absolutely not."

"But he said harsh things to you?" the policewoman pressed.

"Not directly. Not since the restructuring."

"Berit, tell me about the last time you saw Hedvig alive," Lyra asked.

The older woman let out a long sigh.

"I'm sorry, I know this is difficult…" Lyra added quickly.

"No, I want justice." Her eyes flashed. "I hope you will bring his killer to justice—"

"Yes, that's why we're here," Otto butted in, switching to Swedish.

Lyra nodded and added, *"Javisst."*

Berit returned her gaze to Lyra. "But why you?"

"Ah." Lyra explained her work credentials and connection to the Maguires.

Berit's expression opened up, and she sat back in her seat. While she didn't slouch, she wasn't as rigid as before. "You're on our side."

"Uh, yes," Lyra said. By that, Berit clearly meant she was on the Hedvig side of the Sammland corporate politics, as opposed to the Klemens side. If that loosened Berit's tongue, then she was happy to take sides. "Please, back to the day of Hedvig's trip to Helsingor."

"It was a normal day, like any other, or that is what I thought. After lunch, he came into my office, all hurried, and he said he had to go pick up a wedding present for Arvid in Helsingor. This was highly unusual. Why did I not know of this? I thought he was not acting his usual self."

"How so?" Lyra jumped in.

"He was rushing and fussing about, which was not at all like him. I offered to go instead of him and get the present for him—it would be no trouble, and so on. He would have to miss an important meeting and a game of golf. It was unusual for him to go off anywhere in the middle of the day. But no, no, he did not want me to go. He wanted to do it himself. On that he was very clear."

"Did he give any further explanation?"

"All he said was that he had to pick up the present himself, in Helsingor, and that he had to go straight away. It made no sense to me. I confess, I checked out his calendars, and I even talked to Klemens, but nobody could tell me why he had to go."

"And he hadn't ever mentioned the present to you before that?"

"No, the first I heard of it was when he was packing to leave. He asked me to send his excuses to the management meeting."

Lyra exchanged a look with Otto. The police would have checked out the shop in Helsingor for sure, so there couldn't have been any clues there. What they needed to know was why he went on that particular day and in such hurry. Somebody must have contacted him out of the blue.

"Do you have access to his incoming calls?" she asked.

"Only the calls coming through the main switch. Not his cell phone."

Otto sat forward. "We've scanned his cell and the switchboard. Nothing. On email neither." She turned her attention back to Berit. "Was he fond of spontaneous decisions? Could he have been browsing and come across a site that gave him an idea for a present?"

The older woman laughed. "No, oh no, that is not at all something he would do, and especially not during work hours. I'm sorry. It is very unlikely."

Otto smiled tersely. "Who else apart from Hedvig knew about this trip? Anybody in the company?"

She frowned. "I didn't, and of course, Arvid and Olive didn't either, because it was meant to be a surprise for them, so I don't know..." She trailed off.

There was a silence. This was going nowhere. Otto was frowning.

"Berit," Lyra said, "You mentioned two sides in the company, and this is something others have mentioned. Can you tell me your view on the events of the year 2014 in the company?"

Berit fingered her necklace. "You mean when we downsized? Yes, difficult decisions had to be made to keep the company running efficiently."

"You agreed with these decisions?"

"Of course. They were Hedvig's decisions."

"But you're aware that many didn't agree?"

"Business is business," she said in a clipped tone. "There is no room for sentimentality."

"I understand. Did you agree with the reasons for those people being let go?"

"My opinion does not count. I am sure that Hedvig and Arvid had good reasons for everything that they did. Yes, Klemens complained because all his favorite people left...and Virginia Sammland complained, too."

"Really? How?" That was the first Lyra had heard of Virginia's political involvement in the business. As a family company, it made sense but...

"She refused to speak to Hedvig after that, only

Klemens." She sighed. "She played favorites. It is so sad—a mother should not have favorites in any case, but quite soon after that she developed dementia and the relationship was never patched up. Neither Hedvig nor Arvid visit her in Lund. Too busy they say, but I know better."

"Does Klemens visit her?"

"Yes. Although, at this stage, she does not recognize him. I tried to speak to him about it, but he doesn't like to talk about it. It's hard."

Lyra murmured in agreement and made a mental note to check in on the old lady. Even dementia sufferers could be lucid at times, as she knew from her own grandma who could go in an instant from regaling the family with a tale about her mother's childhood antics to not recognizing anybody.

Berit looked between the two of them. "Was there anything else?"

"Not for now," Otto said. "You've been helpful, and we won't waste any more of your time. If you do think of anything, please call my number."

They left Berit to her work. Lyra closed her door as they left. The lack of progress was dispiriting.

"Let's find someplace to talk," Otto said.

Half-way down the corridor they came across a closed door. Lyra shrugged and took out her card and raised a questioning eyebrow at Otto.

Otto nodded.

The door clicked open. Inside, it was empty. Lyra scanned the walls for cameras and the tables for bugs. Clean.

It seemed to be a storage and demo room full of cardboard boxes with lots of marketing samples—bottles and tubes of body wash and shampoo in baskets atop high round tables.

Otto picked up a purple bottle, sniffed, and set it down again. "Ugh, lavender."

"I thought Berit would somehow be the key to this," Lyra said. "Or that she'd offer something new. But all she did was confirm what Hugo said about Klemens being the favorite son of Virginia Sammland. So, there was a company rift in 2014 and a restructuring. What has that got to do with Hedvig being thrown overboard a ferry, or Pronsious being shot through the heart, for that matter?"

She rifled through more samples and chose a paper-wrapped soap that smelled of peach. She moaned. "I want to nick this soap."

Otto gave her a sideways look. "Don't make me arrest you."

Lyra put the soap down. "We need a chat with Big Brother about his extracurricular surveillance activities. Let's see if he's around."

They made their way to the C-Suite. Klemens's door was locked. They knocked, but there was no answer.

"Dodging us, I wonder?" Lyra said.

Otto pressed a number on her phone. After several rings, she grunted. "Yep, playing hard to get. I need to get back to the station—can you drop me off? Don't worry, Eriksson has got to pull him in eventually."

Lyra sighed. "I want in on that interview, too, but I have to go home to Pronsious's funeral."

"Good, you can keep an eye on the happy couple there. Eriksson sure as hell isn't sending anyone."

"Yes, it'll be good to talk to her. I feel she's impossible to get near here. It's almost like she's avoiding me."

"Maybe she feels she can't leave his side," Otto said.

"Or she's ashamed about her liaison."

It burned to have to admit it. Olive had never avoided her before. As little girls camped out in their secret base among the brambles at the end of the farm, they'd sworn to be there for each other forever, no matter what happened in their lives. Turned out, 'no matter what' was relative.

She dropped Otto off and headed back to the hotel.

Liam was waiting at reception for her.

"Oh, hello," she said.

"Don't worry, I'm not going to bother you, Lyra."

"You wouldn't be bothering—"

"I just wanted to tell you that I'm going home. I have to arrange Dad's funeral. We'll get him home today or tomorrow, they said. So, we're looking at Saturday potentially. Save the date."

Wow, another funeral. "That's good, Liam. I'll be home for it."

He nodded, then scowled. "At this rate, I don't know if Olive will."

"What a thing to say! She will, too, of course." She patted his arm. "But you know what, she needs you to be strong and to organize this. She's not in a position to. Your whole family needs you, Liam."

Liam nodded. "Mm, whatever."

Something compelled her to add, "Look, I'm swamped with catch-up stuff for college this coming week, but by the following weekend, I'll have more free time. Maybe come up to Dublin, and we'll go for a drink?"

He made a brave attempt at a smile. "I'd like that." With a nod, he turned and walked out.

In her room, she flopped on her bed and opened her laptop to check email. An email from the adoption agency jumped out among all the junk.

Dear Ms. Norton,
Thank you... blah blah blah.
She skipped ahead.

We are still in the process of determining your case and would ask you for patience. There are many requests for adoption at the moment, and we allocate on the basis of suitability...

What they were *trying* to say was she was pushed to the back of the queue. They'd checked her out, and found her wanting in the parenting department. Couldn't even keep an interview appointment? Clearly unworthy.

She clicked it closed. Looking on the bright side, it put her in an appropriate mood for another funeral.

16

Saturday morning, Lyra was once again in her car, following the M6 west to Kiltomb. Slate-gray clouds hung low with no let up.

Is my life going around in a loop?
No, last time you drove there, Pronsious was alive.

The sides of the N61 were getting clogged even before she reached McNally's on the village outskirts. In Kiltomb center, the scene was chock-a-block. Cars were driven half into ditches to leave a morsel of road for vehicles to pass by. Although Pronsious wasn't extremely outgoing, there was a big turnout—basically the entire village.

The church was packed already when she went in, a huge contrast to Hedvig's rather empty funeral. The air was full of church sounds—the low-level hum of a crowd in their Sunday finest trying their best to be quiet, the clank of heavy bibles against wooden pews, the ear-splitting scrape of wood against stone as a pew moved. Choir members shifted furniture about on their balcony above. For a funeral, the place was teeming with life.

The atmosphere was even more festive at the back. Men who looked like they'd stood there all their lives loitered around the holy water font, no doubt looking forward to being the first in McNally's when this was over. Had they been friends with Pronsious? Probably. Questioning them may provide some insights but ran the risk of being a huge time sink. Better to go to the reception in the Maguire household afterward.

The funeral proceeded with the lulling rhythm of the familiar Catholic sacrament. From her position at the back left, she inspected the important people in the front pews. The first was left empty, as it was too close to the altar for comfort. In the second row sat Una, Liam, Olive and Arvid, and Liam's other siblings, Dermot and Ella. Dermot's kids were there, too, full of antics.

She thought about what Liam had said about his siblings fitting the funeral into their calendars. How could they be so wrapped up in their lives while he and Olive were so deeply affected? Even Arvid seemed affected, head dipped, rigid, as if hewn from stone. Now that he wasn't casting dagger looks at Klemens all the time, he seemed much saner.

At the end of the ceremony, the family trailed out behind the coffin bearers. Liam was one of them, at the front. He caught her eye as he passed, shouldering his burden. Lost in thought, she hadn't been prepared for that. Tears pricked her eyes. She nodded back at him, giving him a sad smile.

Next in the procession came Arvid and Olive. Olive didn't look her way. She was more focused on Arvid, whose eyes darted about, losing contact with anyone who tried to engage with him. He was trembling. It was odd that he should show more genuinely sad emotions here than he had at his own father's funeral. Of course, it may just be delayed grief.

Outside, Lyra took up a position with her back up against the granite wall of the church, taking in deep breaths of air. The crowd formed into groups, chattering in that hushed tone of mourners. The atmosphere couldn't be more different from that of Hedvig's funeral. Here, there was no secrecy; the community had rallied together to see a man buried whose death was a murder mystery. A sense of injustice bound them all together.

Liam was engulfed in his close family group that she didn't want to disturb. She reckoned the best place to stand and talk would be at the entrance to the parking lot, so she headed there.

As she rounded the church, she spied the blond hair of Arvid by the side-chapel. Olive was with him, and they were alone. Arvid was talking, chopping the air with his hand. Olive listened, clutching her hands to her chest.

Lyra shrank back against the wall to eavesdrop. They were arguing in Swedish, Arvid's Scanian accent coming to the fore. She had to strain to understand as the crisp sounds of Swedish got mangled by the dialect—rather like switching from Dublin 4 to a thick Monaghan accent.

"...I can take that one," Arvid was saying.

"No, stay. We'll go tomorrow. Together, as planned." – Olive, insistent, near tears.

"But I can't. This...is torture." –Arvid.

"And what do you call being stuck in that house with the police crawling everywhere? Is that better? God, you're so self-centered!" –Olive.

"Yes, because I need to be."

There was a gap. The sound of a lighter being lit. The smell of fresh smoke.

"It's one day, Arvid. One *fucking* night. I've gone along with everything, so you owe me this." Olive had switched to English, as if her wrath couldn't be contained in Swedish. "It'll look weird if you leave today."

"It's all about image for you," he grumbled.

"Oh my God, you're *unbelievable*."

Lyra's head was spinning. She'd never heard Olive so *angry*. Or cursing—ever! She sounded like a different person. And seriously? Leave Ireland so soon? Today? What on Earth had got into the man?

She slunk away from the wall and made a bee-line for

Una.

Several village women recognized Lyra and gathered around as she hugged Una, forming a cocoon of female solidarity. Lyra bit her lip to stop from welling up. "My deepest condolences. He was a great father and a great husband."

Una simply nodded and offered her a watery smile.

Lyra grappled for words. "It must be good to have the family all home."

"Oh, it is, indeed." Una dabbed her eyes with a tissue balled up inside her fist. "And Olive home at last...and that poor boy."

"Arvid?"

"Yes. The poor lad. He was always quiet. I couldn't get a word out of him when he arrived this morning, all stiff, just like in the beginning when she'd bring him home. Like he didn't know us. Two fathers gone. It's just...too much, too much, for them. I don't know how they'll manage."

Una raised her face skyward for a second and then looked Lyra in the face. "I mean, a cinema for God's sake? He doesn't even *like* the movies. Why would he go there, stupid, stupid man?" Una's voice petered out as if she'd been expecting to be interrupted by now. Pronsious rarely let her string two sentences together, and that was the longest speech Lyra had ever heard the woman make.

There were no good answers, so Lyra was glad when more people came over and drew Una into their midst.

She hung back and headed to the parking lot. As she approached her car, a man walked out from behind a hi-ace van.

"Hey." It was Liam. Red-eyed and worse for wear, but trying to look brave.

"Aren't you going on the procession to the grave?" she asked.

He came in close and hugged her and for a moment, she let herself enjoy being engulfed in his warmth. "Yes," he said, "but I was looking for Olive and Arvid first. Thought they might be in the car, but they're not." He pointed at the Audi behind them.

"They're back there." She nodded to the side-chapel. "Having quite the argument."

"Jesus."

"Liam, I need to talk to Olive on her own." She shot him a meaningful stare.

"Seriously? You want me to take Arvid?" He shot her a long-suffering look.

"Please, Liam." She made a pleading face.

"Lyra. I'm really not in the mood for this."

"I'm sorry, Liam, I know." She grasped his arm. "But I wouldn't ask if it wasn't important. Arvid's trying to get her to go back to Sweden, possibly tonight, but I can't let that happen."

He inhaled sharply. "Tonight?"

"Mm-hm."

He frowned down at her. "Let me talk to her."

"No, Liam. Please, let me try first. You just get Arvid away."

With a grunt, he trudged off over the gravel, his gait becoming slightly less belligerent by the time he reached the couple. He gestured expansively at the surrounding beech trees. Whatever bullshit he was coming out with, seemed to have worked. Olive was on her way over to her. *Good old Liam.*

Olive was smiling, but with every step closer she came, the more strained that smile appeared.

"Liam's asking Arvid something about hunting. I mean, really?" Olive said it in a wry tone that made her seem more like her usual self.

Lyra embraced her hard. "They're just man talking. It'll do Arvid good. What about you, more importantly? How are you holding up?"

Olive let out a harried sigh. "Poor Dad. Poor Mam. Everything's in ruins."

"I know, hon, it's all unspeakably awful for you and

Arvid both, but especially for you."

"Yeah, it's hard."

"It's good you're home with us now, though. Take this time for yourself and your family, Olive. Your mother needs you. All of you."

Olive pulled her coat belt tighter. "But Arvid needs me, too, and he has to go back to Sweden."

"Can't he do without you? Even for a few days?"

"No, he can't. He really can't." Olive's tone was sharp. "The worst thing is, we have to endure more police interviews when we go back. I wish they'd hurry up and just arrest Klemens and close the cases and leave us alone."

"Hurry up? They've no evidence, Olive. Klemens isn't even suspected on reasonable grounds, let alone probable cause. Do you really think he's responsible for your father as well as Hedvig?"

Olive shrugged. "Why not?"

"Be careful. The police have no such evidence. Neither do you, right?" She eyed her friend sternly. "You would tell me if you knew something?"

Olive looked away. "I can't talk about this," she hissed. "It's my father's funeral."

The sounds of men's voices broke the tense moment.

Damn, I need more time alone with Olive.

Arvid and Liam came walking back. Liam's mouth was drawn in a tight line, lines of strain around his eyes.

"We have to join the procession to the grave now, sister." Liam crooked his arm so Olive could take it. She latched on quickly. He flashed Lyra a secret look of apology.

"You coming, darling?" Olive asked Arvid.

He shook his head. "No, I feel out of sorts. You go on ahead. I'll wait in the car."

Liam's face looked thunderous as he regarded Arvid.

"I'll stay with him," Lyra offered.

Olive exchanged a beseeching look with Arvid. He flapped his hands irritably, shooing her away.

"You OK, Arvid?" Lyra asked when the Maguires were

out of earshot.

Arvid held his face to the sky. "No. What is the point of it all? This constant struggle?"

"You've been through a lot. You need help."

"Nothing can help me."

"Time can. Also, perhaps counseling for PTSD. I can ask my police contact for recommendations of good therapists if you wish."

He shook his head and lit up a cigarette. "Go, please. I need to be on my own."

"Fine. I'll be in my car over there if you want to talk."

Lyra trailed back to her car to get some warmth in her bones. Arvid was at breaking point. It seemed to be a cocktail of grief and bloodthirsty revenge against Klemens. Olive seemed poisoned by it. And yet, the police had nothing on Klemens. Otto and Eriksson were due to question him today, but it was still premature to go around accusing the man of one let alone two homicides, as convenient as that would be to everybody else.

*

The kitchen at the Maguire farm was suffocating—packed to the gills with family and neighbors. Condensation fogged up the windows, and the air filled with smells of baking pastries and strong black tea. Una sat at the epicenter, queen-like, at the kitchen table beside a woman Lyra recognized as her sister, Rose. The kids and grandkids surrounded her in huddled groups, never straying too far. The family had come together as one.

Or almost.

Arvid and Olive stood rigidly off to the side, leaning against a defunct stove. From time to time, either one would dip their head to say something, but they declined to engage with anybody.

Lyra took up position by the teapot, serving cups of tea,

which allowed her to observe the room without making it too obvious. When Arvid went outside to smoke, she set down the teapot and headed for Olive.

"Come with me," she said, taking the tea cup from Olive's hand and setting it down on the stove.

Olive's eyes widened, darted to the door, and back to Lyra's face.

"Come on," Lyra repeated.

She led the way out to the hall and sat on the third stair while Olive remained standing at the banister, planting her chin on the polished sphere of wood. She'd taken this exact stance the night twenty years ago when they'd debated at length which boy each of them should invite to their debutantes' ball.

"I wasn't sure this morning," Olive began, "about Mam, but I think she'll be OK. Seeing her there with Rose and all the rest. She's going to be fine."

"But what about you?" Lyra asked. "Are you going to be fine? Look, Sweetie, I know what it's like to lose a dad. You won't feel like yourself for a long while. You have to give yourself the time and the space to process this."

"God, Lyra, you went through this when you were twelve? I didn't understand at the time. I hope I didn't say something stupid or hurtful back then."

"No, no, you were great." Lyra held her friend's concerned gaze. "I'd never have got through it without you. I want to be here for you now. Would you consider staying in Ireland longer? It's clear you have to be back in Sweden for the investigation at some stage, but can't you hang on another few days at least?"

Olive dipped her head. "I would if I could, but Arvid really doesn't want to be here, not even for tonight. I don't get it—he's no more at ease at home. It's like he doesn't even want me to speak with anyone." She sniffed and gestured around the hallway. "It's making this harder...unbearable, actually."

"Is it—do you think it could be because he knows about

you and Hedvig?" Lyra asked in a lower voice.

Olive pressed her hand to her stomach. "He doesn't know. If he knew about that, I don't know what he'd do." Her gaze roamed over Lyra's face. "Could you maybe come back with me?"

"To Sweden?"

Olive nodded.

"I wish I could, but I can't."

"Why not? You were originally coming over round about now for the wedding."

"I know. But I've already taken days off from work earlier this week, and I have to compensate."

It was the truth, but she felt like she was being a pathetic friend. "But I'll be in touch with Otto, and I'll tell her to keep an eye out for you. Plus, I'll call you every night, OK?"

A door in the kitchen opened. Olive flinched. "He's looking for me." She pushed away from the banister. "Call me." She disappeared into the kitchen.

Lyra followed her back in but left the couple alone and made her way toward Liam, who was surrounded by the old cronies of his father. His eyes flashed with relief as she approached.

"Excuse me, gents," he said, breaking out from the huddle. "Lyra, come here—I wanted to show you the new herb garden."

Outside in the fresh air, he shook his head. "I know you noticed. They're acting weird. Did she say anything to you?"

"Just reiterated that Arvid wants to go back today. He's probably already checking flights on his phone in there."

"God, talk about insensitive." He kicked at the gravel underfoot. "If you ask me, she was better off with Hugo. He would have had the decency to hang around."

She shrugged. "At least Olive and Arvid know exactly what the other is going through. Maybe this joint mourning will bring them closer together eventually?"

"She should be here with us. And you should be over there, solving this thing."

Lyra patted his arm. "Much as you'd like to move us about like pawns, Liam, we do have to follow our own paths. Olive needs to be with Arvid. I need to head back to Dublin. Very soon, actually."

She'd had enough of funerals. She'd forgotten how much she hated them. Instead of going back into the house, she walked over the gravel toward her car. When she looked back toward the house, Liam had gone.

17

Monday morning, after a Sunday spent mainly catching up with lecture preparation, Lyra sat in her office in the university—a poky room she shared with a Sociolinguistics lecturer. At the moment, she had the space to herself. Her mentoring session with a Ph. D undergrad was just over, and all that was left for the day was to correct forty essays on language analysis of asylum seekers cases, which she now thoroughly regretted assigning.

The department head, Prof. Yeates, stuck his gray head in the door and gave her his usual goofy smile. "Ah, you're back. Everything OK?"

"Yes, Prof, thanks for getting Sarah to fill in for me at short notice last week."

"You're welcome." Prof Yeates came right in. "I did hear of the tragedy of your friend's father. What dark deeds are happening in Elsinor?"

"Oh, it's the Swedish side, Helsingborg, we have to worry about," Lyra said, adding some late student papers from her in-tray to her pile of work. "The police haven't been able to link the deaths yet and it's all inconclusive, quite a mess in fact."

"I'm glad you're back safe." He shuffled out again.

Yeates's kindly concern just made her feel worse. She should have flown back with Olive to make sure she got settled and had some moral support, because Arvid sure as hell wasn't doing it for her. At least he had finally relented and stayed overnight at the Maguire farm, and they'd flown together yesterday morning, but to think that he was acting like that was some kind of concession to her. It was crazy.

Normally, they should be making the final preparations for their wedding around about now. There would be laughter and lightness and love. Instead, their lives were thrust into this dark, scary hell-hole, unveiling the worst traits of her husband-to-be.

Her phone pinged with a brief text from Otto.

I'm officially off the case. Eriksson taking over from the Helsingborg side. He's taking in Klemens today for questioning about surveillance, etc. Keep you posted.

Her heart sank. She didn't reply. There was nothing to say. Nothing to do but feel the tapestry of the case unravel, like in her early policing days when she'd been shoved off cases abruptly for no good reason other than someone higher up suddenly wanting to get involved. Like back then, she attempted to console herself with positive self-talk: She'd personally gone as far as she could with the case. Eriksson wasn't going to stand for any interference from her. If she'd helped in some small way with finding Klemens's bug and uncovering the Hedvig-Olive affair, then great. She had to move on with her own life, starting with these forty essays.

She pulled the first essay off the stack and started reading.

Three hours later, with half of her essays done, she picked up the phone to call the adoption agency and arrange a new second interview. The same Oscar-nominated secretary from before was on the other end of the line.

Lyra bit her lip. "I can make any time work for an interview."

"Yes, ma'am, you will be called when the committee has decided to proceed with your application. There is a waiting list. Some couples have been waiting more than six months." She put unnecessary emphasis on *couples*. Spiteful, much?

She was having none of this. "Look, I know I missed the last interview, but it was a life-or-death situation. Has that pushed me to the back of the queue?"

"I'm afraid I don't have access to that information."

"All right, can I speak to Mrs. Thompson then?"

"Oh, I'm afraid Mrs. Thompson is not at her desk today."

"How about anybody in a senior role there? I'd appreciate if I could explain my case properly."

"Well…" The secretary let out a pained breath. "I'll see if I can get Mr. Murphy for you. He's the office manager here."

"Thank you, yes, wonderful," Lyra said.

The on-hold music came on—an instrumental version of *"Morning Has Broken."*

But then she saw another call coming in. Otto. *No, I can't take this now.* She clicked to block Otto's call. She'd call her straight after and explain. She wanted to talk to her about the funeral, to fill her in on all the details, including the weird body language of Arvid and Olive.

Back on the main call, the music continued.

Otto called again.

Lyra shook her head. What could be so urgent? She waited five seconds, but Otto didn't call off. She gave in and pressed to take Otto's call.

"Sorry, Otto, I'm on this other call. Can I get back to you after that?"

"No," came the Swedish officer's voice, sounding terse. "You need to hear this."

"OK. Go ahead."

"I…actually don't know how to say this…but we just got a call…" Otto's voice faltered. "I'm so sorry, Lyra.

Dispatch got a call half an hour ago and, uh, it was from Sammland's house. Olive Maguire—it looks like she's...committed suicide."

18

Lyra wheezed in a breath and lurched forward against the desk. "No. No, that's impossible. Not Olive."

Olive?
Dead?
Suicide?

There must be some mistake. She'd just seen her the day before yesterday. With every heartbeat of Otto's silence, the truth seeped further into her bones.

"Lyra?"

"Suicide?" she gasped. "Are you sure?"

"Nothing definitive yet, but she was found in the bath with signs of electrocution. From, uh, a hairdryer. I'm so sorry."

Christ, no…

Sobs racked her body. A keening sound filled the air. She heaved, unable to control it. Her phone slid out of her hand onto the desk with a clatter. She didn't want to pick it up again, ever.

Otto's voice got more insistent. "Lyra…Lyra?"

Numbly, she reached for it and put it to her ear. She didn't have the strength to speak.

"Nobody else was in the house at the time. Uh…Arvid was at work—we interviewed him there, and he has an alibi. I shouldn't be telling you any of this before informing the family, but you have to know. You're practically family."

Lyra's brain felt too sluggish to deal with any of this. She held the phone to her ear, hoping that Otto would say it was prank. She now had to live in a world where there was no Olive. How was this possible?

"Who called it in then?" she asked weakly.

"Their Iranian cleaner who had come in for a regular shift. She's been taken in for questioning and seems legit."

"Don't tell the family yet," Lyra blurted. "It may not be what it looks. We have to know for sure. I just can't do this to them."

How could Olive be dead? They were supposed to grow old together, sharing their stories into their eighties or nineties. How could she take her own life? Olive was stronger than that. She was a fighter. She would never—

"Lyra?" came Otto's voice. "Uh, did you say you were on another call? So maybe you'd better get on that."

"What? Oh…yes." Lyra blinked in confusion at her phone. She cut off the adoption agency's call. No way she was dealing with that. In fact, she'd made up her mind about what had to happen, and pandering to bureaucrats was not part of it.

"Otto? Are you still there?"

"Here."

"I'm going over to you, the next flight out. I can't just sit here."

There was a pause. "Yeah, thought you might say that. As her closest friend, you will have to be questioned, but that can be done by phone or video call."

"I don't care. I want to be there. I need to be there."

"All right. I do have to warn you, though, Eriksson regards this as his case now. I don't have a fraction of the authority I did last time you were here."

"Fine. I'll investigate it myself," Lyra said fiercely. "For

Olive's sake."

There was a rustle and sounds of Otto walking. "OK," she said in a muffled voice indicating she had entered a smaller room. "Here's the deal. Eriksson's prioritized the Pronsious murder, as that's the only clear-cut homicide. He sees Olive's suicide as a reaction to losing both a father and father-in-law in such a short time. As for Hedvig's death, he's erring on the side of it being an accident. He's letting me interview Sammland AG people as long as I stay on top of my other work. I'm bogged down all day, but I'm going to interview Arvid again soon."

"Where's he now?"

"In his office. It was where he said he wanted to be. We've an officer stationed there collecting evidence from Olive's office and a counselor for Arvid."

"I'll book the next flight out. I can make it by six pm."

"Ah—"

"Please, Otto"

Otto sighed. "Call me when you get near Helsingborg. But listen, if you change your mind, that is OK. It might be better for you to stay there and help the family."

Then it hit her. What about the family? Liam. Una... *Christ.* They'd had been through so much, and now this. This would finish the Maguire clan off. First their patriarch. Now their golden girl. And she'd have to be the one to tell them.

But that meant she'd have to do the unthinkable—inform Liam and family over the phone. *Oh, Christ.* The nausea rose again.

"All right," she said, breathing rapid shallow breaths. "But it has to be me that calls the family. Not one of your officers."

"OK, but I'm afraid you can't wait. They need to know before the journalists start poking around."

"Yes, leave it to me."

Lyra stared at Una's contact number on her phone. How in God's name was she supposed to do this? Her training covered informing next of kin but not when both victim and next of kin were someone she was close to. She was thinking of Liam rather than Una. Remembering him as a boy, teasing his younger sister about her dolls, her frilly bedroom, her taste in music, and then her taste in men. She thought of his brown eyes and the way they filled with warmth whenever he talked about Olive. What would this do to him? And what a ridiculous moment to realize how much she cared for someone?

She wiped away the tears, glad that Otto wasn't on the call to hear her blubbing again. The officer was relying on her to get this done fast. Instead, for the past ten minutes, she'd been sitting on that chair staring at her phone screen.

She let out a ragged breath and pressed "Liam". She would tell him, and he'd have the job of telling his mother. The other way around meant that Una might be on her own hearing the news, and that would be worse.

She couldn't do it.

But she had to.

She pressed the green button again.

The phone rang five…six times, the temptation to abort growing stronger with each ring. He picked up on the seventh.

"Lyra?" came his voice, almost cheerful. Like he was glad to hear from her.

Oh, God…

"Liam. Oh, Liam. I have some bad news. Please sit down."

"What is it?"

"It's…oh, God."

"Lyra, what's going on?" he gave a nervous chuckle. "You're scaring me."

"There's no easy way to say this, Liam. I'm so sorry. It's—it's Olive. She's dead."

A silence. An awful silence. She bit into her knuckle, tears flowing freely down her cheeks and into her mouth. She didn't bother wiping them away. A muffled groan came from Liam's side. Cold washed over her skin in waves. She closed her eyes, hating the world and everyone and everything in it, but particularly any notion that there was any kind of fairness in the world.

She sniffed and continued, not even sure he was listening, "I'm so sorry, Liam. I got the call from Otto a few minutes ago. She's been in Fjälastofta, seen her with her own eyes. It—it looks like suicide. It's impossible, but it's true."

"But...no, there's been some mistake. Olive wouldn't kill herself."

His assured tone was the hardest thing to bear. She'd had that moment, too. She hardly had the strength to argue—she just wanted to agree with him. But he had to know as much as she could tell him.

"She electrocuted herself in the bath. With a hairdryer."

"Are you even sure it was suicide?" His tone was harsh. "Because I think it's the serial killer that you still haven't managed to catch yet. The one that's killed Arvid's dad, my dad, and now, my sister."

She winced. She didn't blame him. From his viewpoint, that was exactly what it looked like.

"Look, Liam, I'm going to go. I'm going to call your mother, but I'd like you to be on hand when I do so. Just tell me when a good time is, not that—not that there ever could be a good time. God, I'm so, so sorry."

He inhaled audibly. "No, I'll tell her. I just have to be a hundred percent sure that this is correct."

"It is. The coroner has declared it."

"Arvid drove her to it! He must have."

She wanted to agree with him, but if she was going to help Otto, she had to remain professional. "We don't know that, Liam. He wasn't in the house when it happened. She was alone. Of course, he could have some idea why she did this. They'll take him in for questioning. Please don't delay this, though. This story may show up in the news any time now, and Una could hear about it. She needs to hear it from you first."

Liam was breathing heavily, as if he'd been running. "God. How do I tell her? This will destroy her."

"I know."

"I'm going over there, and I'm going to *kill* that bastard. He's responsible for this. I just know it. He made her this miserable."

"Take it easy, Liam."

"No, I mean it. I've had enough. Arvid's got it coming to him."

"Don't do anything stupid, Liam. Don't make this any harder on your mother than it needs to be."

"Don't tell me what to do, Lyra. Do your job. I'll do mine."

The line went dead.

19

It was 6:30 p.m. later that day by the time Lyra reached Helsingborg Polis station in an airport taxi. Otto was ready outside in a squad car with the headlights on. Lyra bundled into the passenger seat with her only luggage—a hastily packed backpack. They didn't speak as Otto navigated the dark streets out of Helsingborg and into Fjälastofta. Lyra was glad of the silence.

Approaching the house, Lyra scoured the roads, stupidly expecting to see a perpetrator sneaking away. Part of her still didn't believe it could be suicide. Someone could have set it up to look like suicide. She didn't want to voice any theories until she saw it with her own two eyes.

"This will be difficult for you. Are you sure?" Otto asked.

"Yeah. No, turn up this way." Lyra pointed to a turn off ahead. "Quicker."

She felt Otto looking at her. "Look, I'm OK," she snapped.

When Otto cut the engine, the neighborhood had an unearthly stillness about it. No birds, no dogs, cars, or anything, just a dreadful stillness. Lyra's limbs felt heavy.

She didn't feel OK. As a junior police officer, one of her first cases had been a bath suicide. The body had putrefied for four days. The half of the body above water was a sickly green, the submerged part, still pink and the face was turning black. She had nightmares for months afterward.

Otto pulled on latex gloves and handed her a pair. "I'm still not sure it's a good idea for you to come—"

"I'm coming."

They ducked under the tape and entered the front door which was unlocked.

Lyra charged on ahead, aiming for the door on the left at the top of the hall. The bathroom was sparkling clean and...empty. For a split-second, she hoped it was all a stupid misunderstanding.

"Upstairs," Otto said, heading for the staircase.

They were confronted by two youngish officers. Otto explained who they were. A rushed conversation ensued with gesticulations from the taller of the police officers who then hung back and let them pass.

Otto reached the bathroom doorway first. She stood for a moment, immobile, holding the door so Lyra couldn't see in.

"Move back," Lyra said.

Otto pulled the door open wider so Lyra could see.

A floral shower curtain separated them from the bath, obscuring it. Through the translucent material was the dark figure of someone in the tub, too blurred to make out any features. Lyra knew this was the last moment she could kid herself that this hadn't happened. This was the last moment of feeling relatively OK, because the fantasy she'd been building up about this being a stupid error was pretty convincing. She reached forward and pulled back the curtain.

The sight made a scream rise up her throat. Lying in the bath, was Olive, gray-skinned, gaunt, her head slumped against the wall at an unnatural angle. The water covered her up to her collarbone.

Olive…how can this be you? Where is your life? How could you have done this to yourself?

Lyra fell to her knees on the hard tile. The feel of Olive's skin through the latex gloves was of a chicken breast in a shrink-wrapped plastic in the supermarket. Cold.

She backed out, fumbling for the wall because she felt the world rocking.

Otto met her outside the bathroom.

"Why? Why would she *do* this to herself? Why?" Lyra realized her voice was careening out of control. "She has everything to live for. She has people who love her. She put so much *effort* into her life—more than anyone I know. She would never… But what drove her to this?" Through hot tears, Lyra reached out. "Olive…"

Otto's hand landed on her shoulder. "I'm sorry. It must have been grief over her father? Or his father. Maybe both. This wasn't murder. This was too difficult to set up. There were no signs of struggle."

The corridor was empty, but she could hear the voices of the two officers downstairs.

There was a shout from below. "*Vi hittade nåt!*" They'd found something.

"Let's go," Otto said. They thundered downstairs in double speed, into the living room where the officers were chattering.

"Va?" Otto asked.

The shorter one pointed a latex-gloved hand at an open book on the coffee table beside a silver candelabra. The setup was unbearably elegant and so Olive.

"A suicide note," the taller officer translated unnecessarily for Lyra. Then he continued in Swedish, "It was inside the cover of this book on the mantelpiece."

One of the officers went to take the note, but Lyra reached out and stopped him. Nobody was going to read the last words of her dear friend out loud to her.

Lyra picked up the stiff, high-quality card by the edges and read out the message in the neat handwriting.

"Goodbye my love. You know why. Olive."

"You know why," she echoed. *No, Olive, I don't know why!*

Otto spoke gently. "She's lost her father and a future father-in-law. So has he. Maybe that is what she meant."

Lyra shook her head. "No. It's not enough, not for Olive." She paced to the doorway and back to the coffee table. "I-I need to get out of here." She headed out to the hallway, but that didn't feel better. Death had its tendrils wrapped around everything in that house.

After a moment, Otto joined her.

"Alternatively, he could have found out about her affair and given her a hard time about it," the police officer suggested.

"But why would she own up to it now?"

"Death of a relative does things to people—makes them want to face up to things." Otto's voice was calm and steady. "Eriksson could bring him in to the station for questioning tonight, even though it's kind of a mean thing to do—"

"I don't care," she burst out. "We need the truth."

She wasn't being professional, but she couldn't help it. A volcano of rage was building up inside her. "He's basically killed her, Otto. Liam was right. It was his twisted personality that drove her to this. His coldness in the face of the deaths of their fathers. The way he's treated her family, and his own for that matter. God knows what he's been saying and doing. He just couldn't leave her be, could he? What a *bastard*."

"All right, all right." Otto took her by the arm and guided her outside to the porch. There, she pressed Lyra back against the door with surprising force. "Calm down, all right? This is not helping us."

Shocked, Lyra nodded.

"I shouldn't let you near this case. I'm risking losing the small piece of authority I still have left. If I screw up these interviews with the Sammlands, I'm off the case. Eriksson will have it all to himself. If it drags on too long, he'll end up saying Pronsious was a random attack and the other two were suicides, because that's the simplest explanation, and he's a big fan of Occam's Razor. So is his boss."

"But it can't be just that," Lyra said.

"I know that, and you know that, but we need hard evidence to link these deaths, and right now, we don't have it."

I'm too close to the case.

Otto had every right to note that down in the police report. Every right to refuse to work with her. Lyra wiped the wetness of her cheeks; tears she hadn't even realized she was shedding. She must look a total mess.

They stared at each other. Otto's gaze was hard, unyielding, like her hands pressed against her shoulders, holding her back. A different side to this cop.

Lyra felt her breath slowing down. She willed herself to return to professional mode.

"Sorry, Otto. I know I'm a mess, but I can do this. I promise. I can hold it together and help you. That's what I came here to do."

Otto released the pressure on her shoulders. "Good, because we have nobody else on our side. If we don't come up with something very, very soon, Eriksson is going to kick my ass off this and close it up." She frowned. "And by very, very soon, we're talking one or two days."

Through the misery, Lyra appreciated the logic.

Otto reached forward and drew her into a tight bear hug. Lyra felt the power in the officer's arms. Fresh tears prickled in her eyes.

"Life sucks sometimes," the officer said gruffly. "But you can't let it stop you fighting for the truth, for justice."

20

Having taken some minutes to recover, Lyra joined Otto and the other officers who were poring over some items on the kitchen island.

"Found anything?" she asked in Swedish.

They all shook their heads.

"What about her phone?"

The taller officer nodded and gestured toward a large plastic bag with various objects inside—car keys, the phone.

Lyra knew it would be password protected, but she took it out and tried Olive's birthdate, Arvid's birthdate, and then gave up. She put it back in.

She went through the house, scouring every room for personal effects, anything that might tell her what was going on. On the surface, the house was the epitome of a neat, orderly, affluent couple's life.

"Damn you, Arvid," she muttered. "What was really going on between you?" What could be bad enough for the Olive Maguire she'd known since childhood to have taken her own life? Nothing. Unless Arvid had threatened her—perhaps after hearing about her affair with his father.

Otto's radio crackled to life. She pressed it. "Ja?"

An urgent voice rasped out, "He's run away from the office. Heading north toward center in a white BMW – YDB 756."

"Men, va fan!" Otto said, cursing the devil. "Lyra, stay here with Sven." She pointed at the taller of the officers. "I'll take Jonas with me."

"Can't I come?" Lyra begged.

Otto's face hardened with indecision, but then she sighed. "All right, come with me. Jonas, you take the squad."

"Yes," the shorter of the officers said, bounding after them.

"Is this the only way there?" Lyra asked over the wail of the siren as Otto slowed behind a line of traffic.

"Yep."

Her radio crackled out a constant barrage of instructions in rapid Scanian which Lyra had given up trying to follow. The unfamiliar streets made her feel disorientated and worse than useless.

"I'm guessing he knew we were coming to get him," Otto said. "Either Olive called him before she did the deed, or he's got some device bugging his own home, and I wouldn't put that past him."

"Yeah, runs in the family."

"So where are you now?" Otto called into her radio.

"Heading toward the motorway," came the officer's crackled voice. "There's been a sighting of him getting onto Bergalinden. I'm guessing he's headed toward Copenhagen Airport on the E4, or he turned off at Helsingborg Central train station."

Otto shook her head. "He knows he won't win a car chase."

"I'd guess the station then," Lyra said. "The border control will stop him on the bridge if he decides to go that way."

"Yes, but we need to send a squad toward the bridge, just in case. Dispatch will handle that."

Otto swerved sharply into a right-hand turn, making

Lyra's stomach bounce. It didn't help that she was sitting in the seat that was normally the driver's seat back home.

Otto flashed her a wry look that said, "You still want faster?"

Lyra frowned and kept her eyes on the road ahead. Thankfully, they'd entered a long straight stretch with little traffic.

"We're getting a sighting," Otto yelled. "Hang on...hang on." Lyra heard a tinny voice jabbering in the background. "OK, he's heading up Järnvägsgatan. Definitely the station. Hah, we'll get him there."

There was a rush of static then the officer's voice came again. "He's wearing a black puffer jacket, blue jeans. No hat, no bag of any kind. Meet you at Knutpunkten."

"That's what they call the station," Otto explained. "Stay with me because I have the radio."

Otto also had the handgun, which was probably what she meant.

"Understood."

They swerved into the parking lot in front of the station and got out.

While Otto talked in her radio, Lyra scanned the crowds. All around, Monday evening life was going on as normal—commuters wearing headphones walked into the station, like robots. A group of well-dressed people hovered around, staring at the squad cars' flashing lights. A bunch of youths lingered to watch from a traffic island as they waited obediently for the traffic lights to turn green. No sign of Arvid or anyone in a hurry.

The train station blended in organically with the other buildings and shops. It was a nightmare of a place to track someone down in. It combined with the ferry port upstairs. There were too many ways he could have gone.

Otto looked around impatiently for the other officer whose name Lyra hadn't caught.

He waved from the other side of the parking lot. His voice came through on Otto's radio.

"We're going to check the trains," barked Otto. "You check out the ferry exit."

They scanned the main board for destinations. The Oresund train to Copenhagen left in twenty minutes. The next train was a *pågatåg*—a local commuter heading east to Kristianstad on platform 4. Plenty of stops at short intervals.

She and Otto ran for the escalators, Otto muttering, *"ursäkta, ursäkta," excuse me*, and once even, "Polis!" when a gang of middle-aged women wouldn't budge.

Two trains waited on either side of the platform, each filling up slowly with passengers.

"Split up?" Lyra asked.

Otto nodded.

Lyra sprinted toward the train due to leave soonest—in five minutes—She charged up and down the platform, frantically checking the windows on both sides.

Nobody resembling Arvid sat in the nearest seats, but the carriage interiors were too dark to see the far sides properly. He could easily be hidden in one of the doorway sections or in the toilets. She had to get on board. She indicated that to Otto with hurried hand gestures. Otto gave her the thumbs up and signaled that she was going to enter the train on the other platform.

Lyra boarded at the back and worked her way up the aisles, methodically checking seats and outside on the platform. The train was half empty.

The final carriage was the first-class section which seemed identical to the rest. He wasn't there, either.

"First class mess," she muttered.

The announcement over the loudspeakers said the train was leaving. *Aagh, no*. She disembarked and joined Otto on the platform.

"Any luck?" Lyra asked, panting.

"No," the policewoman said, bending over and gripping her thighs. "That would have been too easy."

"Yeah. What next?"

THE SOUND

As the whistles and engine noise of the departing train subsided, Otto patted her radio and asked for an update. A stream of excited Swedish came out

"No luck at the ferry terminal, either," she summarized.

Lyra clenched her fists. These were the actions of a guilty man. Guilty of what, though? If he managed to outrun them for more than 48 hours, then Otto's time was up. Eriksson could well interpret this as the actions of a man half crazed by grief and not read further into it. They had to catch Arvid before he could think up some great cover story.

"He must have escaped out through a shop or something," she said.

Otto nodded, squinting around. "Very likely. We've an alert out for him with all departments."

"Will that work?" she asked skeptically.

"Don't worry. He'll come back to see her body," Otto said.

Her body. A cloud descended over Lyra. For a blessed moment, in all that excitement, she had managed to push Olive to the back of her mind. And Liam. And Una.

"I'm not so sure about that," she said heavily. "It may not be worth the risk to him."

"No. He will," Otto said.

There was a crackle on the radio, and a stream of garbled Swedish rushed out.

Otto nodded and acknowledged receipt. "OK. Lyra, they've found his car in the underground parking here, and dispatch have sent messages out to taxis and public transport. He can't have got too far."

"What about Uber?"

"Don't have that in Helsingborg."

"That makes it easier."

"Time to start questioning all the retailers and catering around here." Otto addressed the officer on the radio. "Jonas, you take the upper level, and we'll do the ground level."

They went from café to shop to kiosk, Otto flashing her

police badge and doing most of the talking. Everyone assumed Lyra was a plain clothes cop, and she did nothing to dispel that illusion.

All their effort was in vain, though. Nobody had noticed a man of Arvid's description. There were many blond men in their thirties in that part of town, and the ensemble of black puffer jacket and blue jeans was practically a uniform.

"Waste of time," Otto said grimly as they came out of the final shop that abutted the station. "Let's get back to the house."

They headed toward Otto's squad car in the station parking lot.

"At least we still have Klemens," Lyra said. "We can question him until we find Arvid. I want to ask him if he ever let Olive know that he was spying on them the entire time. And everything that he heard that might be relevant."

"No, Eriksson already talked to him, and he argued his way out of it. He admitted to the eavesdropping, but claimed it was only to protect Olive from Hedvig's blatant abuse of power. He will be fined, but Eriksson said I had to let him go home. I think he secretly agreed with Klemens's motives."

"I don't believe it!" Lyra held the sides of her head.

Otto threw her a look. "Yeah."

Lyra rubbed her face. "Is there any point in trying to take him in again?"

"Not before we find his nephew."

21

Arvid and Olive's house stood empty, dark and gloomy in the pitch black. Otto cut the engine, took a pair of Latex gloves, and made a move to open the door.

"Hold on," Lyra said, clutching Otto's forearm. "Look. No lights. Where's that guard?"

"Indeed, where *is* Sven?" Otto clicked on her radio. After an intense back and forth, she turned to Lyra. "Unbelievable. They were short-staffed because of our chase at the station—and only had Sven on house duty the whole time. He's taken off, and the next guy is on his way but got delayed somewhere."

Lyra spun her head, checking all directions. "Let's be careful entering then."

Otto took out her weapon. "Pity you're unarmed. Sure you don't want to join the force?"

"Positive."

Otto tried the front door, gun at the ready. It was unlocked, so she crept in, her boots making hardly a sound on the plush carpet.

Lyra's heart raced as they stalked though the hall. Where was the freaking light switch? She grappled around the doorway to the living room where she thought it should be. There it was, lower down than expected.

Four dim wall lights flickered to life in the guise of fake flames, not illuminating the dark as much as Lyra would have liked. If anything, their shadows were eerier now.

She came to a standstill at the bottom of the staircase. Otto's round face stared back at her, moon-like in the dim light.

Was Olive up there on her own? How could the officer have simply left his station with a body in the house?

"Let's check the first floor before we go up," Otto said, a slight waver in her voice.

"Yeah."

Lyra pushed open the living room. Her hand patted the wall again for the light switch. An overhead chandelier illuminated, bathing everything in a dappled light.

A silent scream caught in her throat. Because there, sitting in the center of the sofa, sat Arvid, still as a wax mannequin, a ghastly smirk on his face that was now gaunter than ever.

"Ah," he said in a voice devoid of surprise or any emotion. "I see you've decided to let yourselves in to my house. Please, why don't you sit down?"

"What the hell, Arvid?" Lyra said. "Why are you just sitting there in the dark?" She gathered up her emotions again. Her fear was unprofessional.

Otto stepped forward. "Arvid Sammland, I need you to stand up with your hands away from your body, so we know you're unarmed."

He hmphed, suggesting this was unnecessary. Slowly, he rose.

"I'll do it."

Otto blocked her path with her free arm. "No, you're a civilian."

"Not anymore," Lyra muttered.

"Go on then."

Lyra went forward to frisk him so Otto could keep the

gun trained on him. It made more sense this way.

Arvid kept his hands raised, allowing her to pat him down.

Satisfied, she nodded to Otto. "All clear."

She patted around the sofa cushions, too, just in case he had stashed a weapon.

"Arvid, why did you run?" Lyra asked in Swedish.

"Put down the weapon, and I'll explain," he said in a slow voice.

"Not a chance," Otto said.

"Why did Olive do this to herself?" Lyra blurted. Unprofessional again. She couldn't help it.

Otto frowned at her.

"I don't have to talk to you." Arvid sat down again. "I want my lawyer."

"We're taking you into custody," Otto said.

"Under what charges?"

"For running away when we came to talk to you."

"That is not a crime."

"It is, when your fiancée is found dead in a bathtub in your house with a note saying that you know why."

This provocation had no effect on him.

"Arvid," Lyra said, deciding to appeal to his humanity, instead. "Olive's dead. We need to know why. Won't you help us?"

She paused, waiting for a reaction. He stayed deathly still as if it were a game of who reacted first. Then he flicked a lock of hair off his forehead, sighing, and in a barely audible murmur said in English, "My love, this was too much for you. I should have known. I ought to have known."

"Ought to have known what?" Lyra demanded. Was she role-playing for Olive from another dimension? It was creepy but at this point, she'd do anything to get information.

"How it would be. My judgement was off course. I thought you were stronger, my love. You told me you were. That was before I told you, of course. You told me you could do this, and I believed you. You made it sound so true. But you couldn't."

Gone was all the nervous energy of before. His limbs moved with a new fluidity, and an expression of calm settled over his features. How dare he be calm at a time like this when he went around highly strung his whole life?

"What do you mean by *how it would be*?" Otto barked, evidently just as irked by him.

Arvid pulled his gaze from the coffee table up to her face, projecting surprise to see her standing there. "When the truth came out."

"What truth?" Lyra wanted to play bad cop, but Otto seemed to have bagged that role.

He propped his elbows onto the coffee table and sank his forehead onto his palms, resting his head there for a moment. "Oh, the truth of this rotten world. She was too good for it in the end. It was she who suffered."

"Come on, Arvid. Help us out here. You can't hurt her feelings now." Lyra felt her throat tighten. She blinked back tears. "It must have taken something very serious for her to do this. If you know something, then you've a duty to tell us."

She glared down at him, waves of hatred and impatience washing over her, tempered by pity. Why wouldn't he talk, damn him? She exchanged a look with Otto who nodded back as if to say, *keep going.*

All right, let's try something else. "Look," she said in a quieter voice. "We know about Olive and your father."

She exhaled softly, waiting for the reaction. This was a last resort strategy and a horrible one. Bracing herself for an outburst, she watched his face carefully.

He looked back at her blankly. "Yes. They are both dead. The two best people in my life." He dipped his head.

He doesn't know about them.

Otto looked as surprised as she felt.

They would save telling him about that until later. Arvid was dealing with enough. Besides, if *that* wasn't the reason that he'd thought Olive had killed herself, then what the hell was?

He reached for his cigarettes and lighter on a shelf under the coffee table.

The living room filled with flashing lights as another squad car pulled up into the drive.

"That's our backup," Otto said.

The door opened, and two officers entered.

Otto instructed them to watch Arvid while she hung back to gather up the suicide note and other items in the plastic bags.

"Can I have a few minutes to look around?" Lyra asked.

Doubt played across Otto's face.

"Please, Otto. I may not get another chance."

Otto's gaze wandered to the ceiling then back to her face. "Be quick."

Donning her gloves again, Lyra scanned the bookshelves, half hoping to find another note. No, nothing. She rifled through the plates, cups, saucepans, and food cupboards. On the counter top, a recipe book lay open on a recipe for *coq au vin* along with the herbs and spices mentioned. That was the last meal Olive had cooked—the dinner she was preparing for her father. There was no other evidence of eating. A fresh lump formed in her throat. Her best friend would never cook again, never eat again, never do anything again. Why?

Behind the recipe book sat six sparkling clean wineglasses, in two sizes, for red and white. She looked around for the wine bottles, but there were none.

"Wine cellar," she muttered. Olive had mentioned that Arvid was in the wine cellar choosing wine at the moment she was informed of Pronsious's death. How long did it take to grab two bottles of wine?

She found the door off the dining room and took the bare pine stairs down. It was more than a wine cellar. The basement area opened into a large room with wood-paneled walls, a chocolate brown carpet, with a large semi-circular sofa, a huge TV, and games console. A veritable man cave. With all those distractions, it would be all too easy to take a long time to come down to get the wine. Had he been sitting around playing computer games while Pronsious was shot? She checked the console and the TV. Both were switched off. A slight layer of dust on the game controller suggested it hadn't been used for some time. Nothing in the room suggested it had been used recently.

There was a sauna to one side and a storage room to the other. A half-glass door led out to the back garden. She tried it. It opened. That was interesting. He could, in theory, have left the house without Olive noticing…and come back in again.

She opened up drawers in the storage room. It felt wrong to be rummaging around in her friend's stuff—much of it Sammland PR materials—posters, merchandise containers, t-shirts, but also personal notebooks, planners, calendars, photos.

She stood upright to stretch out her spine. There was a tapestry on the wall featuring a snowy scene with two elks in Lapland. It hung askew—something that would have driven Olive mad if she'd seen it. She pulled the end down to make it straight. Then she noticed that the center of the thick fabric bulged slightly. With flattened palms, she patted the fabric. There was something hard behind it. Spreading her arms, she lifted the tapestry off its hook entirely and laid it aside.

A safe was embedded in the wall. The handles had been pushing the tapestry out in the middle. Her pulse quickened.

The safe used a key. Leaning in closer, she examined the keyhole. It would need a long, circular key. She probably knew where that was.

She dashed upstairs and headed to the counter top. Two bunches of keys lay in a dish beside the recipe book. Without waiting to explain to the officers who were staring at her with mouths agape, she grabbed both sets and dashed down to the cellar again.

It was obvious which key it was—a longer one than the usual door keys. It slid easily into the lock.

What will I find here? It felt doubly *wrong* opening Olive's secret safe as her body lay in a bath of cold water two floors above. Then again, not trying to find out everything that had happened would be even less forgivable.

Inside the safe, there was a black case, bigger than a normal briefcase. Her latex enshrouded fingers fumbled with the latches. The lip opened up to reveal—an all-stainless-steel Smith & Wesson 5906. All her cop instincts told her that it matched the 9 mm Luger that Eriksson had shown around. Something told her this wasn't Olive's. It was Arvid's.

There were nine bullets left in the cartridge out of ten. One shot. One hit.

Shit...

Arvid? A killer? What?

For a moment, she could only stand there, stunned.

No, Lyra, move.

She left the gun and bullets there and marched upstairs.

"Come downstairs," she ordered Otto and Arvid. She led the way down. She knew Arvid would follow, as he had no other option at that point.

"Care to explain this?" she asked him, pointing to the open gun case.

Arvid's face flushed, his scowl deepening. "I—" he began and then thought better of it. He flashed Lyra a dirty look. Then his expression collapsed, all the fight gone out of him.

Lyra searched Otto's expression, hoping the officer would say the words she so badly wanted to hear and yet dreading them at the same time.

Otto nodded. "Arvid Sammland, you're under arrest on suspicion of murdering Pronsious Maguire."

22

Back in Helsingborg police station, Lyra experienced none of the usual euphoria of having found vital evidence and made an arrest. Instead of feeling like a piece of the puzzle had fit, it seemed like somebody had swept their arm across the table and sent all the pieces crashing to the floor. Truth was, she didn't want this to be Arvid. It meant that her instincts had been way off and that the world she inhabited was a whole lot darker and more twisted than she'd previously thought.

"This is messed up," Otto said, lolling against the wall as they waited for Eriksson to come out of the interrogation room. "Have to admit, I didn't think it would be him."

"I'm as flabbergasted as you are." Lyra scowled through the one-way mirror into the interview room where Arvid sat at the table, arms outstretched, examining his fingers. Eriksson was getting nowhere. Arvid was taking him for a ride—doing one of his crazy monologues again.

Lyra turned away from the glass. "This was the reason. This is why she killed herself. She *knew* Arvid killed her father. That was why he couldn't bear to be at his funeral one moment longer than necessary. He probably hadn't wanted to show up in Kiltomb at all with his guilty-as-hell conscience."

"But when did she find out? Before, during, or after her father's funeral?"

"I don't know, but I'd say after. I talked to her at the funeral. There's no way she could have covered up something this horrendous. No, I'm convinced it was after they got back from Ireland. It must have been the tipping point when she heard it."

Lyra shuddered, trying to imagine how she'd have coped with the excruciating situation Olive had found herself in. She'd had the double burden of keeping Arvid's secret from the world and keeping her own secret from Arvid. It would have been too much for anyone to bear. Poor, poor Olive. A wave of cold engulfed her. She pulled her jacket closer to her chest.

"What motive did he have, though?" Otto asked.

"If he'd known about Olive and Hedvig's affair—and it's only an if—then it could have been a sick case of revenge as in, "you screwed my father, so I'm going to kill yours." But if we assume that he didn't know about their liaison, then no, other than a slight animosity toward Pronsious as a pompous father-in-law, I don't know."

Otto nodded. "Reckon he'll tell little old us? Good cop, bad cop?"

Lyra shook her head. "Nah, let's just both be human, even if we want to kill him."

"All right."

Finally, Otto's supervisor rose from the table. He looked straight at them, knowing they were watching. His face was thunderous.

Ten seconds later, the door to their room flew open, and he strode in. "Your turn, ladies. As you've heard, he's admitted to loading the gun. He still insists on us taking in Klemens Sammland for the murder of Hedvig Sammland before he talks. He won't back down on this. Good luck."

"Yeah, Boss," Otto said.

They entered the interrogation room and sat opposite Arvid on the plastic chairs that were still warm. The air was stuffy, and the overhead halogen light too bright. Arvid toyed with his shirt collar, cocking his head to one side, his gaze drifting from one to the other and then to a spot on the wall behind them.

Lyra didn't want him to segue into another monologue, so she jumped in with, "Arvid, as your friend and her best friend, could you please tell me why you think Olive killed herself? What was it that she couldn't deal with?"

"Have you got him yet? I refuse to talk until you get him."

"Who are you talking about?" Lyra asked.

"*Klemens*, of course. Who else?"

"We will get him," Otto said. "Don't worry."

Lyra kept a straight face. Total lie, of course.

"That's not what *he* said." Arvid cocked his head toward the door.

"OK, here's the deal. We'll bring Klemens into custody as soon as you tell us something concrete against him," Otto said. "And don't worry, he won't be going anywhere. He's a main suspect."

Arvid's shoulders relaxed slightly. "All right. Use what I tell you to put him away—for life."

"Sure, sure," Otto said.

"Arvid, all the evidence points to you being the one that shot Pronsious Maguire," Lyra said. "What can you tell us to prove you didn't?"

There was a long pause. She fully expected him to ask for a lawyer.

Slowly, Arvid moved his gaze between them.

"I didn't *want* to kill him," he said in a low voice. "It was an *accident*. What kind of monster do you think I am?"

"An accident?" Lyra repeated.

"Yes, an accident." He exhaled. "And that's where Klemens comes in. I read an email addressed to Klemens saying he should meet the contract killer at that cinema at that time. For payment. It was clear. My uncle was paying them off for killing my father."

"How did you get this message?" Lyra asked.

"I intercepted an email to Klemens's email account. It told him to be at the cinema to hand over payment for the project January 7th. That was the date of my father's murder. What else could it be? It was clear as daylight! Nobody was going to help me. Nobody was going to believe me—because the wretched message had disappeared. I couldn't find it again. I nearly went crazy looking for it. It's a miracle I remembered the details. I decided I had no option but to take a trip there myself and..." He broke off.

Arvid's shifty look told Lyra that he knew he was confessing intent to murder Klemens if he continued. It was only an accident in so far as the wrong person had shown up at the cinema. He was so far gone in his lust for revenge that he didn't care.

"Let me get this straight," Otto chimed in. "You thought Pronsious was Klemens showing up to pay off some hit man?"

"Yes, I thought it. I still think it!"

"And you decided to kill him?"

No answer.

"When did you decide this?" Lyra asked. "When you filled your cartridge? When you loaded your gun? Packed your gun? When you saw Pronsious come in through the door? When you aimed at him? When you pulled the trigger?" She heard her voice careening out of control.

Arvid put his hands to the sides of his head. "Please stop! It's done. I'd give anything to rewind, but I can't. As long as he doesn't get away with this!"

There came a point in every interrogation when the suspect broke down and was ready to confess everything. Arvid's glistening eyes, his slumped posture all suggested the fight had gone out of him, and he wanted it all to be over, come what may. A shudder wracked his body.

His voice lowered to a near whisper. "It was dark. I

couldn't see properly through the glass. I fired off the shot. Why else would it be anyone coming in the door other than Klemens? And why *Pronsious* of all people? It's been driving me mad." He took a harried breath. "There, now I have said it. I'm paying the price now. Why aren't you interrogating the real, *intentional* killer of my father?"

"You mean Klemens?" Otto asked.

"Yes," he hissed.

"For starters, he wasn't on that ferry."

"Because he got a hit man to do it for him! That's what I've been trying to tell you all along!"

Otto leaned forward on the table. "Klemens doesn't have a clear motive. We've no proof of his interaction with a hit man apart from this mysteriously disappearing email. All we know, Arvid, is that you are the killer of your fiancée's father. The question is, did you kill your own father, too?"

Arvid's look was pure agony. "How could you ask me that?"

Regarding him, distraught and defeated, Lyra was convinced Arvid hadn't meant to kill Pronsious, even if, as Liam said, there was no love lost between them. It had been a ghastly mistake. After all, Pronsious and Klemens had similar figures, similar white hair, and were the same height. In Arvid's chronic state of fear and loathing, he was likely to make an error of judgement.

On the other hand, it was clear, too, that he had fully intended to murder Klemens had he shown up.

"We'll try to make this as easy as possible if you cooperate," Otto continued.

He nodded listlessly. "Do what you must," he said in a martyred voice. "What do I have to live for, anyway?"

Lyra threw her head back. "Here's a suggestion," she bit out. "You can live to atone for what you put your fiancée through. That may give your life some meaning."

He refused to meet her eyes, choosing instead to stare at the floor. Again, her outburst had been unprofessional, but

Arvid was really pushing her buttons.

Otto cocked her head toward the door. They'd got what they came for. The judicial system would take over from there.

Lyra's legs felt wobbly as they left the interrogation room and headed down the hallway to brief the others in the main office.

The door opened to the observation room and Otto's boss, Eriksson, came striding out and walked alongside them.

"Karlotta," he said. "Ms. Norton? Good work."

Otto raised a hand in wry acknowledgment. Eriksson marched on ahead.

"That's like a medal of honor from him," she murmured when he was out of earshot. "But if I'm that good he should give me the damn lead on the case."

"Agreed." Lyra folded her arms tight against her chest. "And all we've done is open a can of worms, worms that are wriggling out of control. We need that email message. We have to find this contract killer. We have to figure out why on earth Pronsious would go to a payoff in place of Klemens."

"Did Pronsious know Klemens well?"

"Not even slightly."

"Weirder and weirder." Otto pursed her lips. "In my experience, when people do weird things, it's usually bribery or blackmail."

"Blackmail," Lyra repeated. "Pronsious was a good family man. To my knowledge he's never done anything...wait. What if somebody else knew about Olive and Hedvig..." She looked up sharply. "Then they could have used this to blackmail Pronsious into going there. You know, they could threaten him with destroying the honor of the family or whatever, by letting out this secret."

Otto puffed out her cheeks. "Um, yeah, yeah, that works. Who else knew about this affair?"

Lyra shrugged. "Klemens captured some of it on audio,

for one thing, so if anyone else ever found those recordings..."

Otto snapped her fingers. "Wait right there. I'm going to talk to Eriksson. He'll definitely bring Klemens in again if I tell him this."

She was back within five minutes.

"We're doing Klemens first thing in the morning," she announced.

"Excellent."

They shared weary smiles.

"There's nothing more we can do tonight, so I'll drop you at your hotel."

As Lyra was getting out of the car at the hotel, Otto turned and asked, "You going to inform the family tonight about this latest development?"

Lyra nodded wearily. "I'll have to—before they read it on some freaking website. I bet Liam's sitting there Google-translating all these weird amateur investigation sites that pick up the news before the stations do. This is going to be such a horrible blow to Una. 'Oh, and guess what, your daughter's fiancé killed your husband.'"

Otto winced. "Good luck with that."

"Christ, it's insane. What more can happen to this poor family?"

23

Twenty minutes and one hot shower later, Lyra sat on her spare bed, staring at the case notes, trying once again to imagine what it had been like for Arvid to keep a secret like that all the way through Pronsious's funeral and the family gathering thereafter. No wonder he had shunned the company of others. And then for poor Olive when she found out! At that moment, she must have despised Arvid, and maybe even feared him. She must have felt her whole world collapse in on itself in a manner that no-one should ever have to endure.

Water droplets fell onto the case notes—not from her hair. Tears. She let them flow with abandon. She couldn't erase the image of Olive in the bath—the grayish tinge of her skin, her icy cold skin. That wasn't how she wanted to remember her friend, her bright, vivid, beautiful friend who should have had about sixty more years of awesomeness ahead of her.

She may have reacted the same way as Olive in the same situation, but more likely she'd have taken that Magnum from that safe and put a bullet through Arvid instead. Olive was simply a better person, and she took it out on herself.

But had she taken a single moment to predict the grief of her mother? Her brother? Her best friend?

Tears, hot and salty, flowed down her cheeks. She was so, so done with this case. Once they made a link between Klemens, this mysterious contract killer, and Pronsious, she was out of there, never to return.

She fished a mini vodka out of the mini bar and chucked it back neat, Otto-style. With any luck it would numb her enough to sleep an hour or two. First, though, she had to tell Liam. *Hi Liam, Arvid killed your father…but get this, it was by mistake.* As if Liam didn't hate Arvid enough already. She needed another bottle of this stuff.

Dread pressed against her lungs as she pressed his contact. She wasn't in a suitable state to deal with an outburst of male anger.

"Are you OK?" came his concerned voice.

"Not really." She stalled. There was traffic noise in his background. "Where are you?"

"I'm just outside Malmo. Heading toward Helsingborg."

"You're in Sweden?"

"Yes. I meant what I said, Lyra. I've had enough. I'm going to get him."

"Hold your horses, Liam. He's been taken into custody."

"What? Why?"

"Tell you in person."

He groaned. "Where are you?"

"Hotel Aveny. Room 56. Come as fast as you can."

"Right. See you then." He disconnected the call.

It was then that she remembered the other thing he'd promised to do—to kill Arvid.

Once he heard this news, he wouldn't be able to think of anything else…except possibly killing Arvid Sammland himself. That would land him in jail. Another life lost to this vortex of doom. She couldn't let that happen.

*

Lyra headed down to the small lobby to meet Liam. He'd texted her when he arrived, and when the elevator doors pinged open, the man standing there was much changed from when she'd last seen him. Grief had taken its toll on his rugged features, making him look five years older.

"Oh, Liam." She walked up to him, hesitating at the last moment, but he leaned in and embraced her tightly. She didn't want him to let go.

"I'm so sorry for your loss," she said, cheek pressed against his jacket lapel.

"I had to come see...her. For myself."

She pulled back and met his gaze full on. His watchful, jaded eyes made her heart sink. "Much as I want to, I'm not going to try to put you off. I'll do what I can to arrange that. It won't be possible for at least two days, though."

He released her from his arms. "I'm here until I do."

His tone left no room for arguing the point, not that she had the will to.

"I got a room in this hotel." He gestured back to the registration desk.

"Good. Come on upstairs to my room," she said. "We need to talk."

"Any new developments?" he asked.

"Yes," she said heavily. *You could say that.*

He seemed to sense from her that she didn't want to talk in the corridor, so he followed her in silence down the corridor to the room.

Once inside, she beckoned for him to sit in the chair. She sat opposite him, on the bed. Now that he was here, she couldn't put it off any longer. "Liam, I don't know how to tell you this, but we found out earlier today who killed your father."

He bolted forward, clasping the arms of the chair.

"It was an accident—a terrible, terrible accident. The person who did this did not mean for it to happen. We have this on police record. You must understand this. And I'm sorry to say, but it was Arvid."

He looked at her blankly with his big brown eyes. It wasn't registering…yet.

She hurried on. "He thought it was Klemens coming in the door of that cinema. And he was utterly convinced that Klemens killed his father. So he'd worked himself into a state and took out the gun and fired, even though he didn't even get a proper look at the target. He presumed your father was Klemens. Arvid's in custody now."

She stopped talking and watched him, unease twisting her stomach into knots.

Liam's forehead was a mass of creases. Sheer astonishment was keeping more potent emotions at bay. "What are you telling me? I just…I can't understand this, Lyra. I don't get it at all. How did he *accidentally* kill my father? How?"

"He was armed. He went there fully intending to kill Klemens if he showed up. Because Klemens showing up there was the final proof that Klemens had commissioned some hit man to kill his father. The cinema meet-up was payment for the killing."

Liam's frown deepened. "But what was my father *doing* there in the first place?"

"That's what we're trying to figure out."

He stood up and walked to the window to hide his face. He stood there, gripping the window-sill and staring out, his head shaking. His whole body shuddered. She could feel waves of hatred emanating off him.

"I knew it," he spat without turning around. "I *knew* there was something going on with him and Olive. The way they were carrying on at Dad's funeral. Like zombies. Wait…" He spun around. "She knew, didn't she?"

Lyra nodded. "It's likely that she knew it at some stage, but I think it was later, when she got back to Sweden. The shock was too much for her. That's what I have to conclude from her suicide note."

Liam's fist tightened. "Then he basically killed her, too. This is why she took her own life?"

Lyra sucked in her bottom lip. She couldn't confirm it out loud.

He pressed his fist against his forehead, his face screwed up. "Why did she ever get involved with that bastard? He was trouble from the word go. Everything was fine with her. She was happy in the company. Happy with Hugo. She had great friends, everything. Then one day he swoops in, and takes over her life and makes her miserable. It changed her."

"I know," she breathed, feeling a wave of shame that she'd never zoomed out and noticed the gradual shift in Olive. She'd put it down to the extra responsibilities in her best friend's job—Olive was skyrocketing up the corporate food chain at Sammland. Had she been more astute, braver, she'd have pushed Olive to say more. If she were totally honest, she was too wrapped up in her own issues at the time.

"He was always so cold," Liam said, pacing between the window and the door—a distance he covered in six vigorous strides. "And I remember he kept her away from her local friends. After that rift in the company in 2014, she only got to see him and his father and basically the people he wanted her to associate with. Such a control freak."

"I should have noticed," she said. "She was subdued even if she put a brave face on it. She'd tell me all about her new house, new car, stuff like that. Her conversations had gotten materialistic all of a sudden, and that wasn't her, you know? But it was like she couldn't find any other topic that was safe."

"It was the same when she talked to me," he agreed. "All her idealism was gone. She had her fingers in so many pies in Trinity, chairperson of this and that society. Your typical student eco-warrior, social justice warrior, and all the rest. My parents thought she was going to run for *Taoiseach* or president one day."

"I know. She was so passionate about everything, and she could persuade anyone of anything, even things she didn't believe herself." Lyra realized she was shaking.

She rose and opened the minibar and handed him a tiny bottle of Jameson. He took and sip, nodded, and sank back in the chair.

His gaze landed on the case notes on the bed. "I want to help, Lyra. That's why I came here, to see Olive, to find Dad's killer. Now that we know who that is, all I want to do is..." He glanced over at her.

"Don't say it," she urged.

"What am I supposed to say, Lyra? He killed my father and my sister."

She looked down at the bed sheet. As much as she agreed with him, Arvid's actions weren't the only source of Olive's misery. She fussed with the empty spirits bottles and glasses on the nightstand. "Let's not talk about it any more tonight, OK? It's late."

"Wait. Is there anything more you haven't told me?"

"More? No." She couldn't meet his gaze. Yes, there was something, but there was no way was she telling him about the Olive-Hedvig thing tonight. He was too wrung out. He needed a night's sleep more than he needed another twist in the ever-darkening tale that his life had become.

He reached for her arm, lightly taking her wrist in the crook between his thumb and forefinger. "Come here."

His eyes were soft and inviting. He pulled her into his body, and she let him engulf her in his arms, his warmth seeping into her skin as he tightened the embrace. It felt good. Too good. She didn't want to say it, didn't want to encourage anything. He was a wreck—in need of human comfort, that was all.

"Can I stay here?" he said, pulling back.

"Liam, I don't think—"

"I just mean in the chair. I'm worried something will happen to you."

All the terror of the past week was etched in the lines of face. How could she possibly say no? "All right. But I'm OK on my own, you know?"

"I know. Try to get some sleep. I'll be sitting right here."

24

Liam was still sleeping in the armchair as Lyra left the room at 7:30, heading for the precinct. True to his word, he'd sat there while she slept on the bed. Her fatigue had allowed her to overcome any potential awkwardness by conking out within seconds of lying down, and for this she was glad. She wondered if he'd slept much at all.

The interview with Klemens was scheduled for 8 a.m., and Lyra and Otto were to have the honor of questioning Klemens first because of their success with Arvid the day before.

They took a detour into the bathroom on their way to the interrogation room.

"So, you can stay on the case?" Lyra asked.

"I can interview Klemens. Eriksson thinks we'll wrap it up today and call it a win for Helsingborg. And even if we don't, I have to move on to other crimes."

"All right. So, what do we have on him apart from his surveillance equipment?"

Otto clicked her tongue. "Not a lot. His alibis check out for the dates and times of both deaths." She stared at her reflection in the mirror and tried to smooth out a crease on her collar. "There's no evidence of him receiving an email regarding going to the Bio Royale cinema, nor of him telling Pronsious Maguire to do so, though he did receive an anonymous email on the day of Pronsious's death whose origin we couldn't trace." She handed Lyra a sheet of paper with the details—the email header.

Lyra reached for the other notes Otto was holding. She flicked through them, but there was nothing new there. "Does Klemens know that Arvid confessed?"

"Don't think so," Otto said. "Let's keep it that way."

"Of course. Actually, could I do this on my own? It gives me an excuse to quiz him in English and cross-linguistic comparisons of his answers might prove interesting. Also, I think with two of us, he'd somehow play us off each other. I don't want to give him that opportunity."

Otto held up her palms. "Go for it, Professor. I'll question him after you."

Lyra entered the interrogation room and took her seat opposite Klemens. He sat with the apparent ease of a man with nothing bothering his conscience other than some upcoming missed appointments. The overhead halogens glinted in his glasses as he looked down his nose at her.

"Klemens." Lyra sat and gave him a tight smile in greeting. "Did you hire a contract killer to kill your brother?"

He scoffed. "No. Why would I?"

"But you did receive an email," —Lyra pulled out the correct page—"on January thirteenth with an expiration date on that same date, did you not?"

"If you say so. I never saw such an email."

"I have it on record that an email came into your inbox on January thirteenth. Did you access your email on that date? Bear in mind that we can double check with your IT department."

A faint smile crossed his features. "Haven't you already done that?"

"I'm interested in your reply, in any case," she shot back.

"I did access my email on that date, but I never read such an email. Bear in mind, I read only a fraction of my emails on any given day. I get so much junk and I'm cc-ed on so many unnecessary company matters that it would be impossible to read them all. Rest assured, Ms. Norton, I never hired a contract killer in my life, nor do I ever intend to. Anyone who suggests otherwise is lying."

With an indignant cock of his head, he sat back against the chair.

"Just to confirm, you didn't read this email or even see it in your inbox?"

"Correct."

"Have you any connections with the Bio Royale cinema?"

His sudden blinking told her he'd been caught off guard or didn't know what she was talking about.

"The cinema. I may have gone to see a movie there once or twice, but beyond that, no. What's that got to do with anything?"

"As you're probably aware, that's where Pronsious Maguire was murdered."

"Yes, but you surely don't think I've anything to do with that?"

She gave him a wry look. "Why would somebody send you an email with a limited time to read?"

"I have no idea."

"How would you define your relationship to Pronsious Maguire?" She slapped down a photo of him.

Klemens's face went blank as he regarded it. "Define it? I know him by name, as Arvid's future father-in-law. This is the first time I've seen a picture of him. Truly, I have little interest in that family. I wasn't even invited to the wedding."

His exasperated tone suggested he was telling the truth, but C-level executives were often adept liars, and this guy was the sharkiest of sharks.

"How would you define your relationship with Olive Maguire then?"

He sighed. "Politics aside, she was a fine girl. And a good match for Arvid."

Annoyance rippled through her at this palid description of her best friend. Her dead best friend. "What makes you say that?"

"She was level-headed, on top of things, non-sentimental, ambitious. The kind of person you want as VP of a division."

"And she was on your side, in the beginning?"

The furrows on his forehead deepened, creating a deep tic-tac-toe grid between his eyes. "Yes, if you want to put it like that, I suppose. When she joined she was untainted by corporate demands."

"Untainted? An interesting choice of words. Do you feel that Hedvig was dealing in something dirty? Nefarious?"

"All he and Arvid wanted was to maximize profit. They were hoping that bacteria that biodegraded our microplastics would be developed in some near-future. I always maintained that the responsibility was ours to deal with—in our time."

"And Olive agreed with you?" Lyra prompted.

"She didn't just agree. She was one of the main campaigners. She produced the PowerPoint presentations for the board."

Lyra swallowed. She'd only ever seen Olive's glossy presentations on the amazing the *Freshlife* range of face- and body- lotions. This green activism, however, was much more in line with the Olive she knew from their college days. Strangely enough, Olive hadn't mentioned such activities within Sammland AG. Perhaps she'd signed a non-disclosure agreement.

"At this point, was Hedvig listening to what you had to say?" she asked.

He scoffed. "Of course not. He and Arvid teamed up against me. Slowly but surely, their poison spread throughout the company. Yet, they called me the vermin and many other worse names."

"And you know this because you eavesdropped on them." Lyra gestured to the image of the surveillance equipment.

His gaze skimmed over the image then landed on her face with intensity. "Was it you that found that? How enterprising. Your friends in the police force must be pleased to have an ex-cop from Ireland come over to do their work for them for free. However, I'm afraid you're barking up the wrong tree, Ms. Norton—wasting both their time and mine."

Lyra paused deliberately. No way was he going to derail this line of inquiry. "I can imagine that you got extremely angry at some things you heard your brother say about you behind your back."

"Oh, they said it to my face as well."

"Did either of them ever threaten you?"

His face closed over. "You know what Arvid's been saying since Hedvig's death. He thinks it was me." He shook his head. "It's the grief talking. He doesn't mean it. I don't hold it against him."

How magnanimous of you. "If it wasn't you, then can you describe any particular conversations you overheard that may be pertinent to solving your brother's murder? Had he angered anyone apart from yourself?"

She sat back.

"There was much talk about how the company should be run." Peevishness had entered Klemens's voice. "That is hardly a secret—the news outlets were all over the story in 2014."

"What is your view of the events of 2014?"

He shifted his position. "A spate of unfair dismissals of anyone who disagreed with Hedvig and son. Some protested, but they managed to quash them all. Sometimes using ugly means. I held my tongue for years, but now that he's dead, I see no reason to be quiet about it."

"Ugly means?"

"Planting evidence of misconduct, laziness, you name

it."

"Did they try to get rid of you?"

A faint smile tugged at his thin lips. "Of course."

"How did you survive?"

"Hard work, connections." He tilted his chin up. "Common sense."

Klemens was proving as hard to crack as she'd anticipated. "All right. If it wasn't you, then can you think of anyone who would want to kill both your brother and you?"

"To kill me?" Behind his glasses, his eyes flicked back and forth. "I see no connection."

She believed him. "Think about it anyway."

"If I'm not actually accused of anything, may I please go?" he said querulously, shades of the Sammland temper flashing through. "I have important meetings to attend."

"Mr. Sammland—" Lyra struggled to retain composure. "Your brother has been possibly murdered, your VP of marketing has committed suicide, and her father has been shot dead all in the space of a fortnight. Perhaps this is the most important meeting you could be attending."

"I'm tasked with running the company for those very reasons," he said. "Which is why I must get back."

She gathered the case notes into a tidy pile. "My colleague will question you now."

"Colleague, Ms. Norton?" A mocking smile spread across his face. "So you *have* joined the Swedish police force?"

She smirked back, rose, and walked out.

Back in the observation room, she took a seat and groaned aloud. "Have at him, Otto. Did you get all that?"

Otto whistled. "He has no idea Arvid was prepared to murder him, but just got the wrong guy."

"Nope. I think he was spying simply to keep one step ahead of Hedvig. I'm not really getting the feeling that corporate politics is something he'd murder his brother over but then again, we can't be sure."

Otto rolled her eyes. "This family. Speaking of brothers, can you bring Liam in, too? Might as well get his statements seeing as he's around. But is he—uh, able to talk?"

Lyra nodded. "Yeah. He's pretty stoic. I'll bring him in."

*

Back at the hotel, Lyra pulled the curtains open, letting the low, orange sunshine in. She took a moment to appreciate the lack of worry on Liam's sleeping face as he sat slumped in the armchair. Once consciousness returned, that face would tense up. That jaw would harden and the hundreds of worry lines around his eyes would deepen.

"Rise and shine. Otto wants to meet you. As in, right now."

His eyes popped open. He bolted upright and with the efficiency of a farmer used to sudden awakenings. "Has something happened?"

"No, it's OK, Liam. She just wants to meet you. Well, she wants to question you. I'll wait for you down in the lobby.

"I'll be quick."

True to his word, he was down within twenty minutes, smelling of the hotel shampoo. She handed him a coffee from the hotel bar.

"Nice city," he remarked as they drove down the mostly residential Rektorsgatan. "Shame about the circumstances."

"Yeah, of course, you haven't been here before."

"She never invited me over," he said. "And I'm never setting foot here again."

"Maybe she thought you were too busy on the farm."

"Not in winter."

It was hard to talk about Olive like this, trivially, like all was normal, but the only way to find answers was by talking. She slowed down for a traffic light. "She never invited me either, not after she started seeing Arvid. I did come over the first year when she couldn't speak Swedish well and was complaining about the local dialect. But I guess it can't have been too bad, because she decided to stay."

"Little did she know," he said under his breath.

There was nothing she could say after that. She could only hope that he'd get through this interview and decide to go back home.

At the station, they made their way through to Otto's desk. Before they even reached her corridor, she came walking toward them. The policewoman surveyed Liam's face with that same open curiosity Lyra remembered from their first meeting. Then she removed her right hand from her hip and extended it for a brisk handshake.

"Sorry for your losses, Liam. I know things are shit. We're doing all we can to solve the cases."

"Thanks for that," Liam said, his voice warm. "If I can help in any way, let me know."

"Oh, I will. Of course, you know who killed your father," Otto added. "No mystery there."

Liam nodded.

"Is Arvid here?" Lyra asked.

"Yeah. We have him in a holding cell. We'll keep him on these premises until his trial. He has no possibility to get bail."

"Good," Liam said.

"Liam, I have to borrow Lyra for a minute. Please wait here." Otto pointed at waiting area.

"Of course. Work away." Liam sat down on a sofa and reached for a police department brochure.

Otto guided Lyra away to a quiet end of the corridor.

"What is it?" Lyra asked.

"Listen." Otto held out her phone and pressed the WhatsApp icon. "It's a voice recording from Berit Ehrling."

Berit's precise, and somewhat whispery voice filled Lyra's ear. "It may be nothing, Detective Brydolf, but I believe I have found something that may be of interest to you—a local letter in one of Hedvig's folders. It may be significant, because it was dated the day before he died. The envelope was open in any case."

That was the end of the message.

"The day before he died?" Lyra repeated.

Otto nodded. "Local mail only takes a day to arrive. He could've received it before he went off on that ferry."

"Hm. And she didn't say who it was from?"

"No. I want to go out to her." Otto shrugged. "But this better not be a hoax—"

A loud yell rang out in the corridor.

"Stop!"

"Men, *va fan?*" Otto yelled. *What the hell?*

A young female officer rushed up, hair flying loose from her ponytail. She pointed backward. "He's gone into the holding cells! He barged right past me."

Oh no! Liam.

Lyra sprinted down the corridor.

Liam stood outside Arvid's cell, banging on the door, shouting at the occupant within. "Bastard! You ruined her life. How could you do it to her, you monster? You deserve to hang."

Lyra launched herself at him, using the element of surprise to push him away from the door.

He staggered back. She fell on top of him again, pushing him to the floor with all her weight, her elbow jammed against his chin.

Two uniformed officers rushed up and grabbed Liam by the arms, giving her the chance to climb off him.

"Are you *freaking* insane?" Lyra yelled at him.

"I'm not the insane one," Liam growled and pointed at the holding cell. He writhed in the grips of the officers, but the men were body-builder types, and there were two of them. He didn't stand much chance.

"It's all right," Lyra said to the officers. "He's with me. He won't do anything." She shot him a dirty look that told him he had better not.

The officers exchanged a glance and maintained their rigid grips on Liam.

Otto walked up. "Yeah, let him go."

With wary looks, they released him.

"I'm sorry," Liam said, shaking out his arms and brushing down his jacket.

"Seriously," Otto said, addressing her in the low, menacing voice she remembered from when they'd discovered Olive. "Get him out of here. Lock him in your hotel room if possible, or better still, put him on the next plane home."

Lyra nodded, her face hot. "Right. Sorry. We were just going. But can I—?"

"No," Otto said. "Get a statement from him if you want. As of now, he's no longer useful to the inquiry."

These words felt personally directly at her.

She nodded and guided Liam out who was now docile as a lamb. Curious officers lined the corridor, staring. It was the ultimate walk of shame.

Outside, they stood facing each other on the street. She was still shaking. "What the hell was that, Liam?"

"I'm sorry. I-I don't know what came over me. When she said he was right there...it hit me all at once. I had to see him." He rubbed his hands over his face. "How dare he even be *alive* after what he's done?"

She let it hang there. From Liam's point of view, Arvid would seem like the devil incarnate for what he put Olive through, and she had a lot of sympathy for that, but he'd gone and destroyed the good relationship she had with Otto which was one of the few advantages she had when it came to solving this thing. "Look, Liam, I know this is extremely hard for you, but it was your choice to come over here. I thought that meant you were prepared for what was to come. Clearly, you're not. And nobody would be, in your situation."

"Can we stop talking about this?" He walked ahead on the sidewalk.

"No," she fumed, following him. "We can't stop talking about this. That's the point. That's why I'm here—to talk and talk and talk and figure this thing out by listening carefully and respectfully to everyone involved and that *includes* Arvid. This—this is what I *do*, Liam. And I don't need some ham-fisted farmer to come and ruin it for me just because he can't control his temper."

"Ham-fisted farmer," he repeated. "So that's what you think of me."

"It doesn't *matter* what I think of you," she yelled.

"Well, great for you that you can remain so calm and respectful of Arvid. Because I can't. I'm sorry, I just can't."

"Liam, Arvid wasn't Olive's only problem."

Liam stopped walking and went still. "What...what do you mean?"

She let out a ragged breath. "Olive may have harbored feelings for Hedvig. Intimate ones. Did you have any clue of this?"

His face darkened. "What are you saying? But he was...*old.*"

"And kind and attractive. He had his charms. Any woman can see that. And at a time when she felt isolated, unloved, by Arvid who wasn't connecting to her emotionally, she found solace in this attentive older man, who headed the organization she worked for. He doted on her, praised her, supported her."

"She always spoke well of him, but—" He stared bleakly at the buildings across the street.

"I know it's hard to take in," she said after a full minute of terrible silence.

He groaned and leaned back against a lamp-post. "When you say intimate, did anything...happen?" His expression pleaded with her to say 'no', something she couldn't do.

She didn't have to tell him the exact details. All he had to know was there were some illicit feelings as he may hear rumors from other sources. Raw pain flashed in his eyes. She'd waited too long to speak. Now he imagined the worst.

"Liam..." There was nothing she could do or say to make it easier. She'd probably hit him with this when he was at his weakest.

"No." He turned and strode away.

Shit.

She debated following him, but she had other fires to fight. She went back inside the precinct.

Order had been restored giving the impression that the interruption had never happened. She found Otto sitting with the young female officer who had alerted them, filling out a form.

"That's good. You may go, Sofia," Otto said, scrawling her signature and indicating with her pen that should sit down at the desk. "Thanks for the extra paperwork."

Lyra nodded and took the seat. "I'm sorry about all that."

She got it. Otto was being pushed off the case by her seniors from day one. The Liam incident would be a strike against her for bringing civilians into the precinct *and* telling them where Arvid was being held. They had a man in custody who had admitted killing Pronsious and who had a motive to kill his own father.

"Are you going to lump this all on Arvid?" she asked. "And close the case?"

Otto's gaze was shifty. "I don't get to decide."

"Otto, you can't let this happen."

Otto thumped the stack of files in her in-tray. "There are other crimes in Helsingborg."

"Yeah. Bicycle theft, I know."

Otto sucked in her bottom lip and stared at the desk, her round cheeks flushed pink. Lyra had never seen her flummoxed.

"This—" Otto gestured vaguely between them "—was selfishness on my part. I used you."

"What do you mean?"

"I took advantage of your closeness with the family to aid my investigation. I was desperate. I needed a way in, and I needed it fast."

"But it was what I wanted, too," Lyra said.

"You've been great, but...maybe we can handle this from here?"

"Is it because of what Liam did?"

"No, Lyra. It's because we're not getting further by asking the Maguires anything. It's a matter now of interrogating Swedes in their own language—and I know your Swedish is good, but—"

Lyra held up her hand. "Stop. I get what you're saying."

The officer's sudden about face was clear, drastic, and unbelievably hurtful. Otto was treating her like some kind of hired source. Hadn't it been more than that?

Otto sighed. "I'm sorry. It's nothing personal. For the record, I enjoy working with you. But I do have to move on to other cases, you know, today."

"The Maguires asked me to get to the bottom of this case," Lyra said. "Even if Olive and Pronsious are dead, Liam and Una still want me to solve this for them—hell, they want it now more than ever—so that's what I'm going to do. Because for the record, this case is nowhere near solved."

She turned and headed for the door.

"Lyra, wait."

She turned.

Otto rubbed her forehead hard, leaving red welts. "What are you going to do?"

Lyra sighed. "We never finished going through the people at Hedvig's funeral. I want to talk to Arvid's pals, Marcus and Jasper, again, and visit Arvid's grandmother. Oh, and Berit now, too, of course."

Otto went silent, her eyes flickering back and forth. Then she sat forward over her desk, rummaging in a pile of documents. "All right. I can justify going to Berit because she's got some physical evidence. So why don't you come with me? But after that, you're on your own."

25

Berit Erling's villa with its heavy beams and mix of wood paneling and stone looked like it had been a farmhouse around the turn of the twentieth century, converted into a brochure-worthy abode. It was impeccably painted and decorated in bright pastels. The lawn looked like it had been cut with scissors around the shrubberies. There wasn't a pebble out of place on the driveway, and the little green Opel Corsa parked to the side was gleaming.

"Nice," remarked Otto. "Very nice."

"In an obsessive way," Lyra said.

She was glad Otto was back to normal again after their harsh conversation. They hadn't spoken much on the journey here.

An elegant *bing bong* sounded when they rang the bell. Moments later, Berit opened up. Her lounge wear looked every bit as prim as her workwear—a trouser suit, tightly belted, accentuating her trim waistline.

"Officer Brydolf and Ms. Norton," she said. "How good of you to make it."

Lyra was happy to let Otto guide the conversation in Swedish as they removed their boots in the hall and followed after Berit.

"Can we see the letter, Berit?" Otto asked in her usual blunt manner. She pulled on latex gloves and handed a pair to Lyra.

Berit looked at the gloves and wiggled her fingers. "Oh. I didn't realize, Should I have?"

"No," Otto said, "Your prints are already on it. But we will need to take it in for analysis."

"Understood."

They pored over the letter. It was short, written in an old-fashioned hand with large, slanted letters. Lyra scanned to the signature—Virginia Sammland.

Min kära Hedvig,

"My dear Hedvig," Otto translated aloud, "It is time for your son to get married soon, and I would request that you would do something for me. I would like you to pick up a special gift made of Royal Danish porcelain that I ordered at the Butik Karolina shop in Helsingor and transport it back personally. Otherwise, I am sure it will get broken in the post. You will do this for me, I hope? You should pick it up by the latest Thursday, January 7th before they close at 5pm. The address is Stengade, 41. After that, the proprietors are on vacation, therefore Thursday is the last date. I am sorry to have left it this late, but I trust in you that you can do this errand for me. With much love, Virginia"

"And there you have it," Otto concluded. "It's clear what she was asking him to do. What's not clear, is whether she actually wrote it."

"Also, whether she was aware that by the time he received it, he'd be under immense time pressure to comply," Lyra said.

"That handwriting is unmistakable anyway," Berit said. "And to think of it, it is perfectly logical. You see, Virginia is the only person who could ever have persuaded Hedvig to do anything."

"Even if she hasn't had contact with him for years?"

Otto interrupted.

"Or perhaps because of it," Berit mused.

"What do you mean by that, Berit?" Lyra probed.

"Virginia was disgusted by the way Hedvig conducted himself in 2014, cutting off nearly half the workforce—those employees who didn't agree with him, many of them who were close to her heart. She called him a despot, a dictator, and other names besides. She didn't want to see him again. Oh, the rift between them pained him. He would leap to fulfill her wish if he thought that she would speak to him again. He must have seen this letter, this request, as a peace offering. I am sorry I did not think of this possibility before." She frowned. "Indeed, I did not imagine her even capable of writing such a letter."

"It's eloquent, and there's no evidence of shaking or stopping and starting," Lyra said. "Is she not suffering from dementia?"

"Oh yes. She has second stage Alzheimer's. That is what the doctors said in Helgedomen—her care home. After seeing her at the funeral, I would say she is nearer the third stage."

"But capable of writing such a letter? Of organizing such a present, on the phone, say?"

Berit frowned. "I couldn't see it happening, but I could be wrong. Maybe she was having a particularly good day when she wrote this letter and came up with this scheme. Her nurse did mention that she had good days and bad days."

"Thank you. That's been helpful. We shall take this…and the envelope."

"Would you care to stay for *fika?*"

"No thank you, Berit, we must get back," Otto said.

"Then, good luck."

In the car, Lyra asked, "Is it possible she arranged to have her son killed? But why would she do that? Just because she didn't agree with his corporate politics? Plus, they've been fighting for years, so why now? It doesn't ring true."

Otto started the ignition. "It's definitely a strange turn of events. We need to go ask the old lady herself, hm?"

"You sure you got time?" Lyra asked.

Otto cocked an eyebrow. "No, but I'm doing it. Now, let's see if I can drive out of here without disturbing a pebble."

26

Helgedomen care home was a nondescript low, red-brick building separated from the road by a concrete courtyard. The only thing to suggest it wasn't a tax office or a lawyer's office was the abundance of potted plants in the windows and the chairs and tables placed optimistically in the courtyard, currently dripping. It had begun to sleet, so Lyra was glad Otto had parked right at the front door.

"Helsingborg Polis," Otto said at the reception, which looked a lot more cheerful than the outside—bright and spotless. "We would like to speak to Virginia Sammland."

The attendant—a dumpy, Santa Claus type of man in his early sixties—reared back. "Virginia? Yes. She is here. Are you on the approved list of visitors?"

Otto leaned over the counter, inches from his face. "We're the police. We're approved."

Shock flashed across his face, followed swiftly by annoyance. "I see. Please wait here a moment." He waddled off. "She will need a few moments to get ready."

Lyra glanced at Otto. "Relax there, Wallander. She's not going to jump out the bathroom window."

"Clearly you have not read *The Hundred-Year-Old Man*

Who Climbed Out the Window and Disappeared. By Jonas Johansson."

Lyra smiled weakly. "Clearly, I haven't."

She hated places like these where people were herded like cattle, not because of any individual disrespect, but simply because it was a system that dealt with people like they were all the same. Then again, Virginia Sammland seemed to be treated with the kind of respect one would reserve for a bishop.

"You may come now," the attendant said, returning.

Lyra spotted his name tag: Greger. "Thank you, Greger."

He gave her a weary smile.

They passed a room in which an old man sat staring at a TV. The smell of old people permeated the warm air.

"Does Virginia get many visitors?" Otto asked.

"Oh…I think you should ask her that yourself."

"Hm. I will."

Virginia's room was at the end of the corridor, bigger and brighter than the ones they'd passed. It had a view onto an enclosed courtyard, smaller than the one out the front, but prettier, with shrubs and a small pond. The only windows that looked onto the same courtyard were from the offices next door. She probably had the best room in the place.

Virginia sat erect in her wheelchair, same one as she'd had at the funeral. Lyra remembered the shape of it. Her expression looked haughty and slightly puzzled.

Greger fussed over her, buttoning a cashmere cardigan up to the neckline. Underneath that, she had on a silk blouse—in a startling yellow. The old woman clearly took pride in maintaining her style. Even the blanket laid over her knees looked to be premium quality wool.

"Perhaps she'd like a walk," Lyra suggested, remembering the look of contentment on the old lady's face when Hugo had taken her for a spin around the flower beds.

Greger shook his head. "Not in this weather." He

backed away from the old lady, but to Lyra's annoyance he didn't leave the room. He took a chair by the door.

"Virginia," Lyra began, summoning her best Swedish. "I'm a friend of the Maguire family. You know, Olive Maguire?"

The old lady turned to her, her faded blue eyes icy as she scrutinized Lyra's face, focusing on it section by section, as though examining a painting to see if it were fake.

"Olive?" she said creakily, with a twitch of her upper lip.

"Yes, do you remember her?"

Virginia looked at her witheringly. "You have that same accent...the same as her..."

"Yes, I'm Irish. I'm a good friend of Olive's and her family."

Virginia lowered her eyelids. Red and blue veins were drawn in squiggles on the translucent skin. She made a grunting sound.

Lyra frowned. Was she in pain?

"Virginia," Lyra said gently. "You attended Hedvig's funeral, remember?"

She nodded. "Yes. He died in 1970."

"Her husband," Otto muttered. "Also called Hedvig. No, your son, Hedvig," she said in a louder voice. "You went to his, your son Hedvig's, funeral did you not?"

A faint nod. "Oh yes...killed. Killed." Virginia stared into space. "But one hears too many things these days. I do not believe what those tabloids say. Maybe it's all *fake news*." She seemed proud of herself for using a modern phrase.

"We're trying to help Arvid find out who killed Hedvig," Otto added.

A smothered cough came from the attendant. His presence in the corner was starting to get on Lyra's nerves, and, if her strained expression was anything to go by, Otto's too.

"We need to know if you wrote this letter." Otto produced the letter in its transparent plastic bag and laid it into the old woman's wrinkled hands.

Virginia reached for a different pair of glasses on the night stand and made a dramatic performance out of placing them on her nose and then bending down to read the note.

"Is this your handwriting?" Otto asked.

"Yes. This is my writing."

"Do you remember writing this?"

She nodded proudly. "This is my writing."

"Virginia, the wedding present for Arvid," Otto said. "Do you remember asking Hedvig to get it for you?"

The old lady's eyes opened in surprise. "Did I?"

"Yes. Porcelain from Butik Karolina. Hedvig was going to get it for you."

The old lady put a hand to her cheek. "When is the wedding?"

"It's postponed," Lyra said gently. "There's plenty of time."

"Oh. Oh, I see." Virginia looked around, no doubt seeking to have that confirmed by somebody more trustworthy than her, someone native speaking.

Otto leaned in. "Did you want to attend the wedding?"

Virginia glanced up at her sharply. "What wedding?"

"Arvid's wedding."

"No, no, no. That would be no place for me."

Lyra imagined spiral staircases and treacherous paths, not very wheelchair friendly. "I understand."

"Why did you ask Hedvig to get this present on this particular day?" Otto asked.

Virginia looked around the room again then back at Otto. "I don't know."

"You hadn't spoken to Hedvig in eight years," Lyra said. "Why did you ask him to go to Helsingor for you?"

Her wrinkled face creased into a smile. "I wanted to see if he would do something for me. He doesn't do anything for me anymore. Never, never."

It kind of rang true. A dying woman wanted to see proof of her estranged son's love, and she set up a simple task to let him show it. It would all be perfectly fine—if he hadn't got murdered.

"You have had much more contact with Klemens over the years, haven't you?" Lyra asked.

"Klemens? Oh, yes."

"Did anybody else know of this letter, Virginia?" Lyra asked, pointing at the letter that was balanced precariously on the old woman's lap. Did someone help you with this? "

The elderly woman wagged a gnarled forefinger in the air. "I can still write a letter by myself. I am not useless yet."

"Did you tell anybody about this task you set Hedvig?" Lyra persisted.

"Hm? No, I don't think so."

"This is important, Virginia. Who delivered the letter for you? Who did you give it to?"

She flapped her hand in the orderly's direction. "I suppose I gave it to one of them—Klara, or Greger, or somebody. How do I know?"

Then she started coughing—a rattling cough that wracked her frail body. As it got more intense, Lyra had an image of a bag of bones falling apart.

Greger rushed over with a pinched expression on his face. "She's overexerted herself. Perhaps we should leave it there, if you're done with the questioning?"

"Yes, I guess we are," Otto said in a snappy tone, matching his.

With an affronted face, he moved Virginia's wheelchair closer to the bed, whereupon she stopped coughing. He smoothed down the bedclothes and adjusted the angle of the mattress with deliberate slowness. Although it didn't appear that he was going to put the elderly woman to bed, it was clear he wasn't going to leave the room any time soon, either.

Otto reached forward and fished the letter from the old woman's lap and backed away. "Thank you for your cooperation, Mrs. Sammland," she said.

They left and headed back toward the reception, veering around a cleaning cart in the corridor.

"Did that tell you anything?" Otto asked.

"She was definitely familiar with the letter," Lyra said, "but the style of it and her current level of cognition and speech were different, which suggests she had help writing it."

"Yup. I agree. OK, we need to question Greger on who posted the letter for her."

They passed an open bedroom door. A young woman in her early twenties with black hair and a pretty face looked back at them. She was mopping the floor. Her eyes widened at Otto's uniform.

"Tell you what," Lyra said. "I'll talk to her alone and catch up with you in a few."

Otto frowned, but then nodded.

"Hi," Lyra said to the woman, checking back into the corridor to make sure nobody was listening. "You got a minute?"

The young woman placed the mop into the bucket and frowned. "Uh…ja?"

"What's your name?" Lyra asked.

"Does it matter?"

"Not really." Lyra didn't press. It wasn't worth losing an interview over. The woman's Middle-Eastern accent prompted her to ask, "Would you prefer English?"

"Yeah. I'm only learning Swedish. It's, like, so bad."

"Not the easiest, is it?" Lyra said affably. "Have you been working here long?"

"Half a year."

"How many days a week?"

"Four. Mornings only."

"Good. We're conducting an investigation into that old lady's family. Do you know of her or her family?"

The girl shook her head rapidly and stared down at the linoleum floor.

"Please," Lyra said. "It's extremely important. I'm not the police. Simply a concerned family member."

The girl propped her chin on top of the mop handle.

"She's kind of important, I would say. Greger told me to make sure her room is cleaned best of all. Polished. Not a speck of dust." She rolled her eyes.

"Why do you think she has special status?"

"Oh." The girl made the universal gesture for money with her fingers. "She pays the most."

Lyra nodded. "Why don't you keep mopping as we talk. I'm sure you're on a tight schedule."

She pushed the mop into the plastic wringer. "Yeah. Six more rooms in twenty minutes. I hope nobody's shat their bathrooms today. In Syria, before the war, I was in third year med. I wanted to be a neurosurgeon."

"You're from Syria? Things must be rough," Lyra said. "But don't give up your dreams."

"Yeah. Whatever." The cleaner made a circular swoop with her mop on the floor.

"Has that lady had any visitors since you've been working here?" Lyra asked, stepping out of the way.

"I only ever saw one older guy and one younger guy. They visited a few times."

"Together?"

She considered. "No. Never."

The older guy, can you describe him?

"Rich looking, this weird white hair all swept back."

"Thick black glasses?"

"Uh-huh."

"And the younger guy? Can you describe him?"

"I don't know. Normal?"

"What's normal to you?"

"Tall. Not bad looking. Casual clothes, but designer, you know? Always wore a cap. He looks like a lot of people here."

"Did he come here about two weeks ago? January 6th, to be precise?"

"Oh, I did the morning shift that day. There were no visitors."

"Did either of them ever talk to you?"

The young woman stopped mopping and laughed. "No one talks to me." She indicated her turquoise uniform overall and the trolley. Then she shrugged. "The younger one might if he met me in a bar."

"Did you ever hear his name?"

"Simon, I think." She pronounced it *see-mon*, the Swedish way.

"Surname?"

"No idea, sorry."

"Thanks. If you can remember anything else about him, or any other visitors, I want you to call me. Here's my card."

"No problem." The girl took the card and slipped it into her back jeans pocket. Then she wheeled her cart out of the room, giving Lyra a small wave.

"Who the hell is Simon?" Lyra asked as soon as she got back to the reception area where Otto was standing, reading notices on a board. "Apparently, he comes here regularly to visit her."

"I don't know, and I doubt this lot will tell us even if we ask nicely."

"Then we don't ask nicely. You in the mood to play bad cop?"

"Why me?"

"You're the one in uniform."

Lyra approached the reception desk and gave Greger a smile. "Excuse me, who is Simon, the visitor to Virginia Sammland? This may be important in a police inquiry."

Greger blinked. "Oh. He's a nice young man. A relative, I believe."

"When was he here last?"

"I couldn't say for sure. A few days ago, perhaps?"

"Don't you keep any records?" Otto asked. "Did he have to sign in?"

"No. With people that we know, there is no need. And we do know everyone who comes to visit." He looked at her wryly. "It's not so many."

"Whatever happened to making an appointment?" Otto

muttered.

Greger didn't answer.

"You've no CCTV cameras," Otto remarked, scanning the walls.

"We can't afford it," Greger said.

"Yeah, all right. If Simon comes in again, call me," Otto said, slapping her card down on the desk. "And don't let him know. He may just run away before we can talk to him."

"Of course." He frowned at the card and filed it away in a drawer.

"And who would have posted this letter for Virginia Sammland, dated January 6th?" Otto displayed the letter in its plastic cover.

Greger adjusted his reading glasses and peered at it. "That was me. I handle the post."

"Did she give any instructions? Or make any comment on it?"

"She left it on her bedside table, addressed."

"Stamped?"

"No, we look after things like that."

"You posted it that day?"

"Yes. There's a box around the corner. It was no trouble."

"All right, thank you for your time."

They left and made a dash for it through the sleet to the car.

"We'll get a warrant and take fingerprints in her room. It's a long shot," Otto said when they got seated. "And it doesn't tell us anything except that she has a secret friend. I bet it's some scummy local opportunist angling to get money from her will. I think we've just wasted a whole lot of time. Eriksson's going to be real thrilled. As if he wasn't already mad enough at me."

She let out a long breath and tugged the seat belt across her.

"Yeah. Before you start the car, Otto, I've been thinking."

The policewoman leaned on her steering wheel. "Yeah?"

"Just speculating here. What would make Pronsious go to a disused cinema on a dark afternoon when he was supposed to be on his way to dinner? In a strange country he'd just set foot in for the first time? It had to be something extremely compelling, right?"

"Like a threat...or a blackmail," Otto said.

"Exactly. What if someone knew about Olive and Hedvig, and they threatened Pronsious saying they'd spill the dirt on his daughter if he didn't do exactly as they said?"

Otto nodded. "Yeah, I see what you're getting at. So you're saying somebody set Pronsious up to walk into that cinema at that time."

"Not just that; Somebody set Pronsious up to walk in at the exact time that Arvid was expecting Klemens to show."

"Whoa, because they knew Arvid would intercept that message to Klemens."

"Think about it, Pronsious and Klemens look pretty damn similar...in the dark. Somebody *wanted* Arvid to make this mistake."

"Holy shit, I think you're right." Otto tapped the steering wheel repeatedly. "But who would go to all this trouble? And why have Pronsious killed at all?"

Lyra sighed. "That's the million-dollar question."

"Klemens was never supposed to show up in the cinema, was he?"

"No, once Arvid read the email, it had served its purpose and it disappeared. There's a technology that does that. I'm thinking the sender wanted Arvid only to read it." She watched Otto's face to see if she believed her theory. She seemed to.

Otto looked at the dashboard clock then started the engine in reverse gear. "You may be on to something here. I have to get back to the precinct, though. Eriksson has me on this knife-attack case in Ramlösa and I'm supposed to be there for the briefing. Let's split up."

"Split up?"

"I talk to Arvid and Klemens about this while you go off and question those other funeral guests we didn't get to before. If the point of this was to frame Arvid then find out who hates him that much. Actually, Marcus is quite interesting. He's the head of the foundation that operates a medieval castle near Mölle called Krapperup. Nice part of Skåne. Very picturesque. Japser's place is on the way there."

Lyra nodded. "All right. Send me their addresses."

"Oh, and Lyra? Can you persuade Liam to go home? For his own sake?"

27

Lyra returned to the hotel. She wondered if Liam had cooled down or even if he'd be there. A little part of her hoped he'd be gone, so she'd be free to work on the case. But another part of her was happy to see his answer straight away when she texted him. She picked up two ham sandwiches at the food stall.

She could take him along on this trip and use him as a sounding board for her theories seeing as Otto was too busy. Then, having made him feel useful, she'd gently persuade him to go home, later in the evening. Reminding him of his grieving mother in Kiltomb should be enough to prod him into booking a return flight.

A few minutes after she reached her room, there came a knock on her door. She opened up.

"Hey," Liam said, sounding sheepish. "Sorry for storming off on you earlier."

Despite everything, just seeing him made her smile. "No worries. I'd probably have done the same."

"I would've come earlier, but...where'd you go?"

"I was with Otto. I'll explain in the car. For now, come on. We're going again." She handed him a ham sandwich.

"Breakfast. Bet you haven't eaten for ages."

"Thanks, and no."

Reversing out of the hotel parking, she explained, "We're going out to the countryside to see some friends of Arvid's who attended Hedvig's funeral."

"Oh." Liam bit hungrily into his sandwich. "Why am I not awash with enthusiasm?"

"Come on, make yourself useful." She waved at the navigation. "Type in Krapperup."

"Krapperup? Sounds like it should be an IKEA toilet seat."

She snorted.

"And you really want me to come?"

"No," she said. "But I have to keep you out of trouble."

"Great, you're babysitting me." He finished typing in the address and sat back in his seat, gazing out the window.

"Not just babysitting," she said. "You can help me brainstorm. Has Olive ever mentioned the name Simon or *See-mon* to you?"

"Doesn't ring a bell."

"Hugo, you know, but what about Marcus or Jasper?"

"I barely recognize those names. She may have mentioned them in passing, but they were more Arvid's buddies than hers."

"They said Klemens asked them to come to the funeral to distract Arvid."

"Why would Klemens care whether Arvid was distracted or not?" he mused. "To prevent him causing a scene? To prevent him from openly accusing him by the graveside?"

"Very possible. I'm just hoping we find out something, because once Otto's off the case, I may not get access to anyone."

"You sacrificed a lot to be here." Liam said suddenly.

"I had to take a week off work. I wouldn't say—"

"I was talking more about the adoption."

"What?" She darted a look at him. His gaze was intense, his concern genuine. Why was he even thinking about this?

It didn't feature in her own thoughts. "Maybe it wasn't meant to be."

"Or this is a final test before you settle down?"

She let out a hollow laugh. "Some test. I came here thinking I'd help Olive get over Hedvig's death which I'd thought was a freak accident. I was expecting to be rearranging her wedding with her. Little did I think…"

"I know, Lyra. I know." He placed his hand on her upper arm.

She relished the sudden comfort of simple human contact that lingered even when he took his hand away.

They didn't speak for a long time. Words were useless. She knew he was running through memories of Olive and perhaps his father, too—memories that were much more important than anything she could say at that moment. They shared their pain as they stared through the rain-splattered windscreen at the outskirts of Helsingborg.

They drove to the address of Jasper and Elsa, who lived in a well-to-do suburb.

"Want me to come in?" Liam asked as they parked on the street lined with elm trees.

"Best not. Having you there might make him less willing to be open—if there's something to be open about."

"Yeah, I get it. Believe me, I'd rather not. I was just being polite. I'll be here reading." He took out his phone.

"I won't be long."

There was a small wooden plaque beside his doorbell. *Jasper Lindt. Licensed CBT therapist.*

Jasper met her at the door wearing an orange tunic over skinny jeans. With his curly blond hair flowing loose and bare feet, he looked more seventies' hippy than hipster. His eyes widened. "*Ja så?* —the Swedish expression of mild surprise that covered pretty much every social situation.

"Hej. Remember me? Lyra Norton, private investigator for the Maguire family? We met at Hedvig Sammland's funeral?"

"Of course," he said in English. "Please, come in. Elsa's

out, I'm afraid."

"That's OK. It's more you that I want to talk to. Why's your English so, well, English?" she asked as she took off her boots in the hallway.

"My mother's from Sheffield."

"That would be it."

Jasper led her to a comfortable living room that attached to a kitchen via an arched doorway. Vibrantly colored posters hung on the walls, and the shelves were lined with books, magazine, and wooden ornaments that she associated with Aboriginal cultures.

"Now, why don't you sit there—oh, here, let me go ahead and remove this. We had guests over for a little *soiree* last night, and they made a frightful mess, including that claret stain on the rug. It's bamboo silk, so it'll never come out. Ah, what are friends for, eh?"

Lyra smiled weakly.

Jasper lifted a massive gold ashtray that was filled with butts of joints and a tell-tale lump of hash.

"Can I get you anything? A glass of tea—green or chai?" he said on his way through the arch into the kitchen area.

"No thanks, I'm not staying long." She decided that sitting down would only encourage more fussing, so she remained standing. Her gaze moved to the vibrant poster. It featured an actor in Renaissance costume, gesticulating out to the audience as if in mid-soliloquy. Something about the bearded face seemed familiar. She squinted at it.

"Oh, don't mind the stage name—that's our Hugo," Jasper said, coming back in, beaming at the poster. "In full Shakespearean mode. King Lear. His troupe played at the Göteborgs Stadsteater in 2018. Kenneth Branagh himself called it a tour de force, imagine?"

"Mm." Lyra imagined shaving off the beard and yes, those high cheekbones and glinting eyes were clearly those of Hugo.

Jasper sat on the sofa and indicated she should join him. "It's shocking news about poor Olive. Arvid, too, of course.

Scarcely believable about Arvid."

She hadn't had time to catch up with the news to see what was out there. Clearly, Arvid's arrest had leaked.

"You didn't believe him capable of shooting someone?"

"Absolutely not. But of course until people are put under extreme pressure, you never can know what they are capable of."

"I don't underestimate how painful this is for you personally," she said, aware that she was on shaky territory, talking about emotions to a therapist.

Jasper acknowledged her concern with an affected bow, Japanese style. "You're very kind. So…what would you like to talk to me about?"

"Anything you can tell me about the relationship between Arvid, Hedvig, Klemens, or anyone else you think might have borne a grudge against the Sammlands, including Olive and her father," Lyra said all in one breath. It was best to keep it as general as possible.

"Are you asking me as a therapist or as a friend?"

"Let's go the therapist route first. A professional summary, if you will."

"Hm. There was a difficult situation in that company, an endemic culture of taking sides. It came from the top—from the fighting between the two brothers—ostensibly about green issues—but I don't know much about it. Arvid would never talk about such matters with us. He was the soul of discretion."

Lyra tilted her head. "But he, or someone, did mention problems?"

Jasper sighed. "As a friend now, Arvid is one of those people who tries to carry the world on his shoulders. He was so torn—between his loyalty to his father and what he thought was right—his own values system. I think he may have eventually convinced himself that his father's policies were correct. He may have suggested as much to me in confidence, of an occasion."

With an affected shake of his head, he flicked back a lock

of hair and continued. "Olive had a difficult time during this period, cooped up in the C-suite with them. She had started out on Klemens's side, you understand, and she was talented at marketing, very persuasive. Arvid may have seen her as a Trojan horse that he absolutely needed on his side. I'm sure there was genuine attraction there too, of course, but he had an ulterior motive for turning on his charm when he did."

It stung that Olive's account of falling for Arvid had been so different, and so naive. She'd gushed about Arvid sweeping her off her feet, inviting her on a yachting trip with his cool friends in the Stockholm archipelago where they'd had Champagne and enjoyed exciting sex onboard to consummate the sparkling new relationship. Olive would have been horrified to hear of herself spoken of in this way. Jasper was making her sound like a strategic acquisition, a pawn in a man's game of chess.

"Did she actually tell you this?" she asked, hearing the sharpness in her voice.

"No. We were never that close. It's what I ascertained from observing the dynamics between them. Marcus would know more about that period in their lives. Or Hugo, of course."

"OK, I'll ask them. Jasper, do you ever visit Virginia Sammland, Arvid's grandmother?"

"Goodness, no. I can't stand those places." He wiggled his fingers.

"Do you know anybody who might?"

"Klemens, maybe? I'm sorry, I know nothing about her these days."

"Right." She was keen to move on. Jasper only had second- or third-hand information, and she was getting nowhere.

"Thank you, Jasper. I think that's all. I'll call you if I have further questions."

"You OK? " Liam asked when she got back in the car.

"Yeah. We can move on." She certainly wasn't going to

add fuel to fire by repeating what Jasper had told her about Arvid's ulterior motives with Olive. Anyway, she didn't believe it. Olive was too smart not to have seen through such an act.

"But did you find out anything?"

"Nah, he could only speculate. Moving on. Here's another address to type in." She handed him her phone.

*

The views became picturesque as they drove toward the northwest headland of Skåne. As the countryside turned greener, their conversation dwindled into the silence of awe. They drove along an impossibly long, narrow, straight road with evergreen trees on either side. Liam read out from a site he'd looked up that Krapperup on the Kulla peninsula in the northwest of Skåne had nice palace gardens, but the drive up to it was like entering a fantasy wonderland.

"It looks good now, but it must be fantastic in summer," she said, casting her gaze over the rolling hills of the estate. "But where's the grand house? Ah, here we go."

Straight up ahead through a gap in the manicured trees, a large, dusty-red colored house peeped out. The signs pointed toward a parking lot to the left. She drove past large medieval stone buildings and parked. Theirs was the only car.

"Hm, this could take a while," she said, cutting the engine and turning to him.

"Can I come with you this time then?"

She smiled. "Yeah, why not?"

Liam wasn't going to blurt out anything stupid. Besides, he didn't know much. She hadn't shared her theory with him. Hearing how she thought his dad's death was part of an elaborate set-up to incriminate Arvid wasn't something he needed to know—especially as it wasn't proven.

As they walked down the stony pedestrian path to the main building with incredible gardens falling to either side felt Liam edging closer, as if by accident. She sensed that if she were to slip her hand into his, he wouldn't object, and once he had a grip on her, he wouldn't let go. But she couldn't allow that. Her duty to him, to Olive, to herself, was to solve this case, not to get distracted. She clutched her collar tighter against the biting breeze.

"This Marcus fella, he owns all this?" Liam shouted over the wind, his dark hair rising off his head like a turban.

"No, he's chief operating officer of the foundation that runs it—The Gyllenstierna Foundation." Lyra stopped and pulled out her phone, calling up the Wikipedia page she'd bookmarked. "They support sciences and culture. They run tours in the summer—it's closed in winter. He should be on-site in the museum, as he's doing some work setting up some new acquisitions."

A man had emerged from the house. She recognized the tall, stocky man with the strawberry blond mop of hair from the funeral. He stood bang in the middle of the arched front gate, flanked by two huge, cream pillars. The backdrop of the red castle continued the symmetry behind him all the way back to the horizon.

He was clapping his big paws together. He wore a blazer and shirt that wouldn't protect a lesser mortal from the biting cold.

"Lyra," he said affably as they got close enough to hear him. "Good to see you. And you brought a fellow officer?"

"No," she laughed. "Just a friend from Ireland, Liam. Olive's brother, actually."

"Ah." His face creased with lines of sympathy as he turned his attention to Liam. "I'm so *so* sorry for your loss...losses." He frowned and his chin bunched up in a sympathetic expression.

"Thanks," Liam said gruffly, shaking his hand.

"I trust Officer Brydolf warned you we'd be coming?" Lyra asked.

"She did indeed." Marcus grinned, and his gaze darted between them visibly trying to work out the relationship.

"Is there somewhere we can talk?" Her teeth were chattering.

"Of course. Come with me into the museum building. I can give you a mini-tour along the way. If you can spare the time, that is?"

"Yes, we can." As long as he kept talking, it didn't matter where they were. Shelter from the cold would be nice, though.

"Now," Marcus said, when they reached wind shelter around the corner of the house. He pointed out various facades of the building. "As you can see, Krapperup is a mixture of various architectural styles."

Lyra couldn't see the obvious differences, but she nodded. She caught Liam's eye who was doing the same.

"The main building here is in Rococo style flanked by those two Renaissance wings." Marcus gestured extravagantly toward the moat. "It's built on a medieval citadel."

"Tell me about this foundation you run," Liam asked. "Is it to protect the land?"

Marcus beamed, showing about a hundred white teeth. "Yes, we run Krapperup castle. I'm actually a distant relative in the Gyllenstierna line. You may have heard of them?"

"Mm, vaguely," Lyra said.

They entered a wooden door into a musty passageway which then opened to a long, empty expanse with wooden floors and chairs stacked against the stone walls. "Our function room," Marcus explained.

Without waiting for a reply, he continued, "So in 1964, the so-called liquidation law came into force, which meant that all fideicommissa in Sweden such as Krapperup would be liquidated when the holder died. The very next year, the youngest heir in the family line died in a tragic yachting accident. Unbelievable. This prompted the family to turn Krapperup into a foundation, the main goals of which are to protect the castle and its collections, the surrounding estate environment, and the castle park, and to promote scientific research."

"And you got the job because you were related?" Liam asked.

"Not quite." Marcus laughed politely. "I'm a little too far out on the family tree for that. I applied for the position like anyone else. Of course, my education, background, and interests may have helped me, I suppose."

"I see," she said. It was time to get down to business, and she didn't need another of Liam's questions sending Marcus down another avenue. "Liam, mind if I borrow Marcus here for a few minutes?"

"Hm? No, go ahead."

"Check out the library; it's through there." Marcus pointed out a black oak door.

When Liam had gone, she asked quickly, "You know we've arrested Arvid for the killing of Pronsious Maguire, his father, don't you?" She nodded at the library door.

"I read about it in the *Helsingborg Dagbladet*." Marcus's voice was a near whisper. "I believe it was all a ghastly mistake?"

"I don't want to comment on an ongoing case."

He nodded knowingly. "Poor Arvid. Top guy, you know? Really not many of his kind. Always so loyal and truth-seeking. A bit too intense for his own good, though."

"You and he go back a long way. Have you kept up contact since college?"

"In truth, I hadn't seen him for quite a while before the funeral. Everybody's so busy."

"How did Klemens phrase that request to attend?"

"It was in an email. I can't remember the exact words. Polite."

"I would like to see that email if you still have it."

"Uhm, yes of course. I should." He patted his pockets. "Oh, my phone is in my car. I'll take you there."

"Let's get Liam."

Marcus called into the library for Liam, and they exited the building, walking across the lawn. Massive rhododendrons erupted out of flower beds, spindly and bare in winter. Liam, sensing correctly that she still needed a moment alone with Marcus, veered off to examine the massive shrubs.

"Would you have gone to the funeral if Klemens hadn't asked you to?" she pressed.

"Probably not."

"And, did you manage to distract Arvid?"

"Not during it. But afterward. I invited him to come here for as long as he wanted, as a kind of decompression chamber, if he needed it. He seemed to like the idea. He agreed to coming soon after the funeral, within a few days, so I thought I was getting places with him, but then that godawful thing happened with Olive. That put an end to those plans."

He sighed glanced over at Liam, who was still beyond hearing range. "Awful, awful business."

"Did you ever let Arvid know that Klemens had contacted you?"

"Goodness, no. There has been too much bad blood between them, and I never like to get involved in family affairs. Heaven knows, I have enough of my own. Klemens had his reasons, I am sure. He is a well-intentioned man. But anything that Klemens does is seen as inherently bad by Arvid, and vice versa. That's probably never going to change."

"I got that impression, too," she said. "But you, Jasper, and Hugo must have speculated among yourselves, when you consider that Arvid had recently accused him of murder? Did you not find it strange that he would invite you to the funeral to look after his accuser, so to speak?"

Marcus wrung his hands. "Poor Klemens was probably trying to bring some semblance of civility to the proceedings, as he has always done in this family feud. He could tell that Arvid was going… slightly mad. He wanted us to shield him from other people, and vice versa, something like that."

They had reached his car which was parked in a sheltered spot behind a shed. The Tesla looked like a UFO against the rustic setting. He reached in and retrieved his phone from the glove compartment. After scrolling a while, he found an email and showed it to Lyra. Indeed, it was an email sent by Klemens two days before the funeral asking him to attend "to make things easier perhaps for Arvid", roughly translated.

Lyra scanned it twice then nodded. "Can you think of anyone else who had a grudge against Hedvig?"

"Oh, many held grudges, for sure. But Murder? Heavens, no."

"What do you mean by 'many held grudges'?"

"I meant all the employees who lost their jobs that time. But I'm sure they all got new jobs and moved on. People don't murder their ex-boss just because they lost their job."

"Do you think Klemens capable of it?"

"Not even slightly. He prides himself on solving arguments with words. With intellect. Always has done. Murder would be an admission of Hedvig's superiority. No, absolutely not. Arvid knows his uncle better than that. I am surprised he would fall into such thinking."

"But someone definitely wanted *Arvid* to believe it," she murmured, taking a leap of faith and trusting him. "Can you think who?"

Marcus stared at her, his composure ruffled. He took a step closer to her, his broad forehead creased in worry lines. "Is that what you think? It's positively—" he broke off because Liam was striding over to them.

"Everything OK? " Liam asked.

"Yes," Lyra said, taking a step back from Marcus.

They made their way toward the main entrance. It was twilight at ten to four, the sun casting an orange glow over the water.

"Let's continue around this side," Marcus said with a jovial tourist-guide smile, beckoning them to follow him with impatient sweeps of his arm. "Now, its present appearance is the result of extensive modifications in the 18th century…"

Lyra let Marcus drone on while she watched his body language for any signs of trying to hide something, but he seemed genuinely engrossed in the history he recounted.

Liam shot her a questioning look, but she nodded to indicate everything was fine. Marcus's only crime was being verbose and yes, maybe, a little touchy-feely in a very un-Swedish way.

As they rounded the building, a wall full of bright stars greeted them. It was startling and beautiful—the entire red-bricked façade was adorned with large, yellow, seven-pointed stars. It looked like an imaginative child's painting of a wizard's house.

"Wow. What are all these stars?" Lyra asked.

"The family crest, of course, painted on in the 17th century."

"It's beautiful."

"Yes," he said with a polite chuckle. "These are always a fun surprise to those not expecting it, and I can see from your reaction that you weren't." He cocked his head at her. "Are you alright?"

Lyra nodded dumbly. Her temples were throbbing. Ideas were forming. Her breathing accelerated as insights exploded in her synapses.

"So that concludes our little tour. I hope you may consider coming back in summer when you get to see the gardens in proper splendor and when all this has died down. I wish you both a safe trip home today."

"Thank you," Liam said.

They waved at him as he walked away, around the building toward the car park. Liam turned to her. "Lyra, are you all right? What the hell is wrong?"

She could only stare at him. "That's *it*. That's it, Liam! The stars…" She gestured helplessly at the star-strewn facade.

"Um…what?"

"Gyllenstierna...gold star...*Guildenstern*. This is the ancestral home of Guildenstern. That's what they're called in English."

"What are you babbling about?"

"Rosencrantz and Guildenstern? From *Hamlet*."

"Hamlet? Wh—?" Then he broke off, frowning.

"Have you read it?" she asked.

"No, I told you, we did *Macbeth*."

"But you do know the story?"

"I saw the movie...no, actually I can't remember that, either. So, tell me?"

She waved her hands excitedly. "Here's how it goes—Hamlet, the prince of Denmark, accuses his uncle Claudius of murdering his father, the King. Hamlet kills Polonius, the father of his girlfriend, Ophelia, by mistake. Holy *shit*."

Trembling, she handed him the phone and watched his face go through all the emotions as his eyes scrolled down the text.

"And Ophelia...kills herself!" Lyra pulled the phone off him. "Why didn't I make the connection before? Arvid is Hamlet. Everything revolves around *him*, not Hedvig."

"What are you saying? Someone's riffing off a play? Is this why my father and my sister had to *die?*" Liam kicked the front tire. "Some kind of sick entertainment? What the fuck, Lyra? What's going on here? Explain it."

She reached out and held his shoulder. "There are too many connections for this to be a coincidence. Now, come on. I need you to be calm, to work with me."

The agitation in his dark eyes simmered down, and his mouth drew into a determined line. "I'm all right. I'm just finding this a little bit hard to believe."

After three goes, she managed to type "Hamlet" in the search field and skim-read the plot summary of the sixteenth century play sent in Elsinor. It brought back memories of studying it in Higher level English class nineteen years ago.

"Claudius tells Laertes it was Hamlet who killed Polonius," she read out. "Laertes and Hamlet duel and…Oh."

"Oh what?" he asked.

She took a sharp breath. "Laertes dies."

"Who's Laertes again?"

"Ophelia's brother. That would be you, Liam."

28

"So, I'm next, huh?" Liam said, as Lyra drove through the darkness toward Helsingborg.

The speed limit was seventy, but she was doing way over that. All she could think was that Liam needed to get of there, ASAP. Straight home on the next flight. She was responsible for his life now. She tried calling Otto but only got voicemail. "Damn. Damn. Damn."

"What am I supposed to do? Duel him to the death?"

Liam did not seem to be taking it seriously.

"Read the paragraph near the end. You're supposed to fight Arvid, and you kill each other accidentally-on-purpose with poisoned swords."

"Happy to oblige if you'd just let me at him."

"Liam, this is deadly serious. As in, someone wants you dead. You're going to pack for the airport."

"Airport?"

"Yes, Liam, airport. You're going home."

"No. I'm not."

She swung to look at him. "A killer's on the loose," she said fiercely. "A killer who has successfully re-enacted a play with a high body count. You are going home. I will not,"—

she choked up— "*not* be responsible for yours being the next body."

"Ahh, come off it, Lyra. It's just a coincidence."

She fumed silently. Why didn't he understand? Well, she'd make him go. Somehow. Even if it meant getting a police order. Otto would help her out with that. Speaking of Otto...

She tried her number but it went to voicemail. She was probably in an interrogation room with it switched off. This wasn't something she wanted to leave as a voice-mail. She'd be there soon enough in person.

Liam was quiet, reading on his phone. "I'll grant you," he said in a voice shakier than before. "There are a lot of parallels. There's no queen Gertrude, Hamlet's mother. She died years ago. There's Arvid's grandmother who's still alive. No, that doesn't match up either. And we don't know for sure that Klemens actually killed Hedvig... But that's what Arvid believes, and that's what seems to matter."

She let him ramble on. Her thoughts were too busy churning to speak.

"Maybe Gertrude's not a person, but she's the company, Sammland AG. They were fighting over her. Claudius remarrying Gertrude is like Klemens taking over the reins of the company with Hedvig gone. It certainly enraged Arvid." Liam sounded pleased with his deduction.

"Mm," she said.

"And I'm supposed to sit at home while you tackle this monster alone?" He drummed his fingers against the dashboard. "One thing's for sure. If you're staying, I'm staying."

No, you're going. You just don't know it yet.

With every kilometer, her conviction grew. The Hamlet theory held up. The pattern of events was too distinctive to be anything else. This had to be the doing of some sick mind, a psycho killer, indeed, who had decided to re-enact a Shakespearean tragedy. She wasn't going to let Liam or anyone else be their next victim.

It was Hamlet who eventually killed Laertes in the final act of the play, so did that mean Arvid was supposed to kill Liam? Could the whole thing be Arvid's doing? It didn't make sense. His pain was genuine. He loved his father and Olive. He'd never have done this to himself. It was something done *to* him by someone who must loathe him.

They were hitting the outskirts of Helsingborg. She took the route toward the police station.

"Dump me at the hotel, would you?" he asked suddenly.

"So you're going to pack?" she asked.

"Nice try. No."

"Your mother needs you," she said. It was stooping low, but nothing else was getting through his thick skull.

"There's nothing I can say to her," he said. "She's better off with Rose."

She drove up to the hotel main entrance and turned to him. "Then here's the deal. You're staying in my room tonight, not yours." Before he could make light of it, she continued. "Here, take my card. I have two. Move all your stuff. Might as well check out of your own room while you're at it. Keep the door locked. Do not under any circumstances talk to anyone or let anyone in. Don't even order food. Wait until I get back." She reached into her jacket's inner pocket and took out the can of pepper-spray and handed it to him. "Take this as well."

He looked at the can with a bemused face. "You're really worried, aren't you?"

"Yes," she said, pressing her hands against his chest. "We're dealing with a maniac. I've seen this kind of stuff before."

"How about you be careful, too?" He pocketed the can, leaned in, and kissed her gently on the cheek. "Because I want to be able to do that again."

I'll make sure of it. "Get out of here," she said.

She drove to the precinct as fast as local traffic laws allowed, stretching it at some points. The road was empty at this time of evening.

In the precinct, the front desk waved her through. She bolted down to Otto's office.

But Otto's chair was empty.

"No..."

With fumbling hands, she tried Otto's mobile but got no answer. She tried two more times so Otto would know it was important.

A colleague of Otto's whose name she'd forgotten was at the desk in the corner, surrounded by folders and case files. Lyra approached his desk and read "Andersson" off his name tag on his uniform shirt. The photos depicted a gruesome gang killing. A photo showed a body with a severed arm. Andersson looked about as happy as the victim.

"Officer Andersson, where's Otto?"

"Lyra? What are you doing here?"

"Where's Otto? Please, it's urgent. She's not answering her phone."

"She's out at a crime scene. She got called out, oh, twenty minutes ago. You can leave a message, and she'll get someone to follow up in the morning."

Lyra struggled to control her voice. "I have to talk to her now."

"That's impossible." His voice hardened. "She's out at a crime scene, doing her job like she's supposed to."

"Where is it?"

He peered over his glasses at her. "Come on, Lyra."

"Never mind," she grunted, backing off toward the door. "Is anyone here handling this?" She pointed at the Sammland case board. "Where's Arvid?"

"That's classified."

"Is Eriksson around? Can I talk to him?"

"Please, let us do our job here."

His frosty tone told her she had to give up.

"If either of them comes in, tell them I was here with new information on the case."

"You go get sleep," he drawled. "You look like you need

it."

"Yeah."

She drove back through nearly deserted streets to their hotel. Her eyelids felt heavy. Sleep? Not until she got hold of Otto and finagled a way to force Liam to go home. Maybe he could get a plane ticket for tonight.

Was Arvid OK? Yes, he was in custody. But what about Klemens? The plot of Hamlet dictated he should die and, unlike Arvid, he was roaming around a free man.

She glanced at her watch. He could still be working. She could drive out to Sammland AG and explain everything to him and see to it that he got to safety. But what if he were the mastermind behind all this and decided it was time to silence her? Calling him would give him a chance to run away if he was guilty. Was it worth the risk?

Who else could it be?

And Hamlet's friends—Rosencrantz and Guildenstern, they both died, too. Were Jasper and Marcus in trouble? Or was it Hugo and Marcus? Marcus was definitely Guildenstern, but which one of the friends was Rosencrantz? And what about Horatio?

"Damn you, Shakespeare," she grunted, taking the sharp turn into the hotel parking. "Too many players."

The minute she parked, she regretted it. The underground parking lot was dark with many pillars and alcoves and no cameras that she could see—things she hadn't been conscious of when she'd driven in there with Liam.

She didn't even have her pepper spray, as she'd given it to Liam. *Well, that was dumb.*

How on earth could an ex-cop get herself into a situation like this?

Taking deep breaths, she checked all mirrors—twice. She took her keys and arranged them between her fingers, but she knew it wouldn't be of much use if someone attacked her with a weapon, or from behind. She slipped the room card into her back jeans pocket for quick access. Then she opened the car door. Swiftly, shakily, she closed it shut and belted across the concrete floor to the elevator shaft to the hotel reception.

Bathed in sweat, she took the stairwell, bounding up the steps three at a time. At the top was a door where she could present her room card. Her shaking hands pressed the card to the card reader, but it bleeped red.

"Come on, come on," she urged. She twisted it around and tried again.

The light flashed green.

She collapsed into the bright lobby of the hotel—the plush, brown carpet and tinkly piano music were like balm to her nerves. Dragging a hand across her sweaty forehead, she plastered a smile on her face and headed for the bedrooms.

Get yourself together, woman. No one's following you. You need to get your shit together to solve this. But first things first. Get up there and persuade Liam to go home.

When she reached room 56, there was a sliver of yellow light under the door. She felt stupidly relieved.

She knocked, just in case he was coming out of the shower or something. "Liam?"

No answer. Had he fallen asleep?

She slid in her card and opened the door. "Liam?" she called out.

The bedroom was empty. She rapped on the door of the bathroom. Silence. She tried the door. It opened to an empty room.

Her heart jumped.

She dashed into the bedroom. Empty. His things were gone.

OK, don't panic. Maybe he's gone to the airport like I told him to.

Sitting down on the bed, she pulled out her phone.

Then she saw a letter on the nightstand.

Aha, how old-fashioned of him.

She picked it up and unfolded the heavy paper. There, written in bold typeface was the message:

"If you want to stay alive, you must leave Sweden by ferry. Be gone by midnight. Do not contact the police. Do not broadcast your theory. Stay quiet, and you get to live. If you obey, you may get to say goodbye to your friend. The choice is yours."

"What the hell?" She dropped the note on the bed, but her fingerprints were already on it. She edged it straight again and read it again and again.

Get a grip, Lyra.

If Liam had received that, he would have called her straight away, but he hadn't. So this message had most likely been put there after he'd gone. It was intended for her. So where was Liam? Did he receive a message, too? Same one? Or something different? Did somebody come to him in person? Was it the same person who left her the note? She searched for clues, signs of struggle, anything. Nothing. The bed cover was as smooth as an ice floe. There were no telling scuff marks on the carpet.

Someone knew they'd figured the Hamlet connection. But how was that possible? They'd only just grasped it themselves. Unless somewhere was bugged, either her clothes, Liam's clothes, or most probably, her rental car. She groaned.

Whoever was doing this evidently was in a rush to finish the play tonight—by killing Liam and getting rid of her by sending her home. After all, Shakespeare didn't write anything about Laertes having a female friend, much less one who was poking her nose into everything. So while her fate was unknown, Liam's definitely wasn't, and neither was Klemens's. They were meant to die. As for Arvid's friends, well, Hamlet's friends seemed to be unlucky as well.

She had to stop this. She had to play along if she had a chance of saying goodbye to Liam, whatever that meant. A chill enveloped her as several miserable thoughts sliced through the wave of panic. No, she had to stay calm, act like the cop she used to be—focus on the facts, the things I can control.

Be gone by midnight. It was already 23:11.

Out the window, distant lights twinkled across the black strip of the Sound. "Ferry, ferry." She pulled up the *ForSea* site on her phone's browser. There was one leaving Helsingborg harbor at 23:40. The final crossing. Which left so little time.

She flew around the room, grabbing essentials. "Phone, passport, wallet, keys." Liam's clothes were still there, but he'd taken his essentials.

She had to make that ferry. That was all she knew. It was what the killer wanted, and she had no choice but to obey if she were to have any hope of seeing Liam. The hard-nosed negotiating would come later.

As she bundled into reception, hair flying, huffing for breath, the receptionist stuck her head above the desk like an alarmed meerkat.

"No time to explain, sorry," Lyra flopped against the front desk. "Can I check out by email? You have my credit card details. Oh, and I need stuff I left behind to be sent on to the address I gave you at check in."

The receptionist pushed her massive reading glasses further up her nose and said, "This is not our usual…"

"Please. I need to go. I have to catch a ferry."

The receptionist had the grace to look concerned. "If you could wait, madam, I can ask my manager, if—"

Lyra couldn't wait. She ran.

*

Lyra sprinted downhill to the harbor area and the now almost deserted train station. Remembering the layout of Knutpunkten from the time they chased Arvid there, she knew exactly where to go. She bolted up the wide staircase to the ferry terminal.

She wasn't a police officer, so she had to get a ticket like every other passenger. She ran to the ticketing machines. It was here the fun began. Single ticket? Yes. For now? Yes. Confirm? Yes. Credit card? Yes. Want a receipt? No. *Just give me the damn ticket!*

It was 23:25 when she sprinted past the ticket checker who was just putting up the chain across the passenger chute to the ferry. He nodded wearily at her.

She wanted to grab him by the lapels and scream, *have you seen Liam?* But there was no time for that. Anyway, he would probably assume she was drunk.

Now that she was on the ferry, she realized she was on a ferry that someone had suggested she get on—an uncomfortably similar situation to Hedvig's. Was this how it had happened with him? The black waves with white foam crashing against the sides reminded her, *this is not how I want to die. No—far more likely I'm meant to get out of the way so that the killer can get to Liam.*

That made her even more scared.

As the floor gently rocked, her gaze landed on a duty-free shopping brochure lying on the table before her. She blinked at it. Of course, that was the name of the ferry. The *MS Hamlet*. She'd seen the name on the side of the ferry parked in the harbor on more than one occasion, but it had never registered. Was this planned?

Whoever was behind this was obsessed with details. They also had a sense of style. Clearly, they wanted Liam to die in a duel, like Laertes had done. If not killed by Arvid, which was now impossible, then perhaps by the killer him- or herself. They wanted the last battle to play out in some grandiose manner.

But where? As the ferry gently rocked, the answer dawned. Of course, the *castle*; Kronborg Slot was Hamlet's Castle—another clue that had been staring her right in the face the whole time. She itched to call Otto but couldn't risk it. The killer could be tracking her phone, or Otto's, or they could be watching her right now.

She glanced furtively around, checking behind her and

in the reflections in the windows. The main deck was half full now that the passengers had all come up from the car levels. She did a full circle of the deck, scanning every table. Most passengers were Danish tourists, tired after a day in Sweden, interspersed with energetic Swedes in the first stages of inebriation, heading to Denmark for the cheaper alcohol.

All the signs suggested the killer wanted her to disembark before they met her which meant she'd be confronting them in a cold, dark harbor rather than in this brightly-lit cabin.

I've had enough of this shit. She pressed Otto's number and tried to control her shaking body so that her voice would sound half-way normal. "Otto, it's Lyra. Liam disappeared from my hotel. There was an anonymous note telling me to leave the country tonight hinting I wouldn't see him again if I didn't. I left it there as evidence. Room 56. I'm on the 23:40 ferry to Helsingor and I think the perpetrator is onboard, and I'm pretty sure they've got Liam somewhere. This is—this is all about Hamlet, the play, Hamlet. Arvid is Hamlet. Work out the rest. I can't explain now. Have to go."

She clicked off. Otto was going to think she was crazy, but she'd know what to do. If it wasn't too late.

She did another round. A sweet-sour scent of hot dogs sizzling on the restaurant grill perfumed the entire area. The partygoers' boisterous cheers rose above the constant low rumble of the engines.

She ran to the lounge, crashed the VIP area, checked the toilets—female and male. No sign. Then again, she had no idea who she was looking for. The killer could have been any one of the passengers who had looked her curiously in the face.

That was the thing about ferries. One didn't need an ID to get on. There was no security to pass through. Anyone could walk or drive on board carrying a weapon. She dearly wished she had her trusty old Magnum.

Seven minutes had passed. They were halfway across the

Sound. She tried to put herself in the killer's shoes. This ferry was a small, enclosed world that was inescapable for fifteen minutes. There was no way they wanted her to get off and get lost in the melee of Helsingor harbor. The killer wanted her right there, exactly where she was sitting.

Where are you?

The terrified part of her just wanted to hide, but her only way of getting Liam back was to talk to this maniac using all the negotiation skills she'd learned in police training. She had to check the places that worried her the most—the decks outside.

She pressed against the heavy iron door to the outer deck on the starboard side. The wind whipped her face, mashing her hair into her eyes. Unsteadily, she walked forward across slippery wet, diamond-plate, grasping the handrails. Between the bright spots of the floodlights there was a lone couple kissing, ignoring the bitter cold and the breeze. The man clutched the rail anchoring them both as they continued. Other than that, the deck was empty.

She backed away and entered the ferry again, the sudden warmth hitting her like a full-body hairdryer. She crossed the deck to the other side. This side had a view of the castle. Her gut told her she should have tried that side first.

And her gut was right. Standing alone with his back to her at the rails looking out across the water was a tall, broad-shouldered, slim figure. He turned around at the sound of the door.

His face was in shadow. She moved forward, forcing herself to keep walking.

The figure moved forward into the light to meet her.

Her stomach plummeted.

29

Hugo.

With his artfully distressed hoodie and jeans, and his too-chiseled face, he looked like a stage thug. "You," she said. Then came that dull, nagging sensation that she should have known, a feeling she was starting to get used to.

He smiled his toothpaste ad smile. "Yes, Lyra, me. Come closer."

Her feet seemed glued to the deck. "Why should I?"

"Don't be afraid. I won't toss you in, if that's what you're thinking. If you want to see him, come here."

Him—he meant Liam. That broke the inertia. She stepped forward, bracing herself. She'd gotten Liam into this, and he was going to die because of her.

"Where's Liam?" she shouted, grabbing onto the rail. Although the wind whipped at her and it had to be nearly freezing, her body was burning with adrenalin, fear, and hatred.

"Alive. Give me your phone."

"What?"

"Your phone."

She took it out from her inner jacket pocket but held it

against her chest. "Is this necessary?"

With remarkable speed and dexterity, he lurched forward, wrested it from her grasp, and tossed it over the side into the sea. "Yes, it is. Now they won't track you."

Damn you...

"You've no idea whether they're tracking me or not," she said. "You could be in big trouble as we speak."

He smirked. "I like your spirit."

The wind whipped her hair across her face. She swiped it out of her eyes. "What do you want?"

"What *I* want is complicated. But what *you* want is simple. If you cooperate, you'll see him again."

"Alive?"

"That depends on you."

That meant he was still alive. Her heart hammered so loudly, it almost drowned him out. "What now?"

"Listen carefully to me. We go down to the car deck, and we get in my car. I will drive you to him. Nobody else knows where he is, and if you don't cooperate, he will perish where he is, I can guarantee you that. The choice is yours."

"And if I do cooperate? What then?"

"Then we shall see, won't we?"

"Have you hurt him?"

He shrugged ambiguously.

A fresh wave of horror engulfed her. "You killed Hedvig, didn't you? That was you."

"No. It was his own choice."

Suicide was consistent with the evidence, but she didn't buy it. "You were there."

"Yes, indeed, I was."

She reeled. "Why did he kill himself?"

"Why does anybody? Pride? Weakness? An inability to deal with the sum total of negativity they've caused in their sorry lives?"

"What are you talking about? He had a lot to live for. He was a good man."

Number eleven crinkles appeared on his brow, the first

sign that she was getting through. "Good?"

"You blackmailed him. What did you say to him?"

"I merely presented him with a choice. I told him I knew about Olive. I said I would announce it at the wedding. Should anyone need convincing, I could play them some interesting audio recordings, complete with moaning and breathing and whispering of sweet nothings. Either he could accept this reckoning or he could avoid it—by taking a swim. I promised nobody would ever find out about Olive after his death if he did this little thing. That was all I did—present a choice."

A heavy stone had lodged in her stomach. "Some choice."

"He presented a choice to me so many years ago—leave the company quietly and let Arvid steal Olive from me, or be forced to leave in disgrace. I made my so-called choice. What did they do? They still smeared my name. I was unemployable in any corporate capacity. What gentlemen, eh? Well, I forced Hedvig to make a choice, too. Which he did. At this very spot, in fact." He patted the railing. "It didn't take him long to decide. It surprised me, actually."

"But Hedvig would have known the wedding would be called off anyway because of his death," she argued. "There wouldn't have been any occasion to embarrass him."

"Postponed, merely. It would have gone ahead eventually. He knew there was no escaping. This power couple would never let a trifle like a father's death derail their plans—they had quarterly goals to achieve, an empire to build, a social calendar to conquer, more people to screw over." He lowered his voice.

"The recordings? How did you get them?"

"Hah, I stole them from Klemens."

"Klemens knew the whole time," she mused.

"But he stayed quiet. He is a noble man, after all, a rare thing around here. Vastly different to his treacherous brother." Hugo nodded down to the water. "Hedvig knew he wouldn't last long in that water but that his torment would be long-drawn-out if he decided to live. You see, that was his real gift to Arvid that day."

She stared down at the angry, white-crested waves.

"It's cold here," he said. "We'll go inside as they prepare to dock."

Hugo led the way to the door. She had to follow. She couldn't do anything. If she screamed out *this man is a murderer,* she had no proof. Hedvig had jumped of his own accord. Arvid had killed Pronsious with his own gun. Olive had killed herself with her own hairdryer. Moreover, Hugo's fingerprints were nowhere. It was kind of ingenious.

They stepped into the warmth. Hugo ushered her to a tall round table in the center, away from other passengers who huddled near the sides. There they stood like any other passenger couple waiting for the ferry to reach port. She had to keep him talking, to establish rapport.

"I don't understand. Why wasn't your name on the ferry passenger records?"

"You're referring to Hugo?" he said. "Ah, but I go by my stage name, Simon, these days. I changed it with the tax authority straight after I left Sammland. New life, new name. I wanted no links to that terrible time. Only my old friends use Hugo, and I ask them not to."

"It was *you* with Virginia. You got her to write that letter, didn't you?"

"I'm impressed."

"Especially as the staff were…paid off not to talk?"

He laughed. "I won't even ask how you found that out."

"I didn't. It was a wild guess. Unfortunately, you forgot the cleaner. She told me about you."

Hugo smirked. "All right, you got me there."

"Why this? Why *Hamlet*?"

The actor raised his hands, beckoning in a circle around him. "Oh come on, what *else* could it be?"

He did have a point. After all, she was on a ferry called the *MS Hamlet*, traveling to Hamlet's Castle in Helsingor, aka Elsinore.

"Once Olive's meddling father decided to come over," Hugo continued, "which I totally predicted, by the way, I fired off a little email message to him, letting him know what his daughter had *really* been up to, and to meet me in the cinema. Nothing more was required from me after that, because their pride and paranoia ensured the rest. I just had to sit back and watch the play unfold at my leisure."

She gulped, thinking of poor Pronsious reading those terrible words, swallowing his pride, and rushing to the cinema to face unknown dangers all to save Olive's reputation.

"Admittedly, I didn't expect it to go so well. Arvid intercepting Klemens's mail? Check—he'd been that doing for two years already. Arvid taking his silly gun and deciding to kill Klemens? Check. He thought he could get away with it in an abandoned, soundproofed building and indeed, who would ever suspect him?"

"And Olive?" she asked bitterly.

"I knew Arvid would eventually admit to her that he killed her father and when he did, it would drive her to insanity, especially coupled with her own guilt over Hedvig. I fully expected her overbearing brother to jump across the sea and fight Arvid to the death. Because they'd never liked each other, had they? Except that part of my masterpiece got disrupted by a certain ex-policewoman meddling and putting Arvid in jail instead of letting justice take its course."

"Your masterpiece," she spat. "But you loved Olive once. How could you destroy her like this?"

His eyes took on a faraway look. "Yes, I loved her. Adored her. Would do anything for her. But she decided my best friend Arvid was a better match. She went behind my back. She could have talked to me, broken it off like a decent person, but no, she had to cheat on me while I was away visiting my sick mother. I had to let it go. Day by day, I saw her become more miserable with him."

Hugo's body swayed, enraptured by his own voice. She knew better than to interrupt.

"Oh, I fought myself, worked on myself, took psychotherapy sessions, and I told myself I could forgive her, perhaps even forgive them both. But one day, Arvid decided I was a nuisance to have around. He spoke to his father. They tried to fire me… claiming I had failed to reach fictitious goals, and that I was incompetent, unstable, and addicted to drugs. Bullshit! Klemens stepped in and saved me. But I knew my time was up. No employment law in the world can protect you from a CEO's son on a personal mission. Klemens tried again to advocate for my rights, but he couldn't help me.

"But then came the day when the tables were turned. Klemens and I were out drinking after a theater performance of mine in Lund. He got quite dunk and let slip that he'd bugged his brother's office and that he'd saved a *particularly* interesting recording on his phone. I listened in on Olive and Hedvig Sammland having a cozy moment in his office. A May-December romance was flourishing under all our noses. She didn't tell you this at the time, did she?"

Her hesitation had already given her away.

"Such a great friendship you had," he sneered. "She just kept on eating her way up the food chain until she got to the top."

It took every ounce of her willpower not to claw at his perfect face.

"From that moment on, I was glad I hadn't stayed in that rotten company. Especially not after the ethnic cleansing— only their race of sycophants got to stay. Nobody was spared, not even Virginia herself. She was banished to an old people's home she had no interest in living in. Before you go thinking she's in on this, she's not. She's incapable. But if she had to choose a side, it would be mine. At least I visit her, unlike Hedvig or Arvid."

Judging by the manner in which he spewed details, Hugo clearly thought himself invincible—which was a weakness. But she couldn't attack him while he withheld the information on Liam.

"Please let Liam go. He's innocent. We won't talk, neither of us will. I promise." She hated how wheedling her voice sounded.

"You know how it works. I can't let you go now. You got Arvid to confess too early, and now my main character is locked up. You've stalled my masterpiece."

"I thought the *uncle* got killed in Hamlet. Wasn't that his main goal?"

He smirked. "Poetic license."

"Does Klemens know what you've done?"

"Of course not. That would implicate him. Never. No, you must set him free. He is innocent."

"The Swedish police will decide that. Not you."

He laughed. "Such an insipid, spineless institution. Shakespeare truly understood that the spirit can never rest while injustice goes unpunished. That's how matters were handled in the bad old days—with fairness, and flair, and dignity. There were no fat-cat lawyers protecting the villains with the most money. I called upon his wisdom to sort out the rottenness of the world around me. He and I did a good job, did we not?"

Lyra was spared the need to answer by a voice coming over the loudspeakers announcing that vehicle owners should prepare to go to the lower decks to their cars.

"Come on, down to the car level. If you even look sideways at anyone, I won't tell you where he is, and then it will be your actions that decide his fate."

This maniac was perfectly capable of leaving Liam to starve, suffocate, drown, or bleed to death alone. She had no choice but to follow him.

30

Lyra told herself not to panic, but she couldn't deny that she was in an even more enclosed space with him—the interior of his BMW. Their column of cars was next in line to be ushered out the ferry hatch. Tail-lights lit up in front of them, and Hugo started the engine.

"Seat belt," he said.

"Seriously?" She snapped the buckle closed.

"You've probably never been to Kronborg," he remarked as they drove out of the ferry, following the long line of vehicles.

"So that's where we're going?" At least Liam's location had been narrowed down to the castle—admittedly a large castle with massive grounds. And no, she'd never been there.

Straining to see in the dark, she gathered details that might help—tattoos, his clothes, his jewelry, the exact car model, distance traveled, fuel status. The registration number she'd already noted. She fantasized about yanking the steering wheel from him, crashing the car, throwing him out of the driver's seat, bloodied and unconscious, and speeding toward the castle like a knight in shining armor.

But there were too many variables.

"Isn't the castle closed now?" she asked.

"To tourists, yes. To me, no. I happen to have a key to the casemates."

She knew he meant the bomb-proof underground quarters for soldiers during the war. A dark dungeon? That sounded exactly like where Liam was. Now all she had to do was get out of the car and alert the Danish police. But how?

While she pondered it, she had to keep him talking. "How did you manage to get a key?"

He looked over at her. "You ask a lot of questions. Do you think it'll help you?"

She didn't answer, just mulled over her options as he swerved into a parking lot. She was pushing it by asking him that. She'd nearly blown it.

But Hugo seemed happy to keep talking, comfortable with the sound of his own voice. "After being fired by Sammland, I got a part-time job as tour guide for the casements. I know my way around. Come along, get out, hurry."

She stepped out of the car into the large, empty parking lot. The sea air whipped her face, and the roar of waves made her feel so isolated from the rest of humanity. Any second now, she expected the ghost of Hedvig to appear on the battlements.

Hugo led the way, walking briskly from the parking lot through the expansive courtyard. The castle with its massive earthen moat walls and cannon fortifications rose in the dark—a powerful and menacing presence, commanding over the Baltic. Close up, with its domineering aspect and all its militaristic flourishes, it demanded respect.

"It was used as a prison," Hugo said. "The convicts worked on the foundations."

She let him ramble on. Until she knew exactly where Liam was, she'd play it his way, even if it meant enduring the amateur tour guiding.

"A prince named Amleth," he continued, "who may or

may not have existed in 1100, may or may not have killed his uncle who killed his father and married his mother, may or may not have inspired Shakespeare who never actually came here."

"Right," she grunted.

He pointed toward the water. "Imagine poor Ophelia, throwing herself in there to end her misery."

Lyra swallowed hard as the image of Olive half submerged in the bath reared up in her imagination. In a horribly apt way, she had drowned.

She followed him silently to an inner courtyard. Hugo marched up to a squat, wooden door set deep into the stone wall. A sign above it announced they were at the casemates. She heard a jangle of metal. In the feeble moonlight, she saw he had taken out a bunch of keys that hung off a big, old-fashioned hoop. He singled out a long key and shoved it into the lock.

With a geriatric grunt, the heavy door opened to a dark passageway. She hesitated. It was dark. The walls were two feet thick and made of solid stone. It was exactly the place she did not want to end up in with a killer. Her instincts screeched to break free now.

But if she ran, Liam was as good as dead; Hugo got upset when his plans were interrupted.

"Come along," Hugo's voice echoed out from several feet in front of her.

All other sounds from the outside world were blocked. She could hear his breath—shallow, excited.

"A statue called Holger the Dane is in there," he said, pointing to a door. "Legend has it he'll come alive if Denmark is in danger."

"Denmark *is* in danger with you around," she muttered.

He laughed. "A sense of humor to the end."

To the end. Her foot hit a protruding stone in the uneven floor, and she stumbled forward. She slapped a hand against the wall to steady herself, and it was covered in spider webs.

"Don't try any tricks. Keep up."

She fumbled through the darkness in front of her and above her head in case the ceiling should suddenly get lower. Concussed, she would be of no use to anyone.

Her theory was that Hugo had worked for too long in those damp, gloomy surroundings, seeped in the barbarity of middle ages lore, too soon after his dumping by Olive and dismissal by Hedvig. It had all inspired him a bit too much.

And Liam had thought this guy was nice?

Another door. Hugo stopped, and she heard the jangle of keys again.

Swallowing the urge to attack him from behind, she shuffled in after him. It was too risky. She needed to even up the odds.

31

They had entered a long room with a vaulted ceiling. Hugo switched on a light. She was surprised there was electricity. She spun around, searching the stone floor.

"Where is he?" she yelled.

"There. Beyond that arch."

She raced to the corner, to the body slumped over, and hunkered beside him.

"Liam!" She looked into his face. It was shockingly pale. His skin was cool. He wasn't moving. Was he even breathing? Further down his body, a large patch of black covered his sweater. Blood, wet and sticky, had seeped through to his jacket.

"No!" She took his wrist and felt for a pulse... Seconds ticked by... Where was it?

A wail of agony sounded in the back of her brain. He couldn't be...

But then she felt something, a faint throb. *Yes.*

She struggled to pull air into her lungs. Gently, she laid Liam's arm down by his side again. If he didn't get medical attention soon, he was in trouble. There was no time for sentiment.

"This has happened to you before, of course," came Hugo's voice behind her. "I read about you. Your David got shot, didn't he? All because he was close to you. He bled out."

She didn't turn around. She'd forgotten her situation for a moment but his goading voice was a sharp reminder. She wouldn't rise to it. That was what he wanted. She was now a machine. It didn't matter if she got killed. She had to get this bastard. Outwit him somehow. That was all.

"No," she heard herself saying in a hoarse voice she barely recognized. "You don't get to talk about that."

She heard the gun cocking. He'd had one all along. She turned around and stared at it. A 5-shot .32 Magnum, perfect for concealed carry. She'd owned one herself a decade ago. The picture was clear. He wanted to kill them both. He'd drag their bodies out and dump them over the ramparts. It would be some time before anyone found them—if ever.

It could be the perfect crime.

"In case you're wondering, all I had to do was tell him I would take him to you," Hugo carried on. "Same trick as with you. He was as meek as a lamb. He didn't try anything. In another universe, you were made for each other."

She still didn't turn around. She hunched over Liam, placing one hand against his cheek, feeling where the smooth skin met the bristles of his five o'clock shadow. Her other hand moved toward his right jacket pocket. "Oh Liam," she moaned.

She had only one chance at this. Inside the pocket, her fingertips met the cool surface of the cylinder. Slowly, she pulled it out, eased the safety plastic cap off, and positioned her index finger over the nozzle.

"Take this." She sucked in a breath, whirled around, and pressed the nozzle for several seconds.

The air filled with the foul smell of pepper spray. She dropped the can and backed away quickly to avoid the worst of the mist, yanking her scarf up over her entire face. The important thing was time. The first thirty seconds would only be mildly annoying, and he could still function. The capsicum needed one to five minutes to attack his nose, eyes, and mouth. She felt her own eyes water.

She retreated further until she hit the back wall. Now she could see him through the coarse linen fabric of the scarf—a blurry figure yelling, bending over, clutching his face, coughing.

He stumbled in her direction, grabbing the air in front of him. "Aaagh," he yelled.

She forced herself to look through the tears. The Magnum dangled from his index finger as he mashed his others against his eyes. He clung on stubbornly to the gun despite the agony.

Her life depended on that gun. Thirty seconds had passed. His eyes should be in pain now.

She sprinted forward, swooped her hand in, and tried to twist the gun from his grasp.

"Nej, nej, nej," he yelled, yanking his hand backward. He twisted in a circle, semi-blind, with the fury of an animal fighting to survive.

A blast roared out. The walls amplified the sound. Then another.

Shit! She hunched up, hands to the sides of her head, frozen, as she tried to predict the next shots. He staggered backward, his arms extended stiffly in front of him, waving that gun around, trying to aim again.

Something felt not right. Then she felt a burning hot pain. She looked down. *Oh no.* Her outer thigh was darkening. She felt down her jeans, and her fingers met with a warm stickiness. She'd been shot. The pain came in waves, radiating through her skeleton, getting stronger, becoming unbearable. She let out a gasp that turned into a howl. Nooo, she was at a disadvantage now.

The air cracked. There was a whine near her ear and a blast behind her. He'd shot again. Plaster clattered down from the ceiling. Four shots gone—assuming he'd needed only one for Liam. One left.

Worryingly, he was nearest the door, and he still had the key. All he had to do was lock her up and leave her there. He didn't need his eyesight for that. He could probably make his way out blindfolded. That seemed to be what he was doing. He stepped backward, swinging the gun in a semicircle in front of him. When it swung toward her every two seconds, the weapon was level with her heart. The odds of getting out of there were getting smaller.

She threw a rock to make it sound like she was further away from the door. It paid off. His undulations tended more to his left. She slunk along the wall. They were equidistant to the door.

Now what? Her bleeding leg was going to seize up soon—she couldn't hope to outrun him by much. In the corridor, he'd have a narrow column in which to shoot. He wouldn't miss.

She had to even things up.

She looked at Liam, then back to Hugo.

With a kick of her good leg, aiming high, her boot made contact with his fist and there was a satisfying whacking sound. The gun clattered to the ground.

Hugo yelled, scrabbling on the ground, coughing, nose running, tears streaming down his face.

Hobbling forward, she kicked the gun away further from him and launched herself at it before he could.

She crash-landed on her side on the rocky floor. Her outstretched arm took some of the impact. Pain radiated throughout her skeleton again. She'd broken a rib, she was sure, and maybe a bone in her arm. But she'd managed to grab the gun.

"Freeze!" she yelled. "I'm pointing this gun at you, and I'm a trained officer."

"Then you won't shoot," he said. He raised his hands to chest level in half-compliance.

She disabled the safety switch. "Ex-officer."

Hugo tried to straighten up, but a coughing fit wracked

his body.

"Put your hands up where I can see them," she barked.

She glanced back at Liam. Dying, because of her. If she'd refused the case, maybe he'd have never come there. Maybe Olive would still be alive.

"You deserve to die," she grunted, half at him, half at herself.

"No!" Hugo raised his hands higher. "You can't do this. You don't want to do this."

His tearful voice, his wretchedness, his blotchy face and running nose made her despise him even more. "Where's all your honor now, Shakespeare?"

He was watching her through the slits in his puffy eyes. "You'll regret it if you do. They'll send you to jail."

"I don't care." And she didn't. But her finger wouldn't cooperate. Some remnant of a conscience wouldn't let her pull. "Damn."

She kept the gun poised. Pepper spray residue on the handle seeped into the cuts on her hands, and she felt an odd, disconnected warmth. The pain wrenched her attention away from what mattered. She broke out in a cold sweat. Consciousness was something she had to fight for.

Her gun hand shook. "Put your phone on that stone. No games. I'll shoot if you so much as *breathe* in a way I don't like."

He pulled out his phone, staggered to the stone, and placed it on top.

"Back to where you were." She motioned with the gun. Then, carefully, she hobbled over to the stone, grabbed the phone, and pressed in the emergency number for Denmark 112 on the lock screen—same as for Sweden.

She knew how to phrase it to get immediate help. "Message for Otto Brydolf, Helsingborg Polis. Urgent. Homicide attempts. Casemates, Kronborg Slot."

"Kronborg?" came the astonished voice, but she had already put the phone in her back pocket.

Now she just had to wait. Spend how many minutes not

killing this bastard? She wasn't sure she'd manage. She glanced at Liam again. Motionless. How could she tell Una? How could she live with herself?

"Was it worth it?" she spat at him. "Three, maybe four people? Three of whom belong to one poor family that you had hardly anything to do with. And the one person you thought deserved it most, is still alive and will be released as a free man well before you."

Hugo's puffy face cracked a smile. "But he will suffer, so terribly, and probably go the same way as her."

She pulled the trigger.

First came the blast, then his howl of pain. He rocked forward, hugging his arm, yelping, hyperventilating. She'd grazed the side of his left bicep. Blood spurted out. It wouldn't kill him but it sure would hurt. He doubled over, wheezing, a terrible, inhuman sound.

"That was for Liam," she said. A sudden energy coursed through her body. No matter what happened next, even if she had to sacrifice life itself, she'd done it. She'd solved the crime. She'd made the bastard pay. It was just a pity Olive and Pronsious hadn't lived to see the day.

Liam, meanwhile, was still and silent. Every moment they waited there increased the risk of him dying.

Time entered a different dimension. The distance between seconds seemed infinite. She couldn't tell if she'd been there hours already or only minutes. It didn't feel like it was her experiencing this, holding a gun, pointing at a sniveling man with swollen eyes, and blood trickling between his fingers.

*

Had she been here forever, breathing in this poisoned air mixed with the metallic scent of her own blood, feeling her leg wound in every nerve ending, mourning the potential loss of Liam? It felt like it. She couldn't hold on much longer. The edges of her mind were dark—her body craved to shut down.

Hugo's face had sunk in on itself, and he seemed fully preoccupied by his pain and difficulty breathing.

In between his labored gasps, her ears picked up a new sound—muffled male voices outside in the corridor.

Hugo hadn't locked the outer door to the casemates or this inner door either. His mistake. But what if those were his cronies? Until she saw who it was, she wasn't going to celebrate…or let go of the gun. She grasped the weapon tighter and straightened up.

"Here!" She thought she'd yelled it, but it came out as a pathetic croak.

Just as she'd decided she'd imagined the voices, the door crashed open. Three officers stormed in and pointed guns at her and Hugo as they were trained to do, yelling in the guttural tones of Danish. She had only seconds to establish herself as harmless. She dropped the Magnum and held her hands up high.

The officer nearest her peered into her face. He was young with a sandy beard. "You made the call?" he asked in perfect English. "Lyra? Lyra Norton?"

She nodded. Relief surged through her veins. Otto had done it. She cocked her head at Liam. "He needs medical attention *now*. And he—" she nodded at Hugo, "needs to be arrested for attempted murder."

One officer knelt down by Liam, taking his pulse. Another tended to Hugo. More chattering ensued in Danish. They didn't seem to take Liam seriously enough.

"Is there a medic?" she shouted. "He's critical!"

If he isn't already dead.

"We're taking you all to Nordsjællands Hospital." The sandy haired officer was by her side again. "Luckily, it is just around the corner. The Swedish police will meet us there."

The Swedes would have to get across the Sound somehow, and there were no more ferries. They'd have to take the long way around by car, over the bridge. It would take a while…time they didn't have. She felt the blackness at

the sides of her vision closing in.
> *No, not this. I can't black out... I have to...*
Then darkness took over.

32

Lyra was in a bed, and there were people milling around her—uniformed people. That was the Swedish uniform, not the Danish—POLIS not POLITI.

Vague memories drifted back of being in the back of a vehicle…a blanket…blood on her leg. Then wet cobblestones and a brightly lit building with big windows. She was in a hospital.

Liam!

She tried to bolt up, but her body refused. Only her head tilted up. Her voice when she tried to speak came out as a dry croak. Her throat was still burning, her eyes stinging. Was there any part of her body that wasn't actually hurting?

A blond pixie haircut swam hazily into view. A large round face.

"Otto." Lyra managed a smile.

"Yeah." The tenderness in Otto's voice told Lyra how bad she must look.

"Liam?" It came out as a tearful croak, but she didn't care.

"He's in intensive care. They're doing their best for him."

"But will he be all right?"

"He's stable."

Stable. That could mean anything.

She sank back against the pillows. "How did you get here so fast?"

"Coastguards. Never mind that. The doc says your leg will be fine. Muscle damage. Oh, and two ribs are broken, and you've fractured both your ulna and radius."

That explained why she was feeling like utter shit.

"Tell me what happened," Otto said. "If you're up to it."

"Hugo…He forced me go in the casemates. He'd already shot Liam. He was going to leave us there, dying together, bleeding out. He nearly got away with it."

"But he didn't. We've enough to put him behind bars. As for the rest—the Hamlet thing? I mean, I get it, but that's going to take some explaining."

"Yeah. I feel like I've been living in that goddamn play since yesterday."

Otto hummed in sympathy. "I know."

"Horatio. That's who Hugo is. Hamlet's best friend. He's the only main character in all of this who doesn't die."

"Some best friend." Otto gazed around the ward. "You know, let's save the details until we're somewhere quieter. We're trying to keep a lid on this whole Hamlet business."

"Why?"

"Copycat killers, other little Hamlets running around quoting plays and killing folk."

"Or little Macbeths, or King Lears," Lyra said. "Just what you need."

"How many of these damn things did he write?" Otto asked heavily.

"Ten."

The Swedish officer patted the bed cover. "Get rest."

"The press will figure it out, you know. Some journalist out there is going to connect the dots when they see the pattern of deaths, if they don't guess it from the locations, like I should've."

"You got there first." Otto smiled.

She must have fallen asleep, because next thing she knew, she was opening her eyes and Otto was standing before her once again.

"Did I fall asleep?" she asked groggily. "How long have you been here?"

"Only for a few minutes. I checked on Liam for you. He's doing a bit better, too."

Her eyes snapped open. "Can I see him?"

"Not yet. He's not talking or anything. But hopefully soon enough."

She sank her head back against the pillows. *Damn.*

"I have to get back on duty," Otto said. "Bicycle thieves never rest. And you have to get back to your life. But what next for you, my friend? Quiet life as academic mom in the Dublin suburbs?"

"Not going to happen."

"Uh, which part?"

Lyra managed to sit up a little. Her head was clearer now. "The adoption. Soon as I'm able, I'm going to call them and tell them I'm opting out."

"But why?"

Because a child could get hurt in the crossfire? "I don't think it's for me. I want to continue this. Set up my own gig one day. Help families embroiled in cases the police don't want to get involved in, no offense."

"None taken."

"This case has told me something, Otto."

"Yeah? What?"

The only reason I was on the case was because Olive and I had a close enough relationship that I felt compelled to come over in person. I just happened to have a police background. Only for I came over, she'd have contacted nobody. The case would have fallen apart because nobody was truly devoted to it."

Lyra took a breath and winced as pain seared through her rib cage. "My point is, what about all the other Olives out there? Criminals who are getting away with all manner of shit just because people have secrets and have nobody to turn to that they can trust? Some cases are simply too delicate to want to ask the police to help."

"Yeah, I know. A lot of crime gets hidden that way."

"I want to blow those cases apart, exactly like this one should have been blown apart the minute Olive called me about Hedvig's death."

"I admit, that may have changed the outcome."

"Yes. Olive would be alive, so would her father, and Liam wouldn't be battling for his life in a hospital bed."

An officer called for Otto's attention, letting out a stream of especially staccato Swedish. The Swedish officer turned to her urgently. "Shit, I have to go. But good luck with everything, yeah? Your farm boy there will survive—he's strong. But see you next time you come to Sweden or Denmark?"

Lyra smiled. "I'll try to come on a Friday."

THREE MONTHS LATER

"I remember him, you know?" Liam said.

Lyra glued the finishing period to the gold letters in classic serif font on the glass reading, "Lyra Norton, PI." She stood back to admire her handiwork then glanced over at him. Like his physical condition, his memory was improving. Everything from this year, starting with the time of Hedvig's death, was still missing, but the long-term memories were mostly intact. A Dublin police officer had explained everything to him when he came to in the Mater hospital soon after his transfer from Denmark. She felt glad, but also guilty, for not being there at the time. "Mm, who?"

"Hugo. He came to Kiltomb, just the once. He was so cheerful with everyone. He was one of those people who goes around smiling all the time. He had everyone charmed, even the dog."

Liam didn't sound like a man talking about the killer of two members of his family, who'd put him in a coma for over two months.

"Dad threw everything he had at him, every jibe, every insult, trying to make him crack. Nothing worked."

"Why?" Lyra asked. "I mean, why did Pronsious do that?"

Liam pondered it for a moment. "He was the first she'd brought home. I think Dad didn't know how to act. I suppose I didn't, either. We'd never had a foreigner in the house before. Mam was pumping him full of tea and cakes. He was awfully polite and entertaining…"

"You liked him. I remember you saying that he was fun?"

He frowned, tapping a hammer handle against his chin. "Yes, he was, but there was something about him. I couldn't put my finger on it. When he left us to go back home, I didn't feel anything. That's what it felt like—a hollowness. With Arvid, it wasn't like that. He bugged me, yes, but at least I felt I knew where he was coming from."

"If he ever gets released, would you meet him?"

"Arvid?" He shook his head. "Oh, he'll never want to see me again, but I hope he makes something of his life when he's released, that's all. I don't hate him. Thanks to you, I know he didn't really mean to shoot my dad."

"Yeah, and thanks to Klemens's intervention, nobody suspected him of intending to murder his uncle either." Lyra propped her feet up on her desk, looking around her new office. "Klemens turned out to be an all round nice guy. Not what I was expecting."

The walls were the same blood red as before—she hadn't repainted them, but all the kid-themed stuff was gone, replaced by shelves. Everything was neat and orderly. Ready for business.

The decision to leave her teaching job had come three months ago and, having researched the market, she found potential clients already waiting for her services. It was a viable business. She would be her own boss. She would help the Olives of this world.

But until this moment, she hadn't been able to give up the day job; one thing had been stopping her. Now that thing was resolved. Liam Maguire was awake and talking to her, healthy and getting stronger every day. He had been released from the Mater hospital in Dublin and was going home to his mam within days. That was the final barrier, and now it was down, so there was only one thing left to do. She took one last look at the email addressed to Prof. Yeates with the subject line, "My Resignation." The old dear would understand.

She pressed SEND.

ABOUT THE AUTHOR

Brona Nilsson grew up in Ireland and worked for international tech corporations in several European countries before deciding that Sweden was the quietest place for a switch to writing. She writes in several genres, most recently, Crime and Mystery, blending Irish and Scandi cultures for an international audience.
She lives with husband, son, and dog beside a spooky forest near a body of water that inspired this book. When not writing, she loves making friends and meeting people, and talking about anything other than writing.

Printed in Great Britain
by Amazon